D0237150

LIGHTS IN THE SKY

LIGHTS IN THE SKY

Philip Purser

This first world edition published in Great Britain 2005 by
SEVERN HOUSE PUBLISHERS LTD of
9–15 High Street, Sutton, Surrey SM1 1DF.
This first world edition published in the USA 2005 by
SEVERN HOUSE PUBLISHERS INC of
595 Madison Avenue, New York, N.Y. 10022.

Copyright © 2005 by Philip Purser.

All rights reserved.
The moral right of the author has been asserted.

British Library Cataloguing in Publication Data

Purser, Philip, 1925-
    Lights in the sky
    1. Air pilots, Military - Great Britain - Fiction
    2. World War, 1939-1945 - Aerial operations, British - Fiction
    3. World War, 10939-1945 - Military intelligence - Great Britain - Fiction
    4. World War, 1939-1945 - Sweden - Fiction
    5. Holocaust, Jewish (1939-1945) - Fiction
    6. War stories
    I. Title
    823.9'14 [F]

    ISBN 0-7278-6196-4

Except where actual historical events and characters are being
described for the storyline of this novel, all situations in this
publication are fictitious and any resemblance to living persons
is purely coincidental.

Typeset by Palimpsest Book Production Ltd.,
Polmont, Stirlingshire, Scotland.
Printed and bound in Great Britain by
MPG Books Ltd., Bodmin, Cornwall.

And God said, Let there be lights
in the sky to divide the day from
the night

The Good News Bible,
Genesis I,14

| MORAY COUNCIL | |
| LIBRARIES & | |
INFO.SERVICES	
2O 14 O7 15	
Askews	
F	

I

*W*e *are running out of Jews! A shameful complaint to be voiced by persons who are themselves Jews, but also a fact, and one that can only mean the extinction of the sole flame left flickering within us. All hope, all faith, all desires and all but the most base appetites have gone. Just this one urge remains, like the instinct of the dying elephant to seek out the graveyard of his ancestors. It is to tell the world – no, even more dauntingly, to* convince *the world – of the unspeakable, unbelievable, unimaginable process we attend.*

Even in its humble beginnings, little more than a year ago, when the deaths were counted by the hundred rather than the thousand, and the dead were still being buried, we wondered if people elsewhere in Europe (if there were still an elsewhere in Europe) could know of these things. As more and more human abattoirs were brought into use, as the thousands became tens of thousands and incineration replaced burial, the question haunted us. But all that is left of the country that was Poland has now been occupied for four years. In the camps one is further cut off from all news. Here in the north of the country we did not even receive transports from Paris or Amsterdam or Brussels, with the tidings that they might bring. They went to camps in Galicia rumoured to be cities of death by comparison with which Treblinka is but a market town. Our trainloads came from Poland itself, and continue to do so, if less frequently. Of late they have come chiefly from Warsaw, as the Germans steadily whittle away the Jewish quarter, or Ghetto as it has now become, and deport its inhabitants. Just a few outsiders have reached us by some freak circumstance or eyeblink of the system.

One contingent arrived from a concentration camp at

Theresienstadt, near Prague, confused and aghast as they were herded from the train with kicks and blows by our delightful Ukrainian guards. After the usual preliminaries and deceits they were sent along the 'Road to Heaven', a barbed-wire alley decked with fir branches to make it seem more inviting. It leads to 'shower-baths' which fill not with steam but with the exhaust gases from the filthy old diesel engines of outworn German tanks. Just two men, one a watchmaker, the other a violoncellist, were plucked from the procession to join our precarious 'permanent staff' of inmates.

They told us that Theresienstadt had been like a dream, or as if they had found themselves in some fantastic play. There were little streets and squares, and houses in which Hansel and Gretel might have felt at home. We have our Hansel and Gretel house also, we said, it is long and low and the doors are fitted with strong locks, because it is the armoury where the SS keep weapons and grenades.

In Theresienstadt, they said, there was disease and harsh discipline. But when we asked about the method of killing – was it by gassing or by shooting? – they looked bewildered and said there were no deliberate killings. The worst that could happen was old people being forced to hide themselves for hours in cellars and lofts, out of sight, so that the houses should not seem overcrowded. On these occasions the café would have real coffee, the children would play, there would be dancing in the square. And sooner or later the Commandant would lead a party of visitors through the scene, who would smile at them and exclaim over the little children and make notes in their notebooks. From their voices they were Swiss or Swedish, Spanish or South American.

We looked at each other. No visitors come to Treblinka. It would not be beyond the ingenuity of our turkeycock commandant to stage just as unreal a show – do we not have open-air concerts on summer evenings? But how could he conceal the smoke by day, the flames by night, the stench of burning flesh at all times? Not for Treblinka the refinement and tall chimneys of the crematoria said to be in operation in the Galician camps. The dead are dragged from the 'showers' and burned on improvised grills in the open air, up to 12,000

2

at a time. From last February there was, in addition to the normal traffic, a programme to exhume the corpses which were buried in trenches in the first phase of this hideous undertaking, and have the fires consume them as well. That reclamation is now complete. While it lasted it was a monstrous enactment of that mass-sacrifice of burnt offerings which in religious texts is called a holocaust.

It was what Pickup dreaded more than anything, getting safely down and then being asked to bloody wait. It had happened once before, when he was new to the job, the lights all set out but when he landed, no Joe. *'Cinq minutes, eh?'* He had refused and flown back empty, as laid down in the drill. But in the mess next day the others had winked at each other, and even Tilly had looked a bit wooden when Pickup delivered his report. On top of the times he'd been turned back by the weather, or had sheered off because the field didn't look right, it was no wonder they'd started calling him Pilot Officer Prudence, a variant on the comic butt of the Training Manuals, Pilot Officer Prune.

Not any more, though. He got most of his Joes in, brought some of them out again, and he'd now done it more times than anyone in the squadron except Tilly. The war couldn't last long enough to catch Tilly, who'd just logged his forty-fourth op. This was Pickup's twenty-sixth, which was unlucky times two, and if he'd had any sense he'd have left the motor running while he clambered down for a quick slash before taking off again with a cheery wave.

Instead, in a fit of panic, pique or plain lunacy he had closed the engine down as per drill. The silence crowded in, save for the wind which rustled the trees and nudged little smears of cloud across the blob of the moon. The moon! The moon that had always ruled men's lives, if not often so absolutely as those of the Special Duties squadrons. In the nights of the full moon shalt thou go forth and hope to come back, the rest of the month is for the bull that shitteth. Not content with that, she had bestowed on Pickup the very lunacy he was regretting. The word came from the Latin *luna, lunae*, for God's sake. Here and now, finally, she was past her best as a source

3

of light. This was either the last or the last-but-one operational night in the current moon period, Pickup couldn't remember which.

He shivered, and not from the cold, as they pretended in thrillers. In September this bit of France didn't get chilly even at 01.45 a.m. GMT. He looked at his watch for the umpteenth time to check the exact figure. Well, 01.43. He'd wait until 02.00, not a second later. The Lysander was a solid black presence in the lesser darkness of the field, the motor still wafting out reproachful smells of hot oil and metal. Starting it again was what he most wanted but also feared – supposing its didn't fire first or second time. He could feel the panic welling up already, the urge to keep on pressing the tit and fiddling with the mixture until either he ruined the starter or flooded the whole caboodle.

'*Eh?*' Gaston was looking inquiringly at him. He must have muttered or sworn or something.

'*Rien*,' he called. '*C'est la guerre*, that's all.'

Gaston shrugged. It was Tilly who had ruled that the older Frenchmen who met them, the ones with spectacles and scarves and pongy cigarettes smouldering away, were all called Gaston. The younger ones with glinting eyes were Jean or Jacques or both. One of this crew of Jean-Jacques had already gone, with the wireless operator Pickup had brought in. The remaining three stood huddled in a knot a little apart. He could hear their low voices without catching the words, let alone understand them. He would have liked another fag but that meant offering them around again, and he had only five left, barely enough for the return flight, whenever that was. Soon, that's what it was going to be. Very soon. Not even 02.00 any more, more like 01.50. It was not as if the pick-up – 'your pick-up, Pickup,' as the briefing officer never failed to put it – were an agent bearing priceless information, just some Resistance merchant. He took his hands out of his pockets and scuffed his feet as an overture to making an announcement.

'*Psssst!*' One of the Jean-Jacques was frowning in his direction, finger across his lips. The others had their eyes on a gap in the trees where there was a gate and a track from the D-road which here ran north–south for six kilometres. It was central to the pattern of river and canal and railway line you used to find the right area, before you sought the actual field and lights.

The chap must have keen ears, Pickup thought dully. He could hear nothing – ah, yes, a faint engine whine, the distant thud of wheels or springs as a vehicle bounced along the track. It could always be the Gestapo or the stinking *Milice*, of course, but the Jean-Jacques seemed to have decided that this particular medley of sounds was okay, and were relaxing again. The Gaston blew on the end of his fag to revive it, sending a tiny spark to sail all of two feet through the night.

It was the doctor's Renault again. Pickup recognized the curious boat-shaped body and much-patched hood from the last time he'd drawn this destination, six months ago. In France as in England, or for that matter anywhere in Europe, he supposed, doctors were high on the list of civilians allowed to run a car, next only to tinpot wartime officials like Mr Winwick, his girlfriend's father.

The doctor had jumped out and was hastening towards him, but alone. He was wearing the same incongruously formal hat as before, the same light-coloured silk muffler. He spoke in English and didn't remember Pickup at first.

'I am sorry you have had to wait.'

'Nearly didn't. Where's the passenger?'

'He is here –' he gave a twitch of his head in the direction of the car – 'but I must tell you he has been tortured. He is not well. There is a nurse who cares for him. Is it possible that she may go also?'

Pickup was shaking his head before he'd finished. The Lysander could carry two in the back, three at a pinch, but ever since Brian Merry brought out a character who turned out to be highly dubious there had been a ban on giving unauthorized lifts. He said, 'Sorry, no chance.'

The doctor peered at him. 'Ah! We have met before. Last year. You brought back our brave Nadine. If it is a question of the weight . . .'

Pickup nodded. It was easier to let him think that. The Jeans and Jacques were already helping someone out of the

Renault. He didn't look too bad as he lifted a hand in a sort of apologetic salute, except that the hand was bandaged. So was his other one. Christ, how would they ever get him up the ladder? He sent one of the Jean-Jacques up to perch on the edge of the cockpit, ready to haul the poor sod in. The others lifted him until they could get his feet on the bottom rung, his bandaged hands on the third up. Above this one the ladder curved to follow the shape of the fuselage, so he wouldn't need to hang on grimly. The doctor was manhandling his feet one at a time up the rungs . . . second . . . third . . . the man at the top was already leaning down to grab him under the arm. He grunted as they tumbled him into the rear seat.

An accompanying little gasp or whimper came from close at hand. The girl must have crept up while his attention was all on the bloke. She had short hair and looked no more than seventeen. She was wearing a fur coat and carrying a suitcase.

'Please . . .' It was the doctor. 'She is not his nurse – or not only his nurse, I should say. They were lovers.'

Pickup said, 'What does she weigh?' and wished at once that he hadn't. The doctor was already asking her. The girl gave a tiny shrug. '*Cinquante Kilos, je crois,*' he said in a little-girl voice.

'What's that in pounds, shillings and pence?'

'I am not certain,' said the doctor. 'Not too many.'

Pickup picked her up, another joke that went with his name and the job. She was as light as a child. He could smell her perfume through the musky pong of the fur, and feel the grip of the little hand that clutched the sleeve of his flying jacket.

'And poor Luc is only bones,' said the doctor.

What the hell? Okay. *Ça va.* Nice legs, he thought as he waited to follow her up the ladder. He swung himself into the front cockpit and started the starting drill. All he wanted now was to hear the engine splutter into life. In Biggles stories you could always get the Jean-Jacques heaving on the prop if all else failed, but no possibility of that with a bloody great Bristol Mercury. He closed his eyes for a second in the little prayer he still said to himself when scared or anxious, as he had since prep school, and using the same potty vocabulary. O please,

6

God, make the engine start and me not get into a panic, for Jesus Christ's sake, our Lord, amen.

Okay. Throttle half an inch open, mixture normal, airscrew pitch coarse, fuel on, cowling gills fully open, then the bit Pickup feared most of all, wanking away at the priming pump while turning the engine on the starter with the ignition switched off. Suppose the battery was low, this could be enough to sink it. Sounded all right, though. Shut off primer, switch on ignition, likewise the starter magneto. Deep breath, press the starter tit. *Whirr-whirr*, prop clattering round, count two, three, four slowly, you were never ever to persist for more than ten seconds . . . five, six, seven, eight – and she fired! Blew out smoke, coughed, faltered, picked up again and, Glory Be, was running. He switched off the starter mag and turned off the oil warmer control. You were meant to let her run up for five minutes but not tonight, Josephine, not tonight.

He was already in position for take-off – you taxied back to that immediately on landing. He was just finishing a rapid pre-flight check when, hell's bells, the doctor's head loomed into view, not two feet below his. The idiot was half-way up the ladder.

'What do you want?' Pickup screamed.

The doctor mouthed something about sorry, he'd forgotten, and held up a parcel wrapped in thick paper. Pickup took it. It was quite heavy and clinked as he stowed it, as best he could, under his seat. By the time he'd done that the doctor had vanished. Pickup waved into the darkness, opened the throttle and was airborne at 0202, Not bad. He couldn't tell how they were in the back. There was an armoured bulkhead behind his seat, with a small aperture he could peer through only with difficulty. Tilly had introduced a nice custom of carrying a thermos of coffee laced with rum to fortify the passengers, but the outward-bound Joe had polished off most of it. At 10,000 feet, following the River Saone, he lit the first of the five Gold Flake that would have to see him home.

Then in the month of Tisan in this Year of the World 5703, according to the Jewish calendar, or April 1943 in the

7

Christian – we are now in September, or the month of Ellul – there came, one after the other, no fewer than nine trains bringing people from somewhere strange and distant. At first we thought they must be Romany nobles or Ottoman pashas, so rich and colourful were their clothes, so abundant the luggage they brought, so lordly their manner when they alighted from the train, as if it were the Orient Express rather than a string of cattle trucks.

They were sent along the Road to Heaven just the same, newly bedecked with spring-green branches from the forest. But first they had to undergo the fraudulent routine which we prisoner-servants of the camp staff administer. They deposited their suitcases and valuables in exchange for worthless receipts. The women had their hair cut off, in the interests of hygiene, they were told. On the same pretext all persons were ordered to strip naked, men, women and children alike, before passing the large notice 'To the Showers' and entering the green road to extinction.

Marek, in charge of the hair-cutting detail, contrived to keep one of the menfolk standing by to act as interpreter and reassure the women. The two conversed in French, and from this man, before he became too suspicious and alarmed, Marek learned that they were Jews from Salonika. Until shortly before their deportation they had seen little of the German forces occupying Greece. He was himself a merchant who had continued to trade among the islands, and had been several times to Turkey, which is neutral, and once had even set foot in Cyprus, which is under British rule.

'There you surely heard stories of the Nazis killing thousands of our people?' cried Marek, throwing all caution away. But even as his eyes strayed from side to side in terror the merchant whispered, 'No, never.' Thus did we receive confirmation of a bitter suspicion. The extermination of our race which we witnessed every day was either not known to the world beyond, or if reported, not believed. It was then that we resolved, above all else, to send out someone, somehow, who might force the world to believe.

*   *   *

8

'You felt *sorry* for this female?' The Branch Manager's narrowed little eyes were uncomprehending. Tilly and Pickup called him the Branch Manager because that was how he ran the place, like a provincial bank manager querying every three-penny overdraft.

'Well, mainly for the man himself,' said Pickup. He stood lopsidedly to attention, having somehow missed the last rung when descending the Lizzie's ladder, tired and hungry, at Tangmere, and done something to his ankle as well as ending up flat on his back. Not exactly an arrival to impress the female in question, and more seriously one that had brought a nosy RAF Regiment type beetling over to ask questions. There had been raised eyebrows over the extra passenger, but soon forgotten – Pickup had optimistically hoped – in the bustle of getting the Resistance cove into hospital.

The Lysanders of 161 Squadron were based here at Tempsford in Bedfordshire, but during the moon period they staged at Tangmere, a fighter station on the south coast. This gave an extra hundred miles range, each way, when bound for fields deep in France, and also a certain holiday feeling. You were out of the Branch Manager's scrutiny. Getting back to Tempsford was always a bit like going back to school. It had been extra gloomy this time. The news was that 138, the Halifax and Liberator squadron which dropped supplies and agents by parachute, had just had a fearful run of luck. Eight crews had been lost over three nights. That would be forty or more faces missing, some familiar, a few you had known well and liked.

Perhaps this was what made the Branch Manager particu-larly hostile today. He would be thinking of the heavy brigade trundling off night after night to distant parts – Poland, Norway and the Netherlands as well as France, up to fifteen hours in the air, sometimes still over enemy territory when dawn broke, easy meat for a Ju-88 – while the Lizzies flitted across the Channel like ballerinas, and that not too often.

'So you openly disobeyed a standing order of which you are fully aware,' he was saying. 'Namely that no person is to be carried unless he – much less *she* – has been authorized by the Special Operations Executive and your superior officer?'

9

Pickup shifted his weight to try and ease the throb in his ankle.

'And don't *jiffle*, man,' said the Branch Manager.

'The pick-up was in a bad way, sir. I judged that he needed medical attention on the flight,'

'Hardly much room for medical attention in the rear cockpit of a Westland Lysander. But I shall check with SOE as to the Frenchman's condition.' He put a tick alongside a list of items on the sheet of paper in front of him. 'On another matter, Flight-Lieutenant, it has been reported to me that you have again been putting on overalls and mixing with the maintenance crew working on your aeroplane.'

'Flight-Sergeant Price had no objections, sir.'

'It is not up to Flight-Sergeant Price, whether he has objections or not. You tried to drag him in last time, with your story of wanting to learn how you might make emergency repairs in the event of your machine being damaged on landing in enemy territory. My response was that if this were considered to be a practical measure it would be adopted as a proper training programme. In the meantime you were to remember that you hold the King's commission, indeed that you are no longer a junior officer – difficult as that is for some of us to understand – and not put yourself on familiar terms with other ranks. Did I not make myself plain?'

'Yessir.'

'But you carried on regardless.' It was a statement rather than a question, so Pickup made no reply. The Branch Manager opened a file and perused a document within. He had a square face with a rectangular moustache and those slot-like eyes. Even his uniform had a sober, geometric cut.

'I see you had a spell in Fighter Command.'

'Yessir.' O God, that old black mark again. Lack of aggressive spirit, they said.

'But back to Army Co-operation after – let me see – three months. Then to Training Command. Thence recruited to Special Duties. Now one of our more experienced pilots. A reputation for caution, which I find perfectly sensible but which makes your behaviour last night all the more wilful.' He closed the file. 'Squadron-Leader Tillotson speaks highly of you. Others find you difficult, aloof, not a good messmate. I find you insubordinate, and if you once more compromise the security of our operations, in any way, I shall have you court-martialled. Is that clear?'

Tilly was hovering in the ante-room. He signalled to Pickup to follow him and went swinging down the corridor. Tilly's uniform matched his gait, arms and legs going all ways. His tunic seemed to arrive baggy from Hepworths or the Fifty Shilling Tailors, the patch pockets already stuffed with paper hankies, copies of *Men Only* and packets of the Capstan Full Strength he smoked. The belt made it look exaggeratedly waisted, the trousers flapped, the peaked cap was bashed and bent. The general effect was rakish and, as Tilly himself must have known, a bit chocolate-soldierly. 'Always fly in Service Dress,' he preached, 'so that if you're taken prisoner they'll know you're an officer and a gentleman.'

He was also a squadron-leader at 23 with a DFM and a DFC and the gift of getting on with everyone. Pickup was a flight-lieutenant of 24 who flew in the snug all-ranks serge of battledress, wore a forage cap – or cunt-cap in rude parlance – and wasn't at ease with anyone much, except Tilly and, perhaps, Taffy Price.

'Did you get a date with her?' Tilly demanded as Pickup drew level.

'Who?'

'The little French bit.'

'God, no. Missed my footing and fell on my arse when about to assist her out of the aircraft. Not very impressive. Besides, she was the Joe's *fillette*.'

'As you helpfully told the BM. Do you have to make life so bloody difficult? Why couldn't you say she was his nurse?'

'Thought the love interest might soften the old bastard's heart, I suppose.'

'Fat chance of that, even supposing he has a heart.'

'Anyway, when I did say something about the poor sod needing medical attention, all he said was that there wasn't much room for that in the back seat of a Westland Lysander. What does he know about the back seat of a Westland

11

Lysander? If he ever flew a Westland it would have been a Westland bloody Wapiti, dropping little bombs on tribesmen.'

Tilly led the way into the mess, where tea and uninteresting biscuits were set out on a side-table and you helped yourself, as laid down by the Branch Manager in one of his austerity drives. There was no one else about. Tilly completed what he had to say. 'The fact remains, you have well and truly got on his puny wick. I've stuck up for you all I can. So has the Wingco. The Branch Manager has been told that you're as good as any airman in the squadron when it comes to plonking a Lysander down in the proverbial tennis court, and better than most at finding said tennis court. But if he catches you out once more on security you'll be back to driving sprog navigators round and round the Malvern Hills in an Anson.'

Pickup felt a little clammy spasm of dismay.

'Not that there aren't times when I would happily settle for that,' Tilly added.

'Me, too.' But not now, with another operation notched up and no more possible before the next moon period, in October.

'Meanwhile,' said Tilly, as if picking up the thought, 'boys and girls come out to play, the moon ain't shining bright as day. Fancy a run into Cambridge this evening? Barney and Cobber Ivens are coming. Just room for a skinny one.'

Pickup hesitated.

'Help you wind down,' said Tilly. 'It is your alma mater or masta bater or whatever you call it, isn't it?' Tilly hadn't been to university, just art school for a couple of years before being articled to a printing firm.

'All right, thanks.'

On the way back to his billet, Pickup went round by the hangar where his faithful Lizzie T8865 was being serviced. Taffy Price threw him a cheerful salute. 'Usual mess in the back,' he reported. 'Blood, urine, coffee and rum and a snotty bit of a handkerchief. Otherwise in good order, considering. And how's the Sly Lander today, sir?'

Pickup was wondering if he'd been daft to accept Tilly's invitation. He'd had barely four hours kip since this time yesterday. What the hell, though? Taffy was waiting, his head cocked expectantly. 'Oh, fine, thanks, Flight,' he said. Sly

Lander was Taffy's nickname for him, rearranged from the letters of Lysander, except for the extra 'L'. When Pickup had pointed this out, Taffy had grinned and sucked his solitary front tooth and said aye, but he was Welsh, you see. It was always double-ell in Wales.

It was a good twenty-five miles to Cambridge, but Tilly could do it in under forty minutes in the sporty Lea-Francis saloon he'd picked up cheap from a Hebrew gentleman slinking off to Canada for the duration. And Cambridge was the liveliest town in reach, indeed the only lively town in reach. The colleges were full all the year round, now that the university was working four terms. In addition there was a whole mob of extra students – especially girls – from London University colleges evacuated to Cambridge. Off-duty Bomber Command types flocked in from stations in the area, together with Yanks from the 8th US Army Air Force and the brutal and licentious soldiery of every nationality, all packing into the pubs and picture houses and nooks and corners. Oh yes, there were also WAAFs and ATS galore, a wee Scots ambulance driver reputed to dispense favours in the back of her ambulance, conveniently parked on Market Hill, and a Hungarian queer who haunted the public Gents. It was Saturday night in Sodom and Gomorrah, Tilly proclaimed – half in mockery, half in envy – except that every night was Saturday night.

Pickup didn't really enjoy going back there. It reminded him of his first year in King's, the loneliness at first, the feeling of not belonging, the failure to muck in with others which he had never quite overcome. Chris Bright across the landing would sometimes ask him over for coffee when he and his sort-of-sexy girlfriend from Girton had been making music, but they were denizens of another world. Only when he got taken up by Nick Amering and Co. did he become part of a gang, and even that didn't survive the barmy stunt to Germany in their second year.

But, as Tilly had said, an outing could dispel the heebie-jeebies which sometimes lingered on after a trip, no matter how shagged you were. It was a fine evening, late summery rather than autumnal. Sunlight was trying to force a way through the car's grubby little rear window as the pinnacles of King's Chapel loomed up. Tilly kept his thumb on the horn button as he overtook a string of American trucks, releasing it only to give a cheerful V-sign to the officer who scowled at them from the lead Jeep.

In St John's Street they were held up by a motley procession coming towards them. The chaps were dressed in rough garments apparently made from sacking. On their heads were tin basins sprouting horns. They brandished wooden swords and hauled on a rope to which a number of skimpily dressed girls were tied.

'Stone the crows,' said Cobber Ivens, who was Australian but only since his parents had emigrated there when he was twelve, and liked to ham up his halfway Australian accent with picturesque speech and patter. 'Take a look at those half-naked sheilas. What's going on?'

'Bloody students,' said Tilly. He sounded his horn again.

'It's what you would have called a rag, isn't it, Mickup?' said Barney.

'I suppose so.'

'Did you get up to any?'

'God, no. Left it to the silly buggers who thought it was funny to hang chamber pots on the chapel roof, or set rockets whizzing down the streets on Bonfire Night.'

'Either sounds a reasonable laugh to me,' said Cobber.

Pickup flinched. He was being Pilot Officer Prudence again, if not Pilot Officer Prude. He said hurriedly, 'We did hatch one stunt that was pretty stupid. Could have turned out very ropily. As it was, it put one of us in hospital.'

'What did you do?'

'Oh, I'll tell you another time.' He'd gone off the story before he'd even embarked upon it. Luckily, Tilly was already parking the car. Time to go on the town. They had a couple of pints in the Baron of Beef, a meal in the Indian restaurant in whose dustbin, it was said, the remnants of cats had been found, then more beer in the Spread Eagle, where the craze of American airmen was to write their names on the yellowed ceiling with a candle flame.

Barney got into a cross-talk act with a bunch of them, all

lootenants with a full spectrum of ribbons, on the subject of warm versus cold beer. Cobber was attempting to charm a WAAC officer of hard, intimidating good looks on the edge of the same olive-drab group. 'Why the dark blue?' she asked, pinching his tunic sleeve between scarlet-nailed fingers. 'You navy or sump'n?'

'No, merely Australian,' Pickup interjected before Cobber could answer.

Stony stare from the WAAC. Never mind, in this company he had tried. On his own, he would only have wanted to shrink into the uniformity of uniform.

At closing time they found their way back to the car and Tilly pretended that he couldn't remember where he'd hidden the distributor head, dutifully removed on arrival to immobilize the vehicle. It was part of the routine, just as he always slurred, 'Lift me into the driving seat, and I'll get you home.' In fact he had the hardest head in the squadron, but Pickup couldn't help thinking it would be ironic if, twenty-four hours after touching down deep in occupied Europe, he bought it in Cambridgeshire or, worse still, bloody Bedfordshire.

Wedged in the narrow back seat of the Lea-Francis with twelve stone of Cobber, he listened to the Australian's chat and decided that Cobber was a nicer and gentler type than he had assumed, rather insecure about the English growing-up he'd missed and keen to learn about grammar schools and being an air-minded boy. He was rather literal-minded, though. Pickup kept drifting into sleep, only to be woken by loud double-declutchings and the squeal of brakes as Tilly forged along country lanes in the meagre light from masked and paper-dimmed headlights.

Each time he heard Cobber's voice, and made some suitable remark or guffaw. Finally, Cobber was boring on again about this rag that Pickup had mentioned, when someone got hurt. What was it?

'Oh, it was idiotic. There were four of us involved. One of them had a sister who was at school, sort of, in Munich. She had a boyfriend – well, a man-friend, really – whose old teacher was in a concentration camp. We thought it would be a good stunt to get him out.'

15

'Jesus. And did you?'

'No. He got transferred to another camp just before. All we got was the kid who was going to come with him.'

'What were they in for? Jews?'

'No, just queers. Or the teacher, anyway, reading between the lines. The boy was some kind of Bible-basher.' He thought for a moment. 'As it happened, the Jews were getting it as we beetled off back to Cambridge. Shops smashed, synagogues set on fire.' Suddenly he wished the subject had never come up. Own stupid fault.

They went the last mile in silence. Even Tilly had shut up. Only when the other two had sloped off to their billets did he buttonhole Pickup. 'By the way,' he said, except that it didn't sound like an afterthought, 'I'd like a word with you tomorrow. Nine thirty in the hush-hush room.'

Who should be this bearer of monstrous tidings? And how was he to get out of such a fiendishly fenced prison as ours? There was the possibility of one spectacular opportunity, should that come to pass. But even if he escaped then, would he be able to travel any distance? How was he to reach a country beyond Nazi domination? Then all our deliberations were halted by rumours of something quite unexpected, namely that the last remaining Jews in the Warsaw Ghetto had risen against their German oppressors with hidden arms. How excited, how encouraged were our younger men in particular. A mass uprising and escape had long been the dream of all who clung to some precarious function (and therefore life) in Treblinka. The idea had become more pressing as the supply of victims started to falter. When it dried up altogether, we knew, we would ourselves become the last pilgrims along the Road to Heaven, no doubt stripping out the foliage and rolling up the fence wire as we went.

An Organizing Committee had already been set up under the chairmanship of the saintly Dr Chorazycki, who was in charge of the camp hospital. It included all the Hofjuden, *or Jews entrusted by the SS with positions of responsibility. We who had pledged ourselves, above all else, to get word to the world were ardent supporters of the plot while choosing to*

16

remain outside it. The first and not least daunting challenge facing our messenger would be to get out of the camp. Now he could make his escape with all the others. But until that time nothing must connect us with the plotters, lest they be betrayed or discovered.

Tilly was wrestling with the skylight in the dim little room that was kept for confidential huddles with visiting cloak-and-dagger experts. It had no other office opening off it and no window, just this skylight kept permanently blacked out but which could be opened by cranking it with a hook on a long wobbly pole.

'First things first,' he grunted. 'Did you bring back any brandy? Forgot to ask last night.'

'Sorry, none offered.' There were the two bottles of wine, as they turned out to be, the doctor had thrust at him, but Pickup had already earmarked them for the dread weekend with the Winwicks which loomed.

Tilly clattered the hook into the corner and, as if reading Pickup's mind, said, 'I see you've put in for a weekend pass.' There was a hard edge to his voice, not at all the usual Tilly breeziness.

'Why not? The moon period's over, isn't it?' What was afoot that could only be broached in the hush-hush room?

Tilly was making some sort of calculation in his mind, you could see him doing the same at briefings. Then suddenly he would decide, rule yes or no, and that was that. He was staring at Pickup all this time. He said, 'That story you were telling last night about trying to get some chap out of a concentration camp. . . . was it true?'

'Didn't know you were listening.'

'Couldn't help it. So was it true? Did you really have a go?'

'I'm afraid so. It was stupid, arrogant, achieved nothing very much, got people into trouble and could have started the war a year earlier than it did start.'

'That's what I like to hear, bags of British boast.' Now he had established the facts and made up his mind, Tilly was reverting to his usual style. 'Right, your weekend leave is

17

authorized. Having cocked up prospects with the French bit of crumpet, you will no doubt be pole-vaulting off to your Windmill girl.'

'I'm seeing her, yes.' Too late, he wished he'd sounded more enthusiastic. His failure to join in the rude high spirits of the others was doubtless one of the traits the Branch Manager had been moaning about. He added, 'I mean, we're supposed to be going to stay with her folks.' That would cool anyone's ardour.

'But London first?'

'Just to collect her, then we go to their ideal home together.'

'How about going a day early? Travel on a warrant, collect some modest subsistence?'

'Where's the catch?'

'There isn't one. Just see someone about a possible job.'

'Is this an order?'

'Not yet, old boy. Strictly for a willing volunteer.'

Pickup waited.

Tilly lowered his voice, perhaps unconsciously. He said, 'We have been sounded out about a rather different destination from the usual.'

'Holland?'

'Try again.'

'Denmark.'

'Getting warmer.'

'There's nowhere else in Lizzie range. Except Norway, I suppose, if you went from the Shetland Islands.'

'They do that, actually. But by boat. No, this is . . . well, they'll tell you when you see them.'

'Who's them? Which number Baker Street?' Various premises in and around Baker Street housed the different departments of the Special Operations Executive, otherwise SOE, responsible for sabotage, subversion, liaising with resistance forces, supplying them with arms and explosives and generally setting Europe alight, as Mr Churchill had defined it. Most of the squadron's landings and pick-ups were on behalf of SOE.

'Actually, not Baker Street at all,' said Tilly.

'So it's the SIS.' SIS was the Secret Intelligence Service,

18

old-fashioned spies bringing back military secrets. They were rarer.

'Not them either,' said Tilly. 'This lot is something to do with Political Warfare, whatever that means, but they must have had someone navigating them to the right desk in Adastra House. I'll give you the time and place this afto, as Cobber would say.'

'Why me?'

'The finger of God. Remember that film about the ordinary chap who could suddenly work miracles. There was this giant finger of God that came down from Heaven and lit him up for a second. Last night it picked you out, old son.'

II

Tempsford was supposed to be so hush-hush that no one knew of its presence, least of all the Luftwaffe. Hangars and offices were disguised as farm buildings or in some cases adapted from the real barns of Gibraltar Farm, as the site was still known to locals. When aircraft were on dispersal around the perimeter, the illusion was not so thorough. This morning, as the duty truck bore Pickup to the railway station, two of 138 Squadron's Halifaxes were parked out, likewise one of the Liberators the Poles had acquired for the long flight to deliver goods to their homeland. And down on the south side, possibly even visible – he ought to have a look some time – from the Great North Road, was one of 161's little black Lizzies.

Tilly liked to refer to it as Bad Tempers or, in obscure allusion to its operations being governed by the time of the month, Tamponsford or Tampaxford. But it had been home to Pickup for a year and a half now and for all their binding about the Branch Manager, he knew that it was a friendly station and one that encouraged the anonymity – or girlish modesty, as Tilly saw it – which Pickup seemed to crave. It was changing, of course; in wartime, change was the order of the day. The Poles were rumoured to be leaving, Hudsons were due to take over some of the Lysander jobs, carrying up to a dozen Joes at a time, and thirty miles away, at Harrington, the Yanks were muscling in on the parachute-drops traffic with a whole fleet of Liberators. Sooner or later they would want to start landing and picking up people. What would be left for Lysander Air Taxis, as Tilly liked to call the squadron?

Meanwhile, one definitely good thing about Tempsford was its proximity to the railway. What's more, it was the main line

20

to London. Of course – there was always an 'of course' – only a few trains stopped at such an insignificant hole, and never an express. But thanks to some nifty work by the duty driver Pickup caught the early-morning, slightly faster one that got him to King's Cross just before ten. At Piccadilly Circus he whiled away half an hour over a cup of coffee in Joe Lyons before venturing up Great Windmill Street. The queue outside the little theatre was already a good ten yards, and the first show didn't start until twelve noon. Most of them were Yanks, plus a few Raff types who eyed him warily, as if uncertain whether to salute or not. Pickup looked the other way, hoping they wouldn't.

The stage-door keeper said, 'Blimey, you're early, Squadron-Leader. They've only just come in, some of them. They'll be putting on their make-up and that.'

'Just a quick word with her, that's all.'

'Can't let you go up, sir. Not now. Might see something to make you blush. Hang on and I'll try to get a Tannoy call to her. Audrey, isn't it?'

'Anita, she prefers.'

'And you're . . . ?' He was already fiddling with the telephone.

'Michael Pickup.'

She came down clutching a flame-coloured wrap around her, her feet in fluffy slippers, face a smooth mask of some sort of cream, no lipstick or eye-shadow yet.

'Michael! I couldn't believe it when Charlie said your name. But you'll have to be quick – we've got a run-through of the temple dancer number in twenty min. That cow Vanda showed too much yesterday just when Mr Van Damm happened to be out front.'

'Pick you up tonight, after the last show?'

'Silly! It's tomorrow night we're going to Mummy and Daddy's.'

'I know, I know! Had to come up a day early. Got an errand to do. We could go to a nightclub or something.'

'I *can't*! Five shows today, another five tomorrow. I'd be flakers.'

'I'll get you a room at the Arrol. Save you hiking out to your digs.'

21

She made an angry face, with a twitch in the direction of Charlie.

'Your own little room, just for you. No cause for alarm.'

She ignored his sarcasm and said sweetly, 'Must fly, darling. Look forward to tomorrow. Why don't you see the show tonight? The temple dancer number is really lovely.'

Outside, the queue was even longer. Pickup walked back to the Circus and down Haymarket, switching his valise, heavy with the two bottles of wine for the Winwicks, to his right hand. If a dumb ranker threw him one now it would be doubly awkward, indeed an offence should any budding branch manager happen to see him fail to return the salute. So a bloody great oaf of a guardsman just had to snap one up. Pickup gave a sort of nod and hoped for the best. Luckily a number 13 bus was just drawing up at its stop. Pickup boarded it.

Also luckily, Aunty Milly was on duty at the reception desk at the Arrol Hotel. 'Got your telegram,' she hooted. 'What's all this about there might be two of you? What would your mummy say if she knew?'

'It's not like that, actually—'

'Well, I've kept you a nice double, you devil.'

'Sorry, there's only me after all, Aunty.'

She shrugged. 'So, the usual cubby-hole?'

'If you have one.'

'For the Pickup family, always.'

Partly in fun, especially if she wanted to tease her in-laws for their carefulness with money, and partly because she couldn't help it, Milly was wont to drop into the speech rhythms of the Jews who owned the Arrol and accounted for a lot of its clientele. She was the wife of Uncle Mike, the Royal Flying Corps hero of the last war after whom Pickup had been named. He had married her on the rebound from the approved-of young woman who had jilted him once he shed his uniform and reverted to being a traveller in agricultural machinery. Milly was still not altogether approved of, though this did not deter the family from making use of her. When Uncle Mike went back into the Air Force in 1940 Milly had announced that she was going to do war work too, but instead of becoming a FANY and driving an admiral around, like Aunty Jess, she got this job as a hotel receptionist, and even stern Granny Pickup had been known to avail herself of a sit-down and a cup of tea at the Arrol when in town to see her specialist. Milly would always find Pickup a bed, even if it were only – but advantageously when he was broke – in a tiny converted bathroom at half a crown a night.

Tucked away in a side-street between the Strand and the Embankment, it could hardly have been handier for the appointment with the Political Warfare joker, whomsoever he might prove to be. Pickup had time to dump his valise in his room, go to the lavatory, straighten his tie and compose his doubts about a clearly impossible idea. He still had twenty minutes to spare as he left his key at the desk. '*Mazeltov*,' Milly called with a wink. 'You bet,' he said vaguely. It meant good luck or something. He had only to go to Bush House in the Aldwych, not the bits which were occupied by the BBC but a wing which had no signs or name-plates and in the end took some finding. Finally a messenger with a limp led him to a door, tapped on it and stood aside for him to go in.

There was something faintly familiar about the man who half rose behind his desk in greeting, then sat down again and motioned Pickup into a facing chair. He was maybe fifty, old school tie, and he was looking at Pickup through narrowed eyes as if trying to make a positive identification.

'Yes, it is you, isn't it?' He glanced down at a paper on his desk. 'When I saw the name on the signal I must say I wondered.' He looked up. 'You can't place me?'

''Fraid not, sir.'

'How about Munich, November thirty-eight?'

'Of course! You were the British Consul.'

'Consul-General, to be pedantic. But yes. It was at a rather dreary *soirée* for young ladies at a finishing school.'

'Sister of one of us.'

The Consul nodded. 'And the next day another of your little team thoughtfully called to find out if I were going to be in the office should you need to – er, *consult* me. That was an understatement if ever there was one.' He fixed an eye on Pickup again. 'Luckily for all of us, what could have been an almighty diplomatic incident was eclipsed by the *Kristallnacht* business. Mind you, the Germans still put on a great show of outrage at what you'd done. We had the chief of police on the phone. I told him I was too busy trying to tone down a report for our government on the shameful scenes we had witnessed in the streets to bother about some petty student escapade. Jewish citizens driven from their homes, their shop windows smashed, their synagogue in flames, laid it on thick. He took the hint, probably the only high-up who would have. Of course, they didn't want to admit that someone had actually been spirited out of Dachau. There was that, too.'

He offered Pickup a cigarette from a silver box and took one himself. On the wall behind him hung a map of northern Europe which Pickup recognized as a War Map put out by one of the papers, probably the *Daily Telegraph*, in the very first days of the war. Except for some hatching across Czechoslovakia and Poland all the old frontiers, all the old countries, were still there, a different colour for each.

'One more point before we move on to more immediate matters,' said the Consul. 'The man you had intended to get away was classed as a political, I believe?'

'Or perhaps a queer. Sounded a bit like one to us.'

'Think not, actually. But in neither case was he there as a Jew?'

'No. He'd taught at the university. Got into trouble for his views.'

'And the young chap who did escape was a Jehovah's Witness, but again not one of Jehovah's chosen. He gave himself up, by the way. Did you hear that?'

Pickup shook his head.

'Something about it being God's will that he should suffer with the other Earnest Bible Students, as they call themselves in Germany. No doubt the guards beat the poor kid to a pulp as soon as he was returned to them.' He exhaled a delicate plume of smoke. 'Release from a concentration camp affects people in unexpected ways. There was a businessman, in quite a small way, who contrived some kind of deal, in effect bought his way out. Old contacts he'd dealt with put up the required dollars and pounds. He came here as a refugee but six months later drew the curtains of his bed-sitter and turned on the gas tap. Couldn't stand the guilt he felt. He'd written it all down. Gollancz or someone got hold of it and published it, but people didn't want to read that sort of thing.' He paused, as if considering his own assertion.

Pickup remembered how they had tracked down a scarecrow figure lately released from Dachau when they were planning the stunt. Smuggled him into Nick's home in Chelsea and got him to tell them about the layout of the camp. Could it have been the same man? He was about to chip in when the Consul resumed.

'He was rather prescient, too. Foresaw the day when the camps would no longer be just nasty prisons, but execution centres to eliminate all those reckoned not to fit into the Aryan dream. Which means the Jews, mainly.' He fixed his eyes on Pickup's. 'Or don't you believe all that?'

'I don't know.' It was the honest truth. He didn't. Anthony Eden had made a statement in Parliament, a good while ago now. Other bits in the newspapers. And on one of his landings in France, near Lyon, the Gaston had been muttering about the deportation of local Jews . . . but that was to forced labour in Germany, Pickup had understood, nothing about them being killed.

'Of course you don't,' the Consul was saying. 'No one knows. Because no one can believe the unbelievable. Reason rejects it.' He opened a folder on the desk and turned over a couple of documents before passing a half-plate photograph to Pickup. It was familiar RAF aerial photography, such as they studied for plotting routes across the French coast or identifying landing fields, except that this was high-altitude stuff and pretty smudgy. There was some kind of camp or, rather, a pair of linked camps, enclosed by a fence with watchtowers, just as they had looked – but much closer, much sharper – in the clandestine sailplane shots of Dachau they'd pored over five years ago. There were tiny, tidy rows of huts, and down towards one corner a mysterious geometric pattern.

'Where is this?' he asked.

'Poland. North of, and not too far east. Even so, just about the absolute limit for the Photo Reconnaissance chaps. It's called Treblinka. There are bigger and possibly more sinister establishments down towards Czechoslovakia, but out of range at present. When we get farther up Italy it ought to be possible to reach them from there. Meanwhile, Treblinka will have to do.'

The geometric feature that had caught Pickup's eye was too small and not distinct enough to be identified, but it looked a bit like an array of the elementary steel trusses whose strength he'd had to calculate in Theory of Structures at Cambridge. They were just laid on the ground in parallel, one, two, three . . . six of them, each a good hundred feet long, maybe more. He looked up questioningly.

The Consul handed him another photograph. 'This is it working.'

It was the same location, but an even smudgier view, in fact mostly obscured by smoke rising from the structures and swirling towards the left of the frame. Where there were gaps in the smoke the rails were now hidden by what looked like tiny tick-marks. As Pickup peered at them, the Consul handed him a magnifying glass. It made the picture hellish grainy but the ticks became maggots, piled-up heaps of maggots, writhing, melting, burning.

'Are they . . . ?' Pickup began but didn't complete.

The Consul nodded. 'Yes, the local industry. Burning the dead. They are laid across steel rails supported on concrete blocks or something like that, and fires lit below. Wood, even brushwood, I'm told. The body fats do the rest. That photograph was taken – let me see – in May. The one without anything happening was only last week, September twentieth to be exact.'

He handed this photograph back to Pickup. 'Now, look up to the right. The field with the shadowy lines running across it. Did you know that archaeologists use aerial photographs? Old earthworks that have long disappeared still show up from the air. These, in fact, are recent earthworks but it's the same principle. They are trenches – big trenches, at least four metres deep and six wide. We believe they were full of corpses, thousands of 'em, from before they had the burning programme. Just shot or asphyxiated and tumbled in. Then about eight months ago there was a decision to dig them all up again and burn them, as well as all fresh supplies coming in. The fires burned night and day for a few months, so much so that smoke and smuts blotted out the sun. Likewise the moon. Your chaps dropping supplies to the Poles reported it, which is what put us on to the place.'

His eye held Pickup's. 'Can you accept that?'

Pickup nodded dumbly.

'Even if I tell you to multiply that process by a factor of twenty or thirty or forty? We may be talking about *millions*. The wiping out of an entire race. Not just Polish Jews, but from all over Europe. And now the pits are nearly all filled in and turfed over, some buildings been set fire to, others gone altogether, as if they're getting rid of the evidence.' He glanced at his watch. 'I suggest we now break for a spot of lunch. I've booked a table across the road at Simpson's, if that's all right by you.'

On the way, before they would have to converse guardedly about nothing much, Pickup said, 'You said there was a decision to dig up those buried dead. About eight months ago. How do we know?'

The Consul frowned. 'Intercepted enemy signal. Can't say more.'

Pickup had been to Simpson's-in-the-Strand once before, with Uncle Mike, when he was seventeen and had just hatched the idea of trying for Cambridge. Uncle Mike thought university was a waste of time and had set out, Pickup suspected, to show him the desirable grown-up world of business deals and expense accounts. Simpson's was famous for its great roast joints, brought to the table on a heated trolley, under a shiny hood which the carver flipped open to slice into the smoking meat, and was then rewarded with a silver coin. A brave lone diner might get away with a threepenny bit; a sixpence was better, a shilling if there was more than one or two of you. In wartime, of course, it was pot luck and smaller helpings, but the aroma from the trolley, as the carver sharpened his knife, was rich enough. The hood was opened and – O Christ! It looked like a whole pig, or what was left of one.

Smoking, crackling, melting, it could have been a giant enlargement of one of the maggot-figures in the photograph. A horrible joke of the Consul's? Or some stupid trick-cyclist's test? No, the Consul was busy conferring with the carver, a shilling ready between finger and thumb. And the joint was a leg of pork, not a whole piglet. It had been his bloody imagination, as usual, plus feeling sick and dreading whatever proposition all this was leading up to or, rather, having to make a decision on how to respond to it. He took a swallow of beer and reached for a chunk of bread.

By the beginning of May the rumours from Warsaw had turned sour. The Nazis were said to have sent in an SS division with tanks and guns to clear the Ghetto block by block, kill or capture the rebels and raze the buildings. Confirmation soon followed in the shape of daily transports of survivors reaching the camp. Many were shot or clubbed to death on arrival, so outraged were our Ukrainians by the very thought that miserable Jews should have turned on the masters they themselves served so doggedly – we could only hope these creatures would never guess what was being planned here in Treblinka. All but one of the remainder were sent along the Road to Heaven, though not before they had been able to yell or whisper stories of the days of defiance before the Germans could retaliate, and of the fierce rearguard action from cellar to cellar, ruin to ruin, when the stormtroopers at last burned and blasted their way into the Ghetto. As we sifted through their clothing, and what pathetic possessions they had been able to seize, our fingers were greased with blood.

Back in the office in Bush House the Consul came to the point at once. 'You may be wondering why no Jews have come forward to proclaim to the world what is being done to them. The obvious answer is that those who know the whole truth are behind the wire themselves. In fact, it has been known for people to escape from the camps. The insuperable difficulty is then to get out of Poland or Czechoslovakia or wherever and reach our side.'

It was on the tip of Pickup's tongue to bust in there and

then. If the Consul was about to propose a pick-up, that was plain impossible. A Liberator of 138 or the Polish flight, especially, could get to Poland and back again, just about, but it was way beyond 161's range, even in a Hudson, thank God. He decided not to interrupt. The Consul was saying that just one escaper had made it to the Allies, not from Treblinka actually, but a camp a good way south of there, Belzec. Apparently, he was just a workman, not very eloquent and certainly not eminent. No one took much heed of what he had to say, though the PWE had been glad to make use of it when briefing the Foreign Secretary for his statement to the House. There were also couriers who travelled between the Polish Resistance and the Polish government here. As he could imagine, their journeys were difficult, dangerous and could take months. One of them claimed to have visited both Treblinka and Belzec, disguised as a policeman or Latvian guard or whatever. According to the London Poles, unfortunately, there were some discrepancies in his account of the two places . . .

The Consul paused. 'What I am about to tell you now is extremely sensitive and extremely secret. You understand?'

'I shall forget every word.'

'Good. In this department we have established our own somewhat intricate links with the Polish Home Army and other Resistance groups. If from rather different motives, so has a Swedish humanitarian body with whom we exchange information. They told us of a cell up towards Danzig which operated a little escape line through Gdynia, or Gotenhafen as the Germans have rechristened it. That's the big seaport along the gulf, and it's from there the Germans ship coal to Sweden in exchange for oil.' He made a small grimace. 'We won't go now into the question of how and where the Swedes get that oil. Suffice to say that a hell of a lot of coal is involved in the deal, and it all has to be loaded on to the vessels they send to collect it. The Germans were soon using slave labour to do the donkey work.

'The cell we're talking about set up a stevedoring outfit to insinuate couriers, escapers, anyone on the run, into the pool of slave workers. Provided them with forged identity papers, all that sort of thing. Then it was up to the chap to stow away in the hold, give himself up when they were well out at sea, and with luck be put ashore in Sweden. If the captain was a shit, and turned back, he was out of luck, of course.' He held a moment of silence before resuming.

'We tried to get word into Treblinka about this – apparently there is a sort of permanent staff of skilled or trusted Jews who service the camp – but they have absolutely no contact with the outside world. All we could do was pass the message on to a few key contacts in the Resistance or the Jewish ghettoes in case they ended up in a camp themselves, poor devils. Which is exactly what started to happen, as things turned out. The Warsaw Ghetto was cleared – razed to the ground, indeed – and the whole population transported to Treblinka.

'Then something happened in the camp itself. We can't be sure, but it may have been some sort of uprising, hence the burned buildings in the more recent of those photographs you saw. Certainly some prisoners got away, and eventually – well, just the other day – we heard from the Swedes that three escaped Jews had reached the Danzig cell. At least one of them –' he permitted himself a wry smile – 'was of the eminence desired.'

The smile vanished with his next words. 'The message ended with the news that they had lost contact with the stevedoring people in Gdynia. It is only temporarily, we hope, but for the time being we have to face the possibility of having our eminent Jew at loose in northern Poland and no way of getting him out ...'

Pickup was already shaking his head blindly. 'Not a hope. The big boys can get there and back on a drop, but they can't put down, much less take off again. A Lysander would barely reach the place, let alone get back.' Even a Hudson couldn't manage the return trip, he guessed privately, and anyway it would need a big field—

'Ah! You are assuming I had in mind an operation from this country.'

'Where else is there, sir?'

Without turning his head, the Consul pointed back over his shoulder at the map behind him. 'This is what I meant when

I told you it is a sensitive, as well as secret, matter. We're talking about Sweden again. From the south of Sweden it's a relatively short hop across the narrow end of the Baltic. That may sound a flight of fancy to you, and with reason. Sweden is neutral and goes to great lengths to maintain its neutrality. The Press, the broadcasting service, even the cinemas are required to be impartial. But beneath this equable surface, of course, lurk differing loyalties.'

He passed the silver cigarette box again. Pickup took one automatically. The whole thing was getting too barmy for words.

'There is still, I'm afraid,' the Consul continued, 'quite a substantial section of public opinion which would like to see a German victory. In the last year, however, there has been a growing awareness of the racial persecution and, indeed, racial extermination being practised by the Nazis. Escapers arrive from Denmark or Norway, bringing news of what's going on under the occupation in these countries. Swedish businessmen are no longer free to visit Germany. The rumours mount up. All of which has produced a third party, you might say, which doesn't support either side but is anxious to help any humanitarian efforts.' He paused. 'Such as smuggling out an eminent witness to the full horrors.'

Pickup was waiting for that. 'And we are supposed to land a black Lysander in their country – about as easy to disguise as a witch on a broomstick – fill it up with fuel, buzz over to Poland to pick up this guy, and hope to struggle home with him?'

'No,' said the Consul shortly. Pickup sensed that his mood was changing. 'There is an aircraft already in Sweden which is at our disposal. It will be given RAF markings and a legitimate RAF number. The pilot will wear his RAF uniform, so that no accusations of espionage can be made should anything go wrong. Nor will it be necessary to fly the witness back to this country. Sweden would provide the ideal platform for him to do his stuff.'

All so neat. And so remote from the realities of how they worked. 'I was told that this job would be strictly for a volunteer,' Pickup blurted.

The Consul looked at him bleakly. 'Of course,' he said. 'If, as I sense, you don't have much confidence in the plan, I am sure that we will have no difficulty in finding someone who does, but time is running short.'

'It's just that I'd need to know more about the details,' Pickup heard himself saying, his voice lacking moral fibre in every syllable. 'What aeroplane is it, for a start?'

'A Stinson, I'm told. American. Our American friends have arranged a quick familiarization course, no questions asked, for anyone we send them. I suggest you do that anyway – I'll give you the details in a moment. But you may sleep on the proposal before giving me your answer. In fact, take the weekend if you like.'

Eureka! It was as if a heavy weight was lifted. Pickup's spirits soared. The whole weekend before he need make a decision, and anything could have happened by then.

'But I must know Monday morning, first thing.'

It was Pickup's turn to say it. 'Of course.'

'It would be rather fitting if you did take it on,' said the Consul. 'Almost as if the Almighty had earmarked you for the job.'

Which was what Tilly had said, more or less. We'll see, Pickup thought.

The transport of survivors from the Warsaw Ghetto uprising continued during the month of May. If any more were press-ganged as workers, it was to the unenviable gang who toiled in the Todeslager *or death-camp itself, at the other end of the Road to Heaven. They were confined to that area and not allowed to mix with other prisoners Their task was to drag the dead from the gas-chambers, clean up after them and manhandle the corpses on to the incinerator grills. In slack periods they would dig up old bodies. Except for a small specialist group who extracted all gold or silver teeth and crowns from the mouths of the dead, their lot was hard phys-ical labour, brutally terminated as soon as they weakened or fell ill.*

By comparison, life in the Lower Camp was shamefully easy, even relatively secure. By now the one early arrival from the Ghetto to be singled out had joined us on the scavenging team. He was a man of resolute manner who confided that he was the journalist Leo Spyra, a name some of us remembered from former times. He had edited an underground news-sheet, and played a leading part in the revolt – the Germans had apparently failed to realize that here was a captive they would have liked to torture for information. With our mission much in our minds but so far not disclosed to him, we sought to learn all he could tell us about existence beyond the wire. How effective was the Resistance, for instance?

He replied ruefully that some groups schemed against each other as much as they schemed against the enemy. Nor were all of them sympathetic towards the Jews. Many Poles remained as anti-semitic as they, or for that matter the Germans, had been prior to 1939. On the credit side, there was one underground organization which existed only to urge non-Jewish Poles to help us. Thanks to its influence and, one should add, the true Christianity of many Polish Christians, some thousands of Jews had been able to avoid the ghettoes altogether and led sheltered lives in the country, or in non-Jewish quarters of the cities. Children were adopted into Christian households.

How about travel? we enquired. Could one move about the country? Was it safe to board the trains? With the right documents, he said, it was at least possible. The best recourse was to be able to pass as a slave-worker of the Germans. He had known one young man armed with such an identity who regularly hopped aboard the German troop trains going to and from the Russian Front. Paradoxically, these were less rigorously policed than the civilian trains.

It was at this point that Marek interjected, 'One can cross frontiers, then?'

Spyra was at first puzzled by the question, so Marek rephrased it. 'That is, might a fugitive cross from Poland to another country?'

Spyra shrugged. To reach Czechoslovakia was not too difficult, nor Lithuania, but in either case it would be merely to exchange one province of Hell for another.

And to the north, towards what had briefly been the Polish

33

outlet to the sea, now back in the German Reich . . . ? I was suddenly afraid that Marek's questions would betray our dream. After all, we had no proof that Spyra was who he said he was. How strange that such a thorn in the German flesh had not been recognized. But Spyra was studying us intently. At last he said, 'If it is Sweden you are meaning, I know how to contact an organization which has succeeded in smuggling a number of escapers aboard the ships which carry coal from Gdynia to that country.'

This was news indeed! We looked at each other in wonderment. The last and most difficult obstacle to our plan suddenly seemed surmountable.

'Yep, this is the Stinson L-5,' a lanky, laconic Technical Sergeant informed Pickup, 'L standing for Liaison, five because that's where they've got to in numbering Piper Cubs and Beechcraft and other Sunday fliers' airplanes drafted into the army. The L-5 came outa the Stinson Voyager, and is one of the better ones. Hell, it's the best. They've doubled up the power, that's a one-eight-five horsepower Lycoming out front, the airframe is tougher and the landing gear a whole deal more rugged. In the Pacific they're flying them off 'n' on everything from coral sands to steel-plate strips lashed to the tree-tops. Or so they tell us.'

The Americans had laid on a Jeep to take Pickup out to Bovingdon in Herts. Riding by the side of the driver, looking ahead over the stubby flat bonnet, attracting interested glances from people they passed, especially girls, made a nice Saturday morning outing. Pickup pushed aside the ultimate purpose of the exercise and let himself enjoy it for its own sake.

Bovingdon turned out to be a kind of depot for every kind of US aircraft, from Liberators and B-17s down to the spotter and communications planes the sergeant was appraising. The Stinson certainly looked a bit sturdier than the others. There were two seats in the front of the little cabin, with full dual controls, one seat in the rear. Pickup zipped himself into borrowed overalls. The sergeant waved him into the left-hand seat, officially the first pilot's, and talked him through the starting drill. They taxied round to the runway. Take-off took about 200 yards, Pickup estimated, which was pretty good. They did a few circuits and bumps, then climbed higher to try stalling and then a few steep turns. Neither offered any problems. Coming in for the last time, Pickup cut the landing run down to only seventy, maybe eighty yards, which was really good.

'Sure,' said the sergeant. 'You can fly an L-5 in and out of a nigger's backyard.'

'But how about the Voyager, the civvy version?' – there was always a *but*. The sergeant scratched his nose. 'Haven't had personal experience of that one. Landing roll shouldn't be any different, but I guess the take-off run would be longer, specially with a full load.'

'How much longer?'

'Depends on the engine. Most of them had a Franklin of no more'n eighty horsepower. Like I said, they doubled that for the military. More than doubled it. You could use a thousand feet, maybe twelve hundred.'

A quarter of a mile! 'Thanks,' said Pickup. That settled it. He would say no to the Consul on Monday. Meanwhile there was nothing organized to take him back to London. The Transportation Officer was apologetic, it was Saturday afternoon, all the spare drivers were off base. Pickup got a lift, eventually, to Berkhamsted station. From Euston he took the Underground to Charing Cross, collected his valise from the Arrol, had a bite to eat with Aunty Milly and then strolled through the blackout to the Windmill. They were into the last show of the day, the queues had finally dispersed, and only Pickup knew that you might sneak in unchallenged and see the last few numbers scot free.

He found a seat right at the end of a row, which he didn't mind. The spectacle was always directed at the centre seats, Audrey had told him, and vetted for propriety from the same quarter. From an oblique viewpoint you might glimpse a sliver of flesh you were not intended to see. It was the temple dancer number he was curious to watch, after Audrey's remarks about it. Scuffing noises while the curtains were closed signalled that something more elaborate and possibly more 'artistic' was being set up. The trio of musicians in the tiny pit launched into an oriental number, the curtain rose and after some preliminary shimmying around by the chorus girls and pansies the lights dimmed for Vanda, or whatever her name was.

And cor, she was rather special – long dark hair, or probably a long dark wig, huge black eyes, dusky skin, lots of jewels, virtually naked under transparent shawls she gradually shed. If you needed to pretend that you were appreciating art, she really was graceful and sinuous, and doing elegant things with her arms and hands. At the same time she was sexy, teasing, promising. Which, as the old joke said, made things hard for the wife or girlfriend. Though probably in vain in the case of Audrey Winwick.

III

The Winwicks lived in Surrey or Sussex, Pickup could never remember which, but the railway station was Three Bridges or possibly Four Bridges, anyway n Bridges where n was an integer smaller than 10. As the train from Victoria creaked through the night he had to suppress a furtive longing for whatever London might have offered, or come to that, Tempsford. He peered at his watch. Still only half ten. Tilly and Co. might be beating round Cambridge again. Or if in the mess, singing rude songs and leaping over the furniture. Well, he could do without that. And if it emerged that he had foregone a weekend with a Windmill girl just to be with the boys, he would be counted very wet. Whatever else, Audrey was an enviable judy to be seen out with: silky blonde hair, pretty face, film-star legs. A Windmill company had taken a show to Tangmere back in the spring and one of Pickup's unfulfilled ambitions was that they would do the same for Tampers, with Audrey – or rather, Anita – prominent. He had taken Tilly to the Mill once, and afterwards she had not only gone out with them but brought a friend called Valerie along to make up a foursome. Why was it never like that when he was on his own?

He glanced down at her, curled up by his side in a pose that said: Poor me, exhausted after six days on the trot, five performances a day, don't you dare try anything. She was still a good-looker, bits of the blonde hair escaping from her headscarf, long legs tucked under the seat. Her expression, though, was the forbidding one he knew too well. He wondered if she were really asleep, the few times he had seen her definitely asleep her face had been soft and sweet.

He fumbled for another cigarette as unobtrusively as

possible, just in case. At least the weekend put off the moment when he had to face Tilly and tell him what a pointless, suicidal operation the Polish pick-up would be. He would probably agree, especially as he had never shown any regard for Jews. Didn't he always say of his Lea-Francis that he'd bought it from its Hebrew owner partly to save it from going to another Yid? But there was always the risk, with Tilly, that he might jump the other way. Looking for volunteers was a lousy idea. Orders were orders, that was easier all round. If Tilly was assuming your willingness and you said the wrong thing, there could be a faint curl of the lip, a chill 'I see.'

Mr Winwick was waiting at the station for them, just as he had the time before. His car was parked outside again, an Armstrong-Siddeley with an official sticker on the windscreen and never any shortage of petrol, because Winwick had a wartime government job. He was in charge of all the meat supplies in the county or something like that. He kissed Audrey and extended a wary hand in Pickup's direction. 'You're not favouring battledress this time then, Michael?'

Was he in his narky official mood or putting on the heavy-handed jocularity which was even harder to bear? Pickup played safe and answered, 'No, not tonight, sir.' The previous time he'd been asked for the weekend, back in July, had happened to fall just when he was on his way back from an operation. It had seemed sensible to leave the Lizzie at Tangmere and make the short journey to the Winwicks from there, though the Branch Manager, needless to say, had subsequently disagreed. Mr Winwick, for his part, had seemed quite put out. Officers should be in Service Dress, especially when they went to church on Sunday morning.

'Still on, er, communications, is it?' he now asked, as he steered through dark streets, the Armstrong's weird transmission system sighing like a love-sick WAAF.

'Afraid so, Mr Winwick.'

'I remember you saying you were hoping for a transfer to Mosquitoes, wasn't it?'

'Ah, that would be wizard, but nothing has come through yet.' He reached for Audrey's hand and squeezed it to stop her from butting in. Not that he had ever told her what he really did in the RAF, but she must have got some idea from meeting Tilly that time, and hearing their bits of shop and eyeing Tilly's ribbons. She would know, at least, that there was a bit more to it than stooging round delivering senior officers to Group Headquarters and bundles of bumf to RAF Little Wittering. But she left it at that. Winwick, in contrast, was positively nosy. No doubt it was this poacher-turned-gamekeeper job he had or, to be precise, butcher-turned-bureaucrat. Audrey once let slip that he'd had his own shop – indeed, three shops – and still did, except that they were ostensibly run by her Uncle Derek, while Daddy snooped around like a Gauleiter, directing the apportionment of lamb chops and sausages and making sure that everyone observed the rationing regulations. Despite which, it was a safe bet that there would be a whopping great joint for Sunday dinner tomorrow. Old Scrag-ends ought to be pleased with the wine in Pickup's hold-all.

Old Scrag-ends chose this moment to grunt a request to Audrey. 'Oh, Audrey dear, we've got a Home Guard turn-out tomorrow morning, so if you could help your mother with the table and so forth –'

'Of course, Daddy,' but in her frailest frail voice.

'I shall be bringing the company commander back, all being well, and Mrs Kerr will find her own way to us, so we shall be six.'

'*Yes*, Daddy.'

The moon was just showing up, mistily, if Pickup peered up through his window. Well on the wane now. Ten days before they would be thinking about ops again. Unless . . . unless lunar phases altered as you flew East or West, like sunrise and sunset popping up sooner or later than if you had stayed put, hence the different time zones round the globe. Must find out. No, no point. The job wasn't on. It was crazy.

As may be imagined, the defeat of the Warsaw Ghetto revolt prompted much argument about the armed uprising and escape from Treblinka that our leadership planned. The hotheads were all for launching it without further ado. The pessimists were for abandoning the idea altogether. What chance would unarmed skeletons have against the tanks and artillery the Germans seemed able to whistle up at will? Then a piece of good fortune came along to change the odds dramatically. I have mentioned the cottage the SS built within the camp, indeed in the street between our two lines of huts, and how it reminded us – save for being absurdly elongated – of Hansel and Gretel. It turned out, as I said, to be an armoury and magazine, presumably in obedience to some bureaucratic decree that such premises must be close to hand in case of need, but not where German lives would be endangered in the event of accidental explosion. Our stroke of luck was a dumb Ukrainian managing to damage the lock on one of the doors. Old Czeslaw, by trade a locksmith, was ordered to repair it. He did not find it too difficult to take a moulding of the key and make a copy. The camp warriors would at least have weapons. Indeed, a group of youngsters removed two boxes of grenades, to be distributed among selected conspirators for use in the first moments of the revolt. The grenades proved to lack firing pins and the boxes were returned, fortunately before their absence had been noticed.

Even so, our messenger now had an enhanced opportunity to make his escape from the camp with all the others. If he could reach Gdynia, there lay the possibility of the collier to Sweden. Spyra, now trusted even by me, had passed on all the contact details he knew. Between start and finish there still lay the no man's land of ravaged Poland and many leagues of what had been the 'Polish Corridor' to the sea and now was once more Prussia. How that might be traversed was another matter.

Pickup woke next morning from the stupid dream he'd had, on and off, since infancy. He knew exactly where it came from, a children's story he'd loved but feared in which boys and girls ventured into Witchland to rescue someone and only escaped again thanks to a giant bird which carried them all out on its back. It must have been a long journey because there was a picture of it lying exhausted and maybe dying on the ground, a sort of prehistoric bird with a long neck, and the children standing sorrowfully around him, one of them cradling its head. In the dream the bird was always about to set off and Pickup could hear the other kids calling him, but for one obstacle or another was unable to hurry to the scene. He couldn't get his clothes on, or sort out some toys or bits of paper or guns he had to take, or there were witches or snakes or a rushing river in the way, or his feet were stuck in thick gluey mud.

It wasn't difficult to guess what had prompted it this time. Well, it needn't have bothered. If anyone did have to go on a wild Jews chase it wouldn't be Pilot Officer Prudence. He screwed his eyes shut against the light stealing into the room where he'd tugged the blackout curtains aside to open the window and have a last smoke and wonder what Audrey would do if he sneaked into her room, unfortunately one floor down, next to Mummy and Daddy. As before, they'd put him in a dormer room up in the roof which had been the evacuees' room before the Winwicks had been exempted in 1941 because of Mrs Winwick's nerves. There was a spare room, but it was rather large and they thought Michael would be more comfortable up in the boys' room, eh? He opened his eyes again and reached for his watch. Seven twenty. Somebody was moving about, downstairs. Sounded like heavy boots, presumably Mr Winwick off on his Home Guard call-out. If the Germans actually invaded, they might not be helpful enough to advise date and time in advance. But mustn't be sarcastic, least of all about the Winwicks.

He must have dozed off again, because the next he knew Mrs Winwick was putting a cup of tea on the bedside table. 'Ah, you're awake,' she said. 'Wasn't sure if you would want to be disturbed. I'm going to leave poor darling Audrey to sleep as long as I can. Mr Van Damm works them so hard at the theatre, you know. Breakfast at nine, if that's not too late.' She gave him a fierce smile and was gone. He heard her go down the stairs, then her footsteps fading as she tip-toed past Audrey's door. Shoes, not slippers. And she was quite dressed up, dark blue costume and blouse. Could she be going to early communion? Now he thought about it, she had the time before, leaving Mr Winwick to take Audrey and Pickup to the eleven o'clock service while she got on with the dinner. Down in the bowels of the house a door closed. Pickup slipped out of bed and across to the window. It overlooked the back garden. There was another in the bend of the stairs. He was just in time to spot her heading briskly down the road in hat and gloves, carrying what could be a prayer book.

He started off down the rest of the stairs, remembered something, nipped back to grab a packet of Frenchies and slung his airforce-blue macintosh round his shoulders in lieu of a dressing gown. Should he tap on the door first or simply creep in? He turned the handle softly and pushed. Inside, it was quite dark except for the patch of daylight from the door. It lit up the spread of golden hair on the pillow, the quarter of her face that she hadn't covered with the sheet, the pale, beautiful arm she had reached out to draw up the sheet and hadn't retracted before she fell asleep again. She was breathing sweetly. A faint, disturbing, girly scent hung in the air. He memorized the outline of the bed, closed the door behind him and worked his way silently round to its far side.

All he had to do now was drop the mac and slide in beside her –

She didn't actually say anything, but she awoke with a galvanic reflex that was the equivalent of a shriek in any language. With a flash of bare leg she was out of the bed and out of the room. Pickup caught up with her as she thrust her parents' door open and looked within.

'They're out, they're both out!' For some reason he was whispering.

She turned and stared at him in disbelief.

'Honestly. I just saw your mum go. To church, I think.'

She shook her head wildly.

'And I heard your father leave earlier, on his Home Guard thing.'

She screamed at last. 'It's not that! Or not just that. How dare you think you could just . . . *barge in*. Without so much as a by-your-leave.'

Even as he felt a pang of shame he couldn't help thinking it was a funny old-fashioned turn of phrase. 'I thought it would be a nice surprise,' he said, hoping to make her laugh. But she shook her head again, big slow shakes.

'Just because I'm at the Windmill it doesn't mean I'm a tart, you know!'

'And you know that I've never ever supposed that you were, or for that matter any of your—'

'It means the opposite, as a matter of fact.'

Too bloody true it did, if Audrey or Anita Winwick was typical. He allowed himself to look at her as a Windmill girl, the light from her parents' open door stealing just enough through her nightie to limn the outlines of her body. He put on a boyish smile and took a step towards her. Her hands went instinctively to the vee of the neckline. Her voice was sharp. 'Not now, Michael.'

'Why not?'

'I just said why. Anyway, Mummy or Daddy could be back any second. Last time there was a Home Guard call-out he was back for breakfast.'

'I thought he said he'd be bringing the company commander back for lunch.'

'Then there is Mummy. The communion service doesn't take very long.'

He pointed to his watch. 'If it's at eight, it's hardly started yet.'

'And you expect me to . . . to get up to things while my mother is taking communion?'

He could have laughed a bitter larf but didn't. Just looked abject, which turned out to be rather a good move. She unstiffened and said, 'What you can do, if you like, is run me a bath while I find something to wear.'

She fluttered past him leaving another trace, now mocking, of something in the air. Pickup went into the bathroom and turned on the hot tap and put in the plug, added a handful of bath-salts from a jar of them, thought of something and nipped upstairs to fetch his toilet bag and razor. When he came down again he looked first into Audrey's room. The curtains were drawn now but she wasn't there. He went back into the bathroom, peeling off his pyjama jacket as he went. He'd lathered his face and was half-shaven by the time he heard the lavatory flush next door.

'Oh, will you be long?' He could see her in the mirror as

she hesitated at the bathroom door, eyes wide at the sight of his broad, muscular back, I don't think – skinny and pimply, more like.

'No, just finishing.'

She felt the water in the bath and added a splash of cold.

'Hope it's not more than five inches,' he said. You were supposed not to use more than that.

'I don't care if it is. I've earned it. Now, if you don't mind –'

'Don't worry about me. I'm blind without my glasses.'

'Promise you'll go then.'

'Cross my heart.'

She stepped into the bath with her back to him and, crossing her arms, slipped the night-dress over her head. Even with the outline of the lavatory seat still pink on her bottom, the sight took his breath away. He said, 'You're beautiful,' and the words came out all husky. She turned round to show pale breasts and down below, what could never be revealed at the Windmill, under pain of excommunication. She smiled her holy smile.

'You see, it can be nice, it doesn't have to be all mucky. Shut the door behind you as you go.'

Mrs Kerr, the company commander's wife, arrived first, in a Morris Oxford, a thin woman who retained a thin Scottish accent. Winwick and her husband clattered in ten minutes later. Major Kerr looked huge in a battledress whose trousers were either too short or so hoiked up by his braces that they dived straight into his brief leather gaiters – as opposed to the webbing variety that full-time pongos wore – without any discernible turn-over. He had a big head, greying hair and a medal ribbon on his chest, ahead of the usual Great War ones, which Pickup didn't recognize. He shook Pickup's hand and made some excuse for being in uniform while quite obviously tickled pink by the crowns on his shoulder-straps.

Though what was left of Winwick's hair was untouched by grey, his single pip as a second-lieutenant couldn't but look incongruous. In the ordinary army they were only seen on newly commissioned boys of eighteen or nineteen. He and Kerr had evidently been discussing the matter, because Kerr told Mrs Winwick to have her needle and thread ready, he was going to ring up the adjutant again first thing in the morning. It seemed that Winwick was already the local platoon commander, his predecessor having been moved to the Manchester office of his firm, but promotion was slow in coming through.

Pickup sipped his large, warm Gin and French and wished he had braved Winwick's displeasure and brought civvies. It would have given him extra sneaky satisfaction to be out of uniform altogether while meat-commissar and building-society manager stood in hairy battledress, big boots planted in the carpet, and talked of the war. Never mind, his pristine Austin Reed service dress and absence of medal ribbons were the next best thing. He knew deep-down that it *was* sneaky, a kind of inverted showing-off, but he positively enjoyed the secrecy about the job that you were supposed to practise at all times in Special Duties. Most of them shot some kind of line. He liked being thought of as just a ferry pilot or whatever, stooging around out of harm's way while actually being involved in Biggles-type adventures –

Audrey's elbow was digging into him. He followed her gaze. Kerr was looking quizzically across the table in his direction. 'Sorry, I was miles away.'

'I was saying that my sister's boy Jamie is with the Pathfinders now, on his third tour of operations.'

'He's done awfully well,' chipped in Mrs Kerr. 'A wing-commander at twenty-six.'

'DSO and two DFCs. They fly Mosquitoes.'

'Ah, Michael here was hoping to get acquainted with that species,' said Winwick with a jocularity that Pickup sensed was barbed.

'Gosh, yes. Photo-reconnaissance I was after, actually. For the Pathfinders, as you'll know, you need to have done a tour, or a couple of tours, in bombers already.'

Kerr nodded.

'But I've heard nothing,' Pickup went on quickly, before Winwick could get in again. 'For my sins, I'm just a taxi-driver.'

'Communications,' Winwick said.

'Taxi-driver,' said Pickup.

'So what *do* you fly?' It was Kerr, his question like a pistol shot.

'Oh, all sorts.'

'Such as?'

Pickup hesitated.

'Come on!'

'Well, yesterday it was a little American plane. A Stinson.'

'You didn't tell me,' Audrey yelped from by his side. 'You said you had been moping around town all day.'

Bloody hell, what now? 'It was a couple of hours familiarization, that's all.'

No one said anything. He blundered on about the amusing Yank who'd taken him up, until the situation was saved by Mrs Winwick coming in to summon everyone to the dining room. Audrey had gone glacial again. He simply hadn't thought to tell her. Anyway, she had been too tired to be regaled with service chit-chat. Thank goodness, the others seemed to have moved on to other topics. Just now it was names, prompted by Mrs Kerr's picking up 'Stinson' and asking her husband if they hadn't known a Mr and Mrs Stinson in Caterham and he saying no, it was Stillson, same as the well-known wrench of that name.

'And the wrench was not amused, eh?' said Winwick, and was rewarded with a tinkly laugh from Audrey. 'In our case, what hurts most is being confused with that Jew-boy bandleader who's on the wireless sometimes—'

'If you ask me, they're all Jew-boys,' said Kerr.

'Ah, you mean Maurice Winnick?' said Mrs Kerr.

'The same, except that he's Winnick with two enns and we are the proper spelling, win-wick. It is the name of an estate up Rugby way from which our family originally came, I'm told. And unlike Maurice Winnick and his lot, we have no reason not to eat pork!'

Whether it was a fluke or he had carefully planned it – but he couldn't have, surely? – the maid came in at this moment with the joint. From the savour and the glossy carapace of crackling, it was all too evidently a huge loin of pork again. The Kerrs beamed in admiration and anticipation. As Winwick sharpened his carving knife on the steel, Mrs Winwick hissed something at him.

'Ah, yes, the wine,' he announced. 'Michael has brought us a couple of bottles of the real thing if I'm not mistaken. Perhaps you would do the honours, Michael.'

Pickup would rather have not, but obediently he fetched the first bottle from the sideboard and filled everyone's glasses. More noises of approval, and when he came to Audrey she gave him a forgiving smile. He took a quick sip from his own glass. It was good stuff, you could feel it warming the cockles. Maybe the occasion need not remain as grim as he had feared. Winwick seemed to have settled for jocularity, Audrey was starting to pipe in bits of Windmill gossip, only a periodic frown on Kerr's face was discordant. Not until he had to fetch the second bottle and pour it did Pickup wonder if something was up. As he set it on the table Kerr reached out and studied the label. As if following his gaze, Winwick also peered at it, and the two men exchanged a quick glance.

So what if it was French wine? There was still plenty of that around, if Simpson's-in-the-Strand or the Savoy Grill or, come to that, the University Arms in Cambridge were anything to go by. They had apple pie and custard, then the ladies – would you believe it? – went off to the drawing room for coffee, leaving them to the cheese and what was left of the wine. Winwick ushered out the maid, who had been collecting crocks. 'That will be all for the moment, Elsie,' he said. 'I'll ring if we want anything.' He followed her out and returned with a blackened webbing belt and revolver holster which he handed to Kerr.

'Make sure the door is shut,' said Kerr. Without taking his eyes off Pickup he unbuckled the holster and took out an old Webley which he laid on the table in front of him. 'Right, Flight-Lieutenant, or whatever you are, would you kindly tell us how you came by this wine?'

If it were a story, Pickup thought, this was where he would have to pinch himself to confirm that he wasn't dreaming. He was tempted to say that he'd stolen it but lamely said, 'I was given it,' which in fact was the truth. 'Why, what's the matter with it?'

47

'The matter with it is that it happens to be a 1941 vintage.'

Oh dear! So that was it, the date on the label? He simply hadn't seen it or, if he had, it hadn't registered. 'Sorry,' he said. 'Not a good year then?' but knew even as he said it that these two were going to be deaf to pleasantries.

'Don't play the fool, Michael,' said Winwick sharply. 'You know perfectly well what the Major is driving at.'

'As even a non-combatant warrior might have observed,' Kerr came in on cue, 'France has been occupied by the enemy for three years now, getting on for three and a half. In that time no French wine can possibly have reached this country.' He paused. 'Unless a few bottles were carried in by someone arriving from the other side, eh? You say you were given these. Who gave them to you?'

'A doctor I know.' The truth.

'His name?'

'I can't remember. Gaston something' – he reached automatically for Tilly's standard senior peasantry name. 'He's with one of the Free French squadrons.'

'And when and how did he get here?'

'Don't know.'

Kerr stared at him grimly. Winwick creased his brow as if concentrating hard. The rise and fall of Mrs Winwick's voice came faintly from the drawing room. Kerr laid a finger, without looking, on the unfamiliar ribbon at the head of his ribbons. He said, 'That's the Military Service Medal. I'm an old soldier, real soldier, no one can pull the wool over my eyes. I thought there was something fishy about you when I first saw you, and I still think so. But out of respect to Mr Winwick here and his daughter's feelings, if you will give us the telephone number of your unit and the name of your commanding officer or adjutant who can vouch for you, then that will be sufficient.'

Christ, no! Panic engulfed Pickup, sheer unexpected panic. If the Branch Manager got to know, and you could bet the Branch Manager would get to know, that would be the end, the absolute end, the last straw. Careless talk might just be pardoned. Material security was something else. Never carry any documents or money, never bring back any goods other

48

than those officially sanctioned, and certainly never pass them on to any person outside the squadron. These old fools could get him banished from the weird, shadowy, unarmed warfare that was the only thing he had ever been any good at, that he had ever been at home in.

'The telephone number, Michael.' It was Winwick asking now.

He shook his head wildly. 'I can't. I'm not allowed to. It's secret.'

'Secret?' sneered Kerr. 'What could be secret about a squadron, if I have understood you rightly, that operates far from the sound of the guns? Furthermore, Mr Winwick and I happen to hold the King's commission just as much as you do, indeed more so, I suspect. We are entitled to satisfy ourselves as to your bona fides.'

'Oh, for God's sake—'

'And please do not to take His name in vain.' The capital 'H' resonated.

'The Major is an elder in the Presbyterian Church,' said Winwick helpfully. 'If we could see your officer's identity book, that might help.' He held out his hand.

Panic briefly gave way to temper. 'And how do I know who the hell he is?' Pickup snapped. 'Certainly not!'

Kerr's face darkened. His hand closed on the old Webley. Winwick whispered urgently to him, jerking his head in the direction of the distant voices.

'Very well,' Kerr said. 'We shall take ourselves to company headquarters, where there is a telephone on a military line. We'll tell the ladies that there is a message for you there. We expect to be back very soon but you will take your things with you in case you have to proceed elsewhere. Out of consideration to Mr and Mrs Winwick, not to mention Miss Winwick, I hope you will fall in with this harmless pretence, and keep your shouting for later.'

It didn't fool Audrey, or not altogether, Pickup thought. She was waiting in the hall when he came downstairs with his valise, Winwick close behind. She gave him a quick, apprehensive smile and looked away. They took Winwick's car. Winwick drove, Kerr sat in the back with Pickup, revolver in

49

hand. In the town they drew up outside a building just off the main street which, Pickup guessed, was the old Territorial drill-hall. Kerr handed the Webley to Winwick, squeezed his great frame out of the car and strode through an archway to the entrance.

'I'm sorry this had to happen, Michael,' said Winwick.

'Not half as sorry as I am.'

'He's signalling to us to follow. Stay there and don't do anything stupid while I get out.' Keeping his eyes on Pickup and the revolver aimed unsteadily at him, he fumbled blindly for the ignition key with his left hand and then for the door handle. Pickup said, 'Here, I'll open it for you,' and had his own door open and a foot on the ground before Winwick could object. He tugged the driver's door open and Winwick came almost tumbling out. Pickup stuck out his leg to trip him and he did tumble now, flat on his face on to the pavement, arms flung wide, a great gasp of breath expelled. Pickup kicked the gun from his gun hand and dropped as heavily as he could on Winwick's back to pin the poor sod down while he scrabbled for the ignition key from the other. As he ducked into the driving seat he heard Kerr calling from within the archway, then Winwick shouting hoarsely from the ground. Thanks to the God of Ignition – for the second time in six days – the engine started first time.

He'd watched Winwick operate the pre-selector gear-change, and sensed the flabby take-up of the so-called fluid flywheel. Even so, it was bloody insane. He heard the pounding of Kerr's boots, his voice shouting. But at least you couldn't stall the motor with this system. He wheezed away, juggling the controls until they agreed to pick up a bit of speed. The shouts and thuds were left behind.

Only now did he feel his pulse racing and his breath panting, only now did it hit him that he had burned his boats, shagged things up irrevocably. At the same time there was a calculating department at work on where to head for, what to do. The first priority was to cover as many miles as possible, in as short a time as possible, before they could get a pursuit under way. The car was too easy to track, any car was easy to track when there were so few left on the road, especially if they called in the police, which they would. He'd have to dump it and catch a train, but not from *n* Bridges, from a station up the line or, or better still, another line. It was only just after three in the afternoon, four or five hours of daylight yet.

The street led to what looked like a road going somewhere. He turned on to it. In the absence of signposts – another little wartime handicap – he had no idea where it was going, but from the light and a general sense of direction that was usually fairly reliable he was heading roughly north. The main thing was that he quickly left the town behind him. Apart from a few army and RAF vehicles there was almost no traffic. After about twenty minutes he caught up with an army convoy, big Matador gun-tractors taking up more than half the road and chugging along at twenty miles an hour max. He made to overtake the blue-flagged Jeep bringing up the rear and got a warning flap of the hand from the officer sitting by the driver. With the Armstrong's flabby responses it would be a nightmare anyway. He tucked in again and started to fret. Already there was another car behind him. This was the worst of predicaments, trapped in a traffic crawl in a car whose description and number-plates might already be relayed all over the shop. There was a road junction coming up or, rather, a fork off to the right. The convoy was keeping to the road they were on. On the impulse, Pickup crossed on to the fork.

He was well and truly flying blind now. This road was only a lane, winding through scrubby woods and stubble fields, occasional tiny villages. He saw just one field being ploughed on the Sabbath, a cloud of birds following the plough. At last signs of a township started to show up. The lane came to a main road – and hell's bells! Rumbling by on it was the same bloody convoy. He must have tootled round in a loose arc that brought him back to the road he'd been on. He banged his head despairingly on the steering wheel, making the horn sound and bringing a scowl from the driver of the open tourer stopped ahead of him. Careful, careful, for God's sake. The blue-flagged Jeep went by, then a tail of five or six other vehicles before the tourer could move. Pickup followed. Almost immediately a town began to enclose him, just houses at first, then a garage, shops, a market square, where the hell was the station? He blundered on, past a cinema, past a church, his heart sinking as the centre seemed to be petering out again – then down a side street was a glimpse of pale wood paling, a fretted roof. Just time and space to brake and wrench the Armstrong into the turn, at the cost of an angry V-sign from a cyclist.

There was a gravelled parking area just beyond the station entrance. Pickup nosed the Armstrong into the farthest corner, where with any luck he would be able to see it from the platform. He jiggled the key on its key-ring for a moment, then dropped it into the little cubby-hole in the dashboard and reached for his valise. 'London train?' said the man in the ticket-office. 'Just been signalled. This side, sir.' First lucky break all day.

IV

By the time the train was approaching London his spirits were sinking again. It had seemed the only course open to him, to melt into the hordes of anonymous uniforms in the capital until he could collect his civvies from Aunt Milly. That was the dicey bit. If the police or the military had been questioning Audrey, she might well have remembered the name of the hotel where the villain had proposed to despoil her, and blurted it out. Or been ordered to do so by her father. Then there was Tilly, if they had got in touch with him. They had stayed at an officers' club the time they went to the Mill together, but had called at the Arrol to take Milly for a drink and a laugh. They had got on well, Milly and Tilly, both a bit Bolshie.

Even if he gained the Arrol undetected, he had no civilian identity card, no ration book. Anyway, a deserter was the last thing he needed to be. He must get back to Tempsford and face the music. The only alternative would be to stay in town, call the Consul in the morning as promised – better, go and see him – and see if he could help. But no, he didn't want to do that, either. Out of the frying pan into the chip pan.

At Victoria he resisted the temptation to take a cab. It was only four stops on the Underground to Temple and, approaching on foot, he'd be able to spy out the land, make sure he wasn't walking into a trap. When he was within view of the entrance he walked on the other side of the street, trying to look abstracted. No one obviously planted outside, but there wouldn't be, would there? He caught sight of a telephone box at the next corner. That might be safer. He popped twopence into the slot and dialled the Arrol's number. When he asked for Reception, he got a slightly foreign voice, probably that of the little Austrian refugee Lisa.

'Is Milly there?'

'No, she have day off.'

'Is she in her room?'

'Who is that?'

Pickup had to risk it. 'It's Michael, her nephew.'

'Hello, this is Lisa. Milly won't be back until late tonight. Michael, someone has been telephoning for you.'

'When?'

'The last time one hour ago. I keep saying you checked out yesterday,'

'Okay. Has anyone actually come to the hotel asking for me?'

'Not while I am here.'

'No one waiting for me?'

'Should there be?' She sounded genuinely puzzled.

'Listen, I'm coming round. I'll be with you in a minute.'

She was registering a new arrival when he entered. The other girl was busy on the switchboard. Pickup chafed. They could bowl in any moment, big unsmiling RAF police escorting a Provost Marshal, or CID officers in felt hats. At last the porter picked up the guest's bag and led him off towards the lift.

'Lisa, was it a man or a woman who phoned?'

'A man.'

'He didn't say who he was?'

She shook her head.

'The other thing is that Milly keeps some things for me, for when I'm in town. Change of clothing, you know. I need it now.'

'In her room?'

'Yes.'

She frowned. 'It is Sunday. I am alone but for Judy on the switchboard. It is difficult . . .'

He must have looked a misery. She eyed him speculatively, then reached for a key on a big metal tag. 'Room 605 on the top floor, you must take the stairs from the fifth. That's the pass-key. Do not lose it, please.' He could have kissed her. Should have.

Milly's room had one little window like a porthole, but

54

you could see the Thames from it, she always said. If it were ever cleaned, and the blackout curtain hauled back, you might. Just enough light seeped round the edges to pick out the general shapes of wardrobe, chest of drawers and wash-stand. The electric light, when he found the switch, was not much brighter. Where would Milly have stored his things? On the films you could wrench open drawers and sweep armfuls of clothing off their hangers. He couldn't bring himself to do that, and anyway it probably wouldn't help. At which point the day's second slice of luck came his way. He spotted a faint blue gleam among the clutter of things piled on top of the wardrobe. Please let it be the shiny rexine weekend case his mother had found for him in the loft at home. It was!

He'd just got it down when a phone rang, just once, then silence. It was mounted on the wall, a staff phone. What to do? The call would be for Milly – but no, the girl on the switchboard would know that she was out. It had to be Lisa trying to warn him of something. He grabbed the receiver before she could ring again.

'Michael?' It was Lisa, 'That man is calling again—'

'I'll come down.'

'No, stay there. I think we can put it through.'

Click-click, then 'Mickup? Been trying to find you all after-noon.' Tilly's voice came loud and hoarse over the line.

'They've been on to you, then?'

'You might say so. What's all this about a bogus flight-lieutenant claiming to be stationed at Tempsford?'

'Oh, Christ, who's been asking?'

'Only the police, so far. What happened?' Pickup gave him a terse account. 'I grant you one thing, Mickup, you don't do owt by half measures. Striking a superior officer, albeit of the gallant Home Guard.'

'No, that was the other one, the Major. Winwick's only a one-pipper.'

'Worse. Striking an inferior. Then that wine. If you had brought brandy, like I asked, you wouldn't be in this mess.'

'How bad is it?'

'When the Branch Manager hears of it he'll blow a gasket.

He'll be back at his desk in the morning. Now, where are you? Temple Bar – that's the Strand, isn't it?'

'Just off.'

'Anyone know you might be there?'

Pickup hesitated. 'Only Audrey – Anita, that is.'

'She's also the only one who would have known we're at Bad Tempers?'

'Yeah.'

'Right! Get out. Get out as soon as I ring off. Don't say where you're going. Meet me at – let's see – eight fifteen, King's Cross, the hotel. No, make it that bloody great pile at St Pancras, next door. The beer's better. Oh, hold on! You've got some civvies in your billet, haven't you?'

'No, I keep them here, actually—'

'Even better! Change into them before you leave. Change into them now!'

Who should he be, we were now debating carefully. Who should be chosen from the chosen race to be the apostle to the World? For a start, we decided, there should be two such messengers, so that if anything happened to one, the other might still win through. And as agreed earlier, neither should be drawn from those who would lead the armed uprising. We supported these brave souls, of course, we would help them all we could, and if they succeeded in breaking out of the camp we would take advantage of their feat and despatch one, if not both, of our emissaries in their wake. But until that time, and probably beyond it, we must remain what we had made ourselves, the most conscientious of the slaves who had kept Treblinka a productive and efficient Jew-processing plant.

Only the former underground editor Spyra had reservations about the objective which consumed us. 'Will anyone listen to these messengers?' he asked.

We stared at him as if he had cast doubts on the most fundamental article of a religion we all shared.

'Or if they do listen, will they believe what they hear?' He paused a moment. 'I had hoped not to tell you this, but I must. Last year, when this very hell of Treblinka had not long been in operation but was already killing trainloads of our

deportees, one of them contrived to escape from the camp and find his way back to the Ghetto. No one could believe his account, and I was forbidden by the Elders to refer to it in our newspaper.'

We stared at him now in consternation.

'Another story,' Spyra continued, 'came our way when the SS set up loudspeakers outside the walls of the Ghetto to deafen us with threats and boasts. One early morning they were declaiming about a wretched Jew who had absconded from a labour camp at Belzec.' Belzec, we knew, was in fact another extermination camp, some hundreds of kilometres south of Treblinka.

'He had reached London and then Washington, attempting to spread disgusting lies about killings and gassings,' Spyra continued. 'But even the most ardent warmongers and propagandists refused to believe such nonsense. Or so the loudspeaker voice assured us.' He paused. 'Such broadcasts as we had been able to pick up from America and England seemed to confirm this claim – after one or two references to a talebearer from a Polish concentration camp, no further mention.'

The despair this admission generated among us may be imagined. Was our great resolve doomed to failure? Without much conviction I suggested that the whole episode was a fabrication by the SS, to discourage all such endeavours. Spyra was already shaking his head. The message had been brought out, but the messenger had not been heeded.

At this point an occasional member of our team intervened. He was a chemist called Bader who worked in the camp hospital, but every so often joined us to check over the drugs, pills and patent medicines found in the baggage. Anything that might be of use in a hospital otherwise devoid of supplies he took back with him. What was known of that messenger from Belzec, he wanted to know. What sort of man was he?

Probably an electrician or other skilled tradesman, said Spyra, as apparently he had made his escape while working outside the Belzec camp, in the SS barracks.

Would more attention have been paid to the testimony of a doctor or teacher or politician, Bader then asked, rather than the mutterings of a workman unskilled in rhetoric? This was

57

not a popular sentiment to express in a nether world whose only consolation was that all its denizens were equally wretched. It was especially unpalatable to Marek, who as humble barber in his former life, and very likely a communist, had a great disdain of the rich or famous.

'Is it not enough that he tells of what he has seen and heard and suffered in this place?' he demanded. 'The truth is all that matters, whether it comes from a pianist or a pickpocket.'

Sadly, we had to overrule him. The lesson was plain. We needed an eminence.

Bader was looking in my direction. 'As a distinguished professor your name would be known in Oxford and Cambridge and Uppsala and . . . er, Princetown?'

'Princeton,' I corrected. 'Except that I have not been a distinguished professor, merely an associate or "reader", as they term him in England, and that in abstruse byways of philology. I do not think many Americans or English will have heard of the Karaites people of Vilna.' I was about to add, 'And it would be doubly foolish to send a nobody whose constitution might easily let him down in the exertions of the journey,' but for some reason held back.

'Is there anything we are famous for?' Marek enquired sarcastically.

'Music,' I suggested. It was quite in order for Poles to play the piano.

'And we have musicians here in Treblinka,' said the Rabbi Davidowitz.

Marek sneered, 'You are surely not proposing that we send Artur Gold!' Gold was leader of the camp orchestra. He had been quite a respected Warsaw conductor in peacetime, but hardly a Toscanini or a Klemperer, and in any case was too deeply involved with the camp authorities to be relied upon.

'I was thinking of the Cantor from Grodno,' said the Rabbi with dignity. This fellow was not of our group but we knew him from when, on fine evenings in summer, we heard his rich bass raised both in sacred chants and our old folk songs. He had been a great bear of a man and was still an imposing scarecrow.

But what attention would a mere cantor attract, I dared to

ask. Why not a rabbi at least? The Rabbi Davidowitz had concealed his calling from his captors, but preserved the air of authority that went with it.

'With our own people,' he said calmly, 'the designation might count for a little. To the millions of others we have to reach it would mean nothing.' It was now his turn to cast a net. He looked at Spyra. 'Was your reputation as a journalist known widely,' he asked.

Spyra shook his head. 'Beyond Warsaw I am no one. I doubt if the name of any Polish journalist, or for that matter a Polish writer of any kind, is familiar to the English or Americans.'

Bader intervened again. 'In the hospital,' he said, 'there lurks a medical orderly who not so long ago was one of the most distinguished biologists living – Jan Zielinski.'

I certainly had heard of him, renowned in medical and scientific circles for his work on micro-bacteria, if that is the correct term. He had been featured in the American Life *magazine, and talked of as a Nobel Prize candidate. The others seemed equally impressed, even Marek. We exchanged nods. Bader promised to sound him out on our behalf.*

And to accompany our paragon? The Rabbi was for choosing another figure of stature, to add further weight to the testimony. Bader argued that it should be a soldier or sportsman, more suited to protect Zielinski and handle whatever trials their journey might bring. I suggested, finally, that an additional qualification should be an up-to-date knowledge of ways and means in the divided and occupied world outside. In this respect there was one obvious candidate. We all looked at Leo Spyra. After some thought, he accepted.

Pickup caught his reflection in a giant gilt mirror in the cavernous depths of the station hotel. Harris tweed sports jacket from Watson Prickard, grey hopsack slacks, collar-attached shirt, stripey tie, brown veldt shoes, hair long enough for him to be a junior doctor or university demonstrator. Or a conchie, come to that. Only his airforce-blue macintosh and valise were not quite in keeping with the rest of the outfit. The mac carried no rank badges, and he had folded it inside-out to show as much as possible of the lining. Slung over his carrying arm it even helped conceal the valise, but just the association of ideas could arouse suspicions in the beetle-browed. If Tilly hadn't been so impatient to ring off he could have asked him exactly what he needed.

In the streets, he had begun to feel safe. Here he could be cornered. He found a deserted bar, a lounge empty but for a few old ladies, but no sign of Tilly. He heard deep voices behind him and dodged into a side space which led to double doors. Someone further back called what could have been his name. He pushed one of the doors open and found himself in a brightly lit room with a table set as for a meeting, with sheets of paper, glasses and water-jugs. Two or three men in black were already seated. Another was hovering over a side table. They stared at him. The doors opened again and the owners of the deep voices marched in. There were two of them, also in black hats and overcoats, deep in conversation in some language Pickup couldn't even guess at.

He backed out mouthing, 'Sorry,' and there was Tilly shambling up in his raffish uniform, raffish cap on head, likewise clutching a valise.

'Didn't know you were one of them,' Tilly said.

'How do you mean?'

'Our chosen friends. If you'd got your Boy Scouts badge for observation you'd have seen the sign in the foyer. "Board of Guardians" or something like that.' He said it rather studiedly, Pickup thought, as if toying with a little signal. 'Signs and portents, eh?' There, he'd run it up to the masthead.

'I found the bar,' said Pickup. 'Not exactly pulsating with life.'

'Yeah, I looked in, too. The dining room ought to be livelier, if you haven't eaten already.'

They left their macs and bags at the cloakroom and found their way there. In fact, it was quite crowded. Who were they all? Pickup wondered.

'Bods on their way here and back from there,' said Tilly. 'Bods going on leave, bods going back off leave, bods staying at the hotel with other bods' wives.' He looked down with some distaste at the boiled fish before them and took a swig from his tankard of Fuller's. 'And people catching a night sleeper.'

60

Again that deliberation. Sometimes you had to decode Tilly, but this time it wasn't difficult. Pickup said, 'What are you driving at, master? What's afoot?'

Tilly reached into his right breast pocket to extract some flimsy documents. 'As I told you on the phone I had been trying to find you before we knew anything about your dust-up with the gallant Home Guard – which rumbles on, by the way. And where you are going is Leuchars.'

Pickup nodded and held out his hand for the papers. First-class rail warrant to Leuchars Junction, first-class sleeper reservation. The date was today's, as he had expected but still could not quite believe. 'Tonight?' he wailed.

'The sooner you're on your way, the sooner you'll be out of reach of the Branch Manager. More to the point, the little operation they told you about on Saturday has been brought forward. It could now happen in – well, as soon as the moon starts to oblige.'

'Tilly, how much do you know about it? Do you know exactly what's involved? Flying into heavily occupied bandit territory you have never seen before to pick up a couple of clients who may or may not be there, then doing it all again in reverse – flying back into a country whose defences will be equally keen to shoot you down.'

'You should be used to that, Mickup, if you've come across the Channel into Tangmere lately when our brave Ack-ack are pooping at anything that moves in the sky –'

Pickup acknowledged the joke with a grimace.

'– whatever pretty lights you provide for their delectation,' Tilly finished. The drill was to fire the colours of the day from a Verey pistol as you hit the coast, but they weren't always registered.

'At least you're heading for home and beauty, with 800 horse-power in front and armour-plate behind you. The Stinson's an Austin Seven by comparison. And all for the sake of bagging witnesses for some propaganda exercise. If you can find them, that is. It's . . . it's a wild Jews chase.'

Tilly smiled. 'I like that.'

Pickup paused to make sure he really wanted to say what he was going to say next. 'It's not as if we even like them much.'

'Who?'

'The Jews. All the stories we used to hear when the war began, about them scuttling off to America. Or anyway, off to the seaside for the duration. Southport or Llandudno, it was in my part of the world.'

'Don't blame them,' said Tilly. 'If they had no need to stay in town and be blitzed, only sensible to get out.'

'Well, your story then. What made you buy your Lea-Francis from a yid, to save it from going to another greasy yid? Now it's the greasy yids we're supposed to save.'

He shouldn't have brought that up, he saw too late. Bad form to trot out a man's own ugly wording against him. He suddenly remembered Winwick and Kerr and their talk of Jew-boys, and how he'd winced to hear it. But Tilly seemed not to mind. He was frowning to himself more than at Pickup.

'We're taxi-drivers,' he said. 'You know that. We carry who we're ordered to carry. I'll tell you something, Mickup. I was going to do this job myself. Wanted to do it. I was ruled out at the service end because I'm flight commander and couldn't hang around Sweden for weeks, while at the cloak-and-dagger end they were asking for you – or anyway, enquiring about you – because they somehow knew of your thrilling past. As I said at the time, the finger of fate sought you out. But if you're unhappy about it, things have changed a bit. The date is now close. I haven't flown a Stinson yet, but I soon can. There is no reason why I shouldn't go instead. We'll do our best to placate the Branch Manager. You'll probably end up in Training Command again, but there are worse fates in life –'

Pickup realized he was shaking his head busily. 'Forget it, Tilly. I'm sorry. It's my job. My name's on the rail warrant. I'm on the way.'

'No more binding?'

'I wasn't binding actually. Just a couple of middle-of-the-night doubts I thought you would want me to share with you.'

Tilly relaxed. 'Of course, dear boy. Now – marching orders. You travel to Sweden in civvies, you wear civvies there. You fly the operation in uniform. With the help of your unsavoury batman – what's his name?'

'Doggett.'

'With his help I've brought your battledress, plus that bloody great white pullover you like to wear, strictly against regs. You can't take flying suit and boots. Too bulky, and they might give the game away to nosy Swedish Customs. For the same reason you won't be on the VIP service, riding in the bomb bay of a Mosquito, two and a half hours. The Jerries keep a check on everyone who arrives that way. You'll be on the regular Dakota run, more like five hours, along with the cypher clerks and radio operators and other salt of the earth, because that's what you're going to be as far as most people at the other end are concerned. You'll get your documents, and a briefing on exactly who you're supposed to be, at Leuchars. You're wearing your identity tags? Right, you keep those, wear them at all times, leave everything else behind when you take off on the trip, as per usual. No cheque book, no letters, money or diary. But I don't need to tell you that.'

'Scout's honour,' said Pickup.

Tilly's brow was furrowed in thought. He opened his mouth and sang, quite loudly, '*Hutsut rosen on the rilera, and a brola. brola suey*, or however it went.'

It had been a bit of a hit on the wireless and in the dance-halls, the summer before last. '*Rosen is a Swedish town*,' Pickup chipped in, '*rilera is a stream.*'

'*Hutsut is a boy and girl.*'

'*And the brola is their dream.*'

'Or is *suey* the bloody dream?'

'We ought to know, it was on the Forces Programme often enough.'

'Never mind,' said Tilly, 'it's Sweden. Where the boys and girls swim naked.'

'In October?'

'Naked under their diving suits. Oh, there's one other thing. As per usual, even if the operation is not quite usual, it has been allotted a code-name. It comes with acknowledgements to your Flight-Sergeant Price. It's SLY LANDER.'

They retrieved the two valises from the cloakroom and swapped various effects between them. Pickup's service dress went unlamented into the one Tilly would take back to base.

63

He kept the battledress, the white submariner's jersey he had cadged from his cousin in the Navy, and all the clean shirts and socks and pyjamas and underpants they could find, service or civvy, which wasn't a lot. 'If you run short, you'll have to pinch some off a clothes-line,' said Tilly helpfully.

They walked the short distance to King's Cross. Tilly's train, the last back to Bad Tempers, was soon to leave. 'You ought to be able to get on the sleeper by now,' he said. 'They usually let you on early. And in the morning you'll wake up amid mountains and stags and blokes in skirts, you lucky sod. Wish it was me.' They shook hands and Tilly went through to his platform. It could just have gone the other way, Pickup thought. It could have been him on that train, Tilly on his.

It came as a blow to learn that Dr Chorazycki had killed himself. An attempt of his to buy arms from a Ukrainian was betrayed, and rather than risk giving away the names of his fellow conspirators under torture he chose to take cyanide. The engineer Galewski succeeded him as leader of the committee planning the revolt. There was still no date set for this, although it was now July. As regards our own interest in it, the choice of Zielinski to be principal messenger filled us with hope. He had a quiet but assured presence. He was fluent in both German and English. And he was fit to make the journey. At which point I have to make a gruesome confession.

By some strange whim of the commandant, we scavengers were allowed to keep and distribute all foodstuffs we found in the baggage of the damned. Perhaps he never realized that the Jewish impulse, especially among the wives and mothers, is to take luxuries rather than staple commodities when faced with an unknown journey. We were not surprised to come across jars of caviar, dried fish and whole cooked fowls amongst the rye bread, bagels and coffee beans. Leo Spyra said it was a better diet than they had ever had in the Ghetto, let alone as prisoners. Thanks to this manna from Heaven or, rather, from the Heaven-bound, both he and Zielinski were incomparably stronger than the poor skeletons who had to depend solely on the camp diet of watery soup.

Other than food, we were not allowed to hold anything back, on pain of death or at best a savage beating. The guards kept constant watch on us as we toiled, with frequent checks on our persons at the end of the day, when often we were stripped naked to make sure we had not secreted some knife or pocket-file. Valuables we ignored for most of the time. In a death camp they had no value. A special squad known as 'the Jewellers' sorted out the gold and diamonds and Cartier watches, to be sent away for sale on behalf of the SS. Only as we started to make preparations for the escape did we dare to slide a gold coin or a Reichsmark note into the wrappings of some foodstuff or another. Our messengers would need money on their journey.

Also abstracted were two items of still greater value to them, or to the purpose of their mission. One was a folding map of Eastern Poland and 'Greater Germany' up to and including the old corridor land and Danzig. Spyra spotted it soon after he joined us. Braving the stare of a suspicious guard, he contrived to cover it with a fine shirt from the same suitcase until he could seize the opportunity to slip it down the seat of his striped prison trousers. There it attracted no attention because it was – is – common practice to stuff down newspaper against the dysentery rife in the camp,

The other find came some months ago in the baggage of the exotic Jews from Salonika. As a philologist I have never been impressed by the old Chinese saying that one picture is worth a thousand words, but photographs could certainly add powerful support to our testimony. To see the huddled masses spilling from the train, being sent along the Road to Heaven and then burned in outdoor pyres – surely that would convince the sternest doubters? But even if we had a camera, which we didn't, how to take such photographs without being observed? Stefan, usually a rather silent member of our group, told us about a tiny camera called the Minox, hardly bigger than a box of matches. We hoped one might turn up. None ever did, nor any other camera for that matter. Then one day I heard a faint grunt from Stefan himself, and saw him dart a look towards the nearest guards before pushing something into the hiding place we kept ready for just such a discovery,

65

under a bucket into which we threw all rotting food. It proved to be a small roll-film camera of French manufacture called an Eljy.

'Not much more than a toy,' said Marek when we examined it later, and indeed it may have been the precious possession of a child of some cosmopolitan Smyrnan family. But it had quite a good lens and a three-speed shutter, and though hardly to be described as tiny it could be cupped, as Stefan demonstrated, in a man's hand. Further furtive rummaging in the particular suitcase had yielded two little rolls of film. There was a partly used one already in the camera. Depending on the number of exposures each roll held, we could take possibly fifteen pictures, twenty at the most.

We started out very carefully, very cautiously, aiming by guesswork, never more than one snap at a time, the camera then immediately hidden away again. We took it in turns, Stefan and Marek and even I, once, to lessen the risk of one man setting a pattern of behaviour that would be noticed. We caught the arrival of a crowded train from the Warsaw Ghetto, one guard killing a woman, another dashing her infant to the ground. Marek got his barbers at work from within the group, Stefan the pilgrims setting off on the Road to Heaven.

Where we could not go was with them to the Todeslager, the fume chambers, the burning of the bodies. Those who worked there were never allowed out, those of us who worked outside were not allowed in. Just one of the 'dentists' who pulled out the teeth of the dead would be escorted down to us with his pail of bloody golden crowns and fillings. This brave man agreed to smuggle back the Eljy, loaded with the last roll of film, take what pictures he could and bring it back the next time.

If there was a next time, we had soon to say. No more trains came from Warsaw. No trains came from anywhere. The last remaining thousands of buried dead had been dug up and burned. A strange repose descended on the camp. The greenery of the Road to Heaven wilted as if it knew its deception was no longer needed. The pall of smoke died away, and for the first time in many months we could see the heavens clearly.

66

Looking up in wonder one morning I saw a fine white line drawn slowly across the blue sky, as if by a finger.

'The finger of God,' I suggested to Leo Spyra, not wholly in jest. More likely the trail left by a giant rocket, he countered. German scientists had been experimenting with such machines for years. Now they were rumoured to have a full-scale research establishment on an island off the Pomeranian coast. There were stories of a rocket big enough to carry a man. 'To take Hitler and Goering to the Moon when the Reich is finally defeated,' I said.

'Not Goering, no rocket could lift him. Goebbels, perhaps.'

Seriously, had the run-down of the camp robbed us of our last chance to capture the holocaust on film? But that was surely not a subject for regret? In the dark watches of the night it was difficult to know what to pray for, what to dread.

V

Pickup alighted from the sleeper to a bright, clear morning. The wind was cold and unwavering. A camel-coated man who'd followed him on to the platform clutching a suitcase in one hand and a portable typewriter in the other made a loud *Brrrrr*. 'Starts up in Siberia,' said Pickup, 'and this is its first stop.' It was what people said of the Cambridge wind, but it fitted this end of the world equally well. They watched the four or five other passengers who'd left the sleeper board the little branch-line train waiting to chug down to St Andrews, and as wartime strangers always did when decanted together at a new camp or barracks, exchanged speculations as to what happened next. Finally a porter pointed them to the airfield, even closer to the station than Tempers; indeed you could see the entrance.

At the gate the sentry asked them to wait while he whizzed the handle of a field telephone. Inside, a little way off, lay the familiar RAF cluster of hangars and admin. offices and control tower. A separate line of green-painted huts looked faintly out of place. Beyond the extravagant expanse of airfield, to one side, was a river estuary with flocks of sea-birds clearly visible on the sandspits. Straight out to the East, a blue-green sea twinkled away to the horizon. Beyond that was Norway and then Sweden. Mmmmm.

An RAF Regiment warrant officer, very smart and soldierly, arrived and steered them into the guardroom. 'Just to put you in the picture, gentlemen, in case you don't already know, the Royal Air Force shares this establishment with British Airways, whose personnel you will recognize in due course by their becoming dark blue uniforms. Those are their offices –' he jabbed a thumb at the green huts – 'but as it's a civilian outfit, not a soul is to be found there at this hour.' He drew a service pocket watch from the flap below the faded peacetime ribbons on his breast – including, for God's sake, the MSM which old Kerr had shown off only the other day. No, yesterday! It seemed like ages past.

'There should be someone in about ten,' the W.O. said, pushing the watch back into his pocket. With that ribbon he must have been one of the army sergeant-majors lured into the Air Force when it decided to set up its own airfield defence mob. 'Meanwhile I'll take you to the mess for a bit of breakfast, and afterwards you both have to see the passport wallah here.' He peered at a paper in his hand. 'Mr Nesbit?' Camel-coat nodded. 'You'll be first. Then I suggest you go into St Andrews and get yourself a hotel room, just in case. The Dakotas haven't flown for twelve days now, and it doesn't look too likely for tonight—'

'*What?*' Pickup couldn't help it. The W.O. was staring at him frostily. 'I mean, isn't there a flight this morning?'

'No, sir. The service is by night, and only dark nights at that. Too much moon or starlight and it's not on. I don't need to tell you why, gentlemen. Just look at the map.'

Nesbit was nodding agreement. Pickup said, 'I'm sorry. I wasn't thinking.' Of course! It was the logical ploy if you had to fly through enemy skies in an unarmed Dakota but could look forward to a nice brightly lit airport at the other end, the very opposite philosophy to that of Lysander Air Taxis, Ltd. He had been assuming he would be on the way before the Branch Manager could recall him. Now he had to fight flutters of panic that it was already too late, any minute the guardroom phone would ring with a summons for Flight-Lieutenant Pickup to report to the station adjutant at once.

The W.O. was rounding off his homily to Nesbit. 'It's vital that you keep in touch. You'll be given a number you can ring. They'll keep you informed, and at all costs be back here by whenever they say. All right?'

Nesbit nodded again.

'Now if you wouldn't mind waiting outside a moment . . .'

Or had the long arm of the Branch Manager already reached

out? Was this the moment of truth? Pickup held his breath as Nesbit gathered up his things.

But all the W.O. said was, 'Ah, Flight-Lieutenant Pickup, sir? There will be a billet for you in the officers' quarters, it goes without saying. There is, however, a difficulty about using the officers' mess. You've brought your uniform with you, I gather, but it has to go into the diplomatic bag before that's sealed. Also, I understand your journey is as a wireless technician or similar, who would be a non-com in the service, and it is felt that you should accustom yourself to that status. By and large you may prefer to go into town with Mr Nesbit and perhaps buy a screwdriver and some wire to mend your spectacles.'

Pickup laughed, mainly in relief, also because he warmed to this comedian.

'But watch what you say, sir. He's a gentleman of the Press.'

'What?'

'Yessir. Not sure what newspaper, but they're all the same, I say.'

'Thank you.'

'And the same applies to your good self about keeping in touch. Only more so.'

We need not have fretted. Treblinka Todwerke AG was soon back in full production. Another ghetto was being emptied, this time one lying in the opposite direction. It was the turn of the Jews of Bialystok, on the Eastern border, plus those from other cities and shetls *who had been herded into its walls. Train after train shuddered into the camp station, mountains of luggage accumulated, mounds of shorn hair. The workers of the* Tarnunskommando, *or camouflage detail, had been marched into the woods at dawn to collect fresh branches with which to decorate the Road to Heaven. Other woodsmen, many more in number, resumed the felling of trees and sawing of logs to feed the cremation fires. The pall of smoke hung over the camp again. It was quite like old times, said Marek sardonically. There would be no shortage of subject matter for our dentist to photograph, if he had the chance and the courage.*

And as in former times, a few of the arrivals were singled out to become workers. All were assigned to the hard and horrifying labour of the Upper Camp, but later in the day just one man reappeared in our Lower Camp. Beyond giving his name as Tarrutis, he kept himself to himself. He had a bearing, a distinction about him which in Nazi hands you soon learned to disown. The only hope of survival was to fade into the mass of shaven, downcast humanity. This Tarrutis – a Lithuanian name – seemed to choose to stand out.

Marek stared at him across the shed until he scowled back. 'I know that face,' hissed Marek. 'I've seen him somewhere, but I can't remember when or how.'

As the transports from Bialystok continued, day after day, week into week, we found something rather more serious to wonder and worry about. How would this renewed activity affect preparations for the uprising? Still no date had been set for it, and in the Upper Camp, the Todeslager, *the workers had become so impatient, we heard, that they were threatening to turn on their hated guards without waiting any longer for orders from below.*

They caught the same train to St Andrews. There, Nesbit insisted on taking the station taxi, in fact a weird vehicle, half bus, half taxi and looking more like a wooden-bodied hearse than either of those. 'I want to get the hotel room sorted out before anything else,' he explained. 'Taxi drivers always know which to go to.' The one to go to turned out to be Rusack's, a stately pile near the famous golf course. Nesbit said he'd just check in and park his stuff, wouldn't be a minute.

Pickup looked at his watch for the seventeenth time, at least. It was 10.35. The Branch Manager would have been in his office for two hours by now, must have been told something. He felt a real gnawing in his vitals. Should he ring Leuchars to check? No, the buggers would find him soon enough if they wanted to.

Nesbit emerged from the hotel. He was in his late thirties, Pickup gauged, a bit jowly but with a brisk voice and decisive manner. Presumably it was as a reporter he was going to Stockholm, though Pickup didn't like to ask.

Where now, the driver wanted to know. The university, Nesbit said promptly. 'If that's okay by you,' he added, turning to Pickup. There was his wife's kid brother he was supposed to look up if he had time, and if the boy had arrived already. 'Are the students up yet?' he called to the driver.

'The most of them. The rest next week. Mind you, with the four terms they have for the war we're never without a fair crowd of them.'

'And the service cadets?'

'Aye, they'll be here.'

'He's on an RAF short course,' Nesbit told Pickup. 'Six months and then God bless. You're RAF, aren't you?'

The question caught Pickup on the hop. 'Sort of,' he said lamely.

Nesbit gave him a quick, curious glance but didn't pursue the matter. Well, it was true. His RAF battledress had duly been examined for any give-away clues and set aside to go into the bag, but in his inside pocket was a brand-new diplomatic passport identifying him as a Foreign Office wireless telegraphy assistant, grade II.

They were entering the university quarter, with a first sighting of students in their long scarlet gowns. 'So that's what they're like,' said Nesbit. 'Look a bloody sight more practical than ours,' said Pickup. 'Warmer, that is.' Otherwise it was like a miniature version of Cambridge, he thought as the hearse drew up by a gatehouse leading into a grassy enclosed court, only all in dour grey stone, none of the golden – or anyway sandy – glow of King's. He had a sudden sharp memory of trying to mug up structures in his rooms overlooking the Backs while listening uncomprehendingly, enviously, to the dry, skinny music that came on Sunday afternoons or summer evenings from Christopher Bright's set across the landing. He played the violin, his girlfriend Sarah the oboe or something. They belonged to a world Pickup knew only from novels. They had been to progressive co-ed schools, Bedales or Frensham Heights, their homes were in Hampstead or Highgate and they went to recitals in the Wigmore Hall. Yet they were always friendly and interested when Chris poked his head round the door to ask him over for tea or coffee, and

72

for a Girton girl Sarah was really very sexy with her black hair and dark eyes and long slim legs, especially in summer when they were bare and she wasn't over-careful with her skirts. What had maybe prompted this particular memory was a bit of news of her he'd heard only last year.

He said, 'There is someone I might look up, come to think. Only she's a lecturer or demonstrator. How would I find her?'

'By asking,' said Nesbit. 'Same way as I am going to track down young Robert. It's what I do for a living. What's her name?'

'Friedlander. Sarah Friedlander.'

'Any relation to Victor Friedlander? Churchill's pet boffin?'

'Daughter.'

'What's her subject?'

'Natural Sciences, it was. She's gone on to astronomy, I believe.'

'Oh, the RAF cadets get that. Well, not astronomy with a capital "A" but astro-navigation, or so my kid brother-in-law told us. We'll find her.'

At last the date was set. It was only a few days off, the second of August, or the day of the New Moon in the Jewish calendar. We had already secreted suitable everyday clothing for our envoys. Now we found strong boots which they surreptitiously tried out and then continued to wear. We thought their need to cover considerable distances outweighed the risk of a guard spotting too good a pair of shoes on a Jew.

And the brave 'dentist' from the Upper Camp duly returned the Eljy camera in another bucket of gold and shattered ivory. Stefan removed the tiny roll of film and wrapped it, with the other two, in waxed paper that had held a costly cheese. The package was entrusted to Leo Spyra, as one more skilled in the arts of subterfuge. As if by some surrealist association of ideas, the mystery of the Bialystok arrival was solved on the same day. Though his stubbled skull and gaunt features were much distorted from the face which had once stared out from cinema posters and the pages of 'fan' magazines, Marek and Stefan and even the Rabbi were convinced that he was the film star Kurt Westermann. Our 'dentist' accomplice

73

*confirmed that this had been the supposition of Upper Camp
workers during his brief stay there. The commandant had been
seen to draw the man aside and engage him in conversation
for several minutes, after which he had been transferred to
the Lower Camp.*

*We pooled what knowledge we had of Westermann. Marek
had been the keenest filmgoer, I suppose, and I the least
addicted, but I did have acquaintance with his ancestry.
Westermann was the name of one of the Hanseatic families
which had settled along the Baltic coast from Lubeck to the
Russian border. All were merchants originally. Some became
bankers or lawyers, others took root as landowners and farmers. A minority was Jewish. The film star Kurt Westermann,
Marek said, was always rumoured to be a Jew.*

*Towards the end of the Kaiser's war of 1914–18 he had
been a youthful air ace, awarded the highest decoration for
bravery, the* Pour la Mérite. *In the gloomy aftermath of defeat,
heroes counted for less. After various vain starts he became
an actor in the once-royal, now provincial, city of Konigsberg.
There he might have remained but for the lucky accident of
a cinema company setting out to film a story set in that same
part of the world. Westermann was given a small part but
played it well enough to be taken up regularly by the studios
in Berlin. Until in 1938, on the eve of another war, he landed
the leading role in* Storm of Steel, *and stardom the world
over. And here he was in Treblinka, on the eve of our war.*

She'd answered the phone herself when Pickup rang the
number that Nesbit had found for him, but after sounding
genuinely pleased to hear his voice had hesitated when he
proposed lunch at Rucksacks – Rusacks, she corrected him –
or any of the big hotels. Stuffy, and anyway she wasn't wearing the right clothes. Also, the observatory was some way out
of town. If he could find his way back to the station there
was a little hotel with quite good food. One o'clock? He was
there in good time and had a beer in the bar while reflecting
that life held few pleasures to compare with waiting – though
not too long – for a date.

When she came in, for an instant he couldn't be sure it was

her. A headscarf hid her hair, her face looked narrower than he remembered. Had she always worn glasses all the time? Only when reading, he'd supposed. Worst of all were her flat shoes and thick woollen stockings. But as soon as she spotted him and clawed off the headscarf there was at least the glossy dark hair he used to dream of nuzzling.

Once the usual exclamations were out of the way, and Pickup had bought her the Votrix so-called vermouth she surprisingly asked for, she said there was a dreary little dining room if he liked, but they could probably have something here in the neuk. The what? The neuk. She glanced at the barman as she said this and he nodded.

'Would you like to try something really Scottish?' she asked. 'Something you wouldn't get in Rusacks in a month of Sundays?'

'I'm game.'

She had another word with the barman and led the way to a little table in the corner which a lumpy girl presently set with a cloth, spoons and forks and some hunks of bread. Neuk, said Sarah, was a nook, a corner or, for that matter, the whole of this promontory of Fife. The lumpy girl returned with big bowls of creamy soup with bits in it, more like stew.

'It's delicious!' said Pickup. It really was. 'What is it?'

'Partan Bree, they call it. Crab, mussels, odd and ends of other species.'

'But I thought shellfish weren't. . . .' He fizzled out, embarrassed and angry with himself.

She smiled the first big warm, faintly mocking smile such as he had hoarded in Cambridge days. 'Weren't allowed, you were going to say? Dietary laws and all that. I'm afraid they were never heeded in our household. Practical hygiene when plodding to the Promised Land, Daddy would say, but not theologically relevant.'

'I put my foot in it all the time,' said Pickup, affecting to slap the offending limb. 'Talking of Daddy, he's rather busy now, it seems?'

'Oh, the Churchill connection, you mean? The old boy likes to have a whole troupe of scientists at his beck and call. Lindemann, Lockspeiser and Friedlander are only the Jewish

75

end, I guess. Sounds like a carpet business, doesn't it? Daddy is mainly consulted on things like secret death rays, which don't exist. I thought you were in the RAF, by the way.'

Again Pickup was caught off guard. 'Sort of,' he said again. It had worked before. 'What about Chris? Where's he now?' He should have asked much sooner.

'You didn't hear, then?'

'No.'

'Killed at El Alamein. I'd just started here. Nearly a year ago now.'

'Oh gosh, I'm sorry, Sarah. If I'd known . . .'

'Why should you have known?' She was looking down, didn't continue for a moment. 'He was going to be a conscientious objector, he always said. In fact he would have been if he'd been called up sooner. As he was doing Mechanical Sciences he was allowed to finish.' She looked up at Pickup. 'But hey, you were too, weren't you?'

'Which do you mean? Conscientious objector or that I did Mechanical Sciences?'

'Oh, the Tripos.'

'Didn't go back for the last year. Own silly fault. Will have to do so when this lot is over, as the erks say. Chris did, obviously?'

She nodded. 'Got a First. By then he had decided the war was necessary. Still didn't want to take life, etcetera. Happy to join the Royal Engineers, assuming he could go into bomb disposal, but by the time he was commissioned the raids were tailing off and he was posted to a field company, whatever that is. Wrote me rueful letters about bayonet drill and being issued with a revolver, until I told him to be more careful.'

'He could have been clearing mines when it happened. That's saving lives, too.'

'Perhaps. What about you?'

'I did the same but the other way round. Started off with the heroics, i.e. not going back to Cambridge, joining up to be a fighter pilot. Discovered I lacked the killer instinct, and switched to a non-combatant job.' If not the whole truth, nor a whopping lie.

'But you're a pilot still?'

76

'Communications. I hurt no one, no one hurts me.' The standard cover, but oh, the temptation, stronger than it ever was in Audrey's company, to shoot a line, to bask in some admiration. In fact she looked at him reflectively and asked what he was doing at Leuchars, then, and why the civilian clothing? He tossed off something about having to have his uniform cleaned after an oil-spill and changed the subject. She told him about the astronomy department, set up only just before the war under yet another Jewish-German refugee scientist, which was how she got to know about the job. Daddy knew him from the old days. She had been his first research student and demonstrator, now junior lecturer. It was fun, being in on something from the beginning, even the little observatory was new, and the job had its war-effort side, too, in the classes for RAF cadets. A new lot had just arrived.

When they had finished the meal she asked if he'd like coffee, in which case it was no good expecting anything drinkable here. If he had time, she could make some in her flat. It was not all that far away.

'Don't you have to get back?' Pickup asked dumbly.

'No, we're actually doing a little real observation just now. Early in the morning. You should see me pedalling through the streets at three a.m. But it means I finish early. Incidentally, that's why I'm dressed as Mother Courage, if you were wondering.' She flashed the big smile again.

As she walked her bike and he walked beside her, Pickup politely sought more about the observation. Oh, it was Venus, about which practically nothing was known, not even the length of its day. The Prof was trying to test a theory of his that it was much longer than anyone supposed. The planet was very big and bright at the moment. 'So big and bright,' she added casually, 'that it even throws shadows, like the moon.'

'That reminds me,' Pickup said. 'I'm supposed to ring Leuchars.'

'What for?'

'Check on something.'

'If you had said, there was one at the hotel.'

'I forgot.' But something different had suddenly occurred

him, an obvious question he had thought of on the night train but had not yet been able to put to anyone.

They walked in silence for a minute, then he put it. 'The moon.'

'What about it?'

'Is it the same everywhere? I mean, if it's a full moon here is it a full moon in – say – Russia?'

She shot him a sideways glance. 'The phases, yes, are the same everywhere. They have to be. I'll draw you a diagram if you like. The only difference is in the times when the moon is visible, because that depends on the local sunrise and sunset. Oh dear, I'm not being very lucid—'

'You are, you are!'

'Why do you need to know?'

'Just wondered, that's all.'

After a bit she said, 'If Annie is in, you can use her phone. To ring Leuchars, I mean. She's my nice landlady.'

But inside a narrow vestibule the main door was shut fast. Sarah unlocked a smaller door which led to a narrow stair up to the flat. 'It's only wee,' she said with a half-hearted attempt at a Scottish accent, 'but awfy cosy.' In the little sitting room she said to excuse the mess, and lit the gas-fire before disappearing to make the coffee. Well, yes, it was a jumble of books and papers and a music stand and a gramophone and lots of records. Pickup idly picked up a thin, smudgily printed newssheet, from the wording at the top something to do with anarchy. Presumably it was another of the Left-wing journals her kind liked to read. He glanced over a bit in black type on the front page. Crikey, Left wing-tip at that. On what moral grounds were we incinerating German cities? Was that what Sarah thought? Meanwhile, he wished he had sought out the Gents at the Station Hotel, which reminded him that he had also omitted to telephone Leuchars while they were there. He went out on to the landing to look for the smallest room and through the only other door, half open, saw one long leg already bare, and the other fast becoming so as Sarah, sitting on the bed turned away from him, tugged off the second of the thick stockings. He pulled back, at once embarrassed and excited, and called out, where was the lavatory.

78

Downstairs, she called back. He emerged from it to meet her descending. She was wearing velvet slacks now, and a sloppy angora pullover.

'I needed to slip into something more comfortable,' she said with a half-smile. 'The kitchen's down here, too.' She busied herself setting a percolator on the gas, the meanwhile extolling the absent landlady. 'She knows someone who keeps hens. Every week she brings me an egg off the ration, sometimes two,' and with another stab at the accent, 'always telling me that they are straight from the hen's tail.' Back in the sitting room with the coffee, she curled herself into a big squashy armchair. Pickup, in a lesser chair the other side of the fireplace, began to feel happier. She wasn't wearing glasses. Her face hadn't got narrower. It was simply an even truer heart shape than he remembered, the cheekbones higher, the mouth softer, the eyes darker, the frame of hair glossier, altogether more beautiful and alluringly less and less English.

Another question he had been harbouring surfaced. Without thinking, though immediately regretting it, he said, 'Does your father hear anything about the persecution of . . . your people? You know, those camps . . .'

Inevitably the light was snuffed out from her eyes. Christ, he should have known better. She said stiffly, 'Mr Churchill tells him what he knows, which is not a great deal more than bits there have been in the papers. Says that the best hope is to win the war as soon as possible, and devote all ends to that.' She thought for a moment. 'A man arrived from Poland – a messenger of some sort – who had actually been to a camp, he said, which only existed to kill people. He went on to America and was seen by Roosevelt, but other Poles said there were inconsistencies in his story. We don't know what to believe. We none of us know. Nobody wants to accept what's happening, so nobody does accept it.'

Pickup said, 'Have you got relations who might have . . . ?'

'Oh God, yes. Cousins, aunts and uncles, great-aunts and one old grandmother. I used to help her with the washing when I stayed with her as a little girl. She was forever washing – sheets and shirts and endless shifts. I loved stirring them in the tub with a wooden paddle. I suppose she could have died naturally, but not all the rest. Their letters still came last year, via friends in Switzerland. Who write now to say that nothing more has reached them.' She shook her head violently and said, 'Talk of something else. Something nice.'

Pickup searched for inspiration. From below came the sound of a door opening and shutting. 'That's Annie now, if you want to phone,' said Sarah.

'In a minute. Just now the nicest thing I can think of is trying to work for the bloody Mechanical Sciences Tripos on Staircase "S", King's College, four years ago, while across the landing you and Chris – oh God, I'm sorry, there I go again.'

'It's all right. Go on.'

'While you were tootling and sawing, I was going to say. It could have been a foreign language for all it meant to me, the music. But it was sort of special.' Steady, now he was getting soppy. How would Tilly cheer things up while continuing to pitch the woo if he were in Pickup's underpants just now? 'The sun would be shining,' he blundered on. 'From the river there would be lascivious sounds as a chap in a punt, with reclining blonde, poled by in the hope of some, er, pleasure.'

Dark eyes flicked up warily. Back to the sop, then.

'But I had ears only for the sound of your oboe—'

'Recorder, actually.'

'And Chris's violin—'

'Viola!'

Now she laughed, a lovely silver laugh. He had an impulse to leap from his seat and kiss her. He didn't, but perhaps gave something away in his expression. She went serious again. Dark eyes looked into his, needing to make something plain. She said, 'It wasn't as if . . . I were head over heels for Chris. He was the one that was serious. I liked him as a friend, someone to make dire music with, someone with his head in the same silly clouds, that was all. I was going to tell him, but then he was about to be sent overseas and I simply couldn't.'

'And I loved you and couldn't tell you because you were Chris's girl!' It wasn't wholly true but it bounced out spontaneously enough.

'I did wonder,' she said.

'You might have tipped me the wink.'

She shook her head, eyes closed. 'Nor did I tell Chris what I should have told him. So in the end I think he guessed. His last letter from the Desert was . . . different. I felt terrible when it arrived, after we'd heard that he was dead.' She uttered a little sob, it could have been. 'Which is why I don't want to let anyone else down, ever.'

'I'll take the chance.'

At which point, with life about to go into a controlled spin, they heard sounds below, louder sounds, closer sounds, finally a crash on the little front door. Sarah grimaced and went tripping down the stairs. Low, urgent voices, and then heavy steps hastening up them.

'Pickup?' boomed Nesbit.

'Yes!'

'You didn't know?'

'I never asked.'

'So they told me. Never mind, the Old Pals' Act has come to the rescue. It's on for tonight. And we have to be back in twenty minutes.'

'Oh, shit.'

'Lucky we had discussed your friend's name – oh, excuse me, Miss Friedlander. Under a bit of pressure, the university disclosed this address. And I have a taxi outside, paid for by Mr Edward Hulton.' With which he diplomatically backed out of the room.

Sarah's face was bleak. 'I'm sorry,' Pickup muttered.

She shrugged. 'Why didn't you say you were on the Stockholm flight?'

'I thought it was supposed to be a secret.'

'Not in St Andrews, it isn't, with strangers forever hanging around the streets waiting for the right conditions. Anyway, the Airways people have been ringing us up at the observatory to ask how long Venus is going to be so bright.' Her expression softened. 'I should have guessed you were up to something from all those questions you kept asking. What ever it is, take care. You must go now. *Lyckan commer.*'

'What?'

'It's the only bit of Swedish I know. *Lyckan commer, Lyckan* something else which I've forgotten. It means "Happiness comes, happiness goes, Whom God loves, happiness knows." '

'All I know is *Hutsun rosen on the rilera.*'

She laughed and kissed him goodbye.

It was a day of wrath, a day of vengeance, a day of hope, a day of despair, a day I have no need to memorize in case I should ever need to describe it. It is burned into my memory. The revolt started badly and half an hour too soon, after a routine search of a prisoner revealed he had money about his person, ready for his escape. Fearing that he might tell all under torture, the leaders gave the signal to start straight-away, before all the guns and grenades from the armoury could be distributed. Many of the guards were nevertheless overcome and killed, especially in the Todeslager, *where they were most numerous. Gaps were cut in the barbed-wire fences and buildings set on fire. By nightfall half Treblinka was ablaze or already destroyed.*

How many prisoners had made their escape was not clear. Several hundred, we knew, had tried. At least a hundred had been caught and killed before they even got out of the camp. Many others died in the minefields beyond the wire, or were soon recaptured. Perhaps two hundred got away. Whether devout Jews or old sceptics like me, we besought God to enable Jan Zielinski and Leo Spyra to fulfil their task.

Around midnight Pickup was woken from a fitful doze by Nesbit, in the seat alongside his, fidgeting and wheezing under his oxygen mask. He seemed to be trying to reach inside the layers of rugs and flying-suits in which each passenger was enveloped against the petrifying cold. Pickup hoped he wasn't having a seizure or something, but in total darkness there was no way of telling. Eventually there was a muffled grunt of satisfaction and the rustle of the wrappings being rearranged.

At Leuchars they had gone straight into a lengthy routine of customs, passport examination, security checks and God knows what else. Then the pantomime of everyone – Pickup counted nineteen passengers, including two women in trousers

– pulling on flying suits and fur-lined boots and gloves and helmet, not to mention parachute and Mae West before waddling out to the plane. Pickup resisted the temptation to display a casual familiarity with the gear and rather enjoyed feigning bewilderment. In truth he hadn't been decked in the full Christmas tree since flying on a couple of Whitley parachute drops when he first joined Special Duties. The bomber crews were stuck with it regularly, and he felt a sudden pang of compassion for them, setting off night after night, still kids, some of them, with no great odds on coming back.

Aboard the Dakota, the windows proved to be completely blacked out, but at least there were the cabin lights, however dim. At 10,000 feet they donned oxygen masks. Peering over his shoulder at the grotesque congregation Pickup had reflected how far removed it was from the advertisements for the DC-3, the original civilian version of the plane, he used to see in *Life*. The bright cabin would be filled by clean-cut men in lightweight suits, smart women and cute children, variously playing with dolls, chatting or extracting important-looking documents from a briefcase. And advancing down the aisle, a smiling steward or stewardess with a tray of drinks.

At which point in the current reality even the cabin lights had been switched off. They were entering enemy air, initially while still over the sea, later it would be over occupied Norway. In three years a couple of planes on this run were said to have gone missing, never heard of again, and a third was definitely known to have been shot down. Pickup closed his eyes feeling strangely indifferent to whatever might transpire tonight. The odds were incomparably better than those of a Lancaster crew en route to Hamburg, and anyway, he was in no hurry to reach Sweden and be staked on a very long shot indeed. Meanwhile the sound of the Pratt & Whitney Twin Wasps maintained an even, reassuring, muffled note. He thought again of Sarah and her teasing smile and onyx eyes, and the glimpse of her peeling the thick woollen stockings from her long bare legs.

The next time he woke, the cabin lights were on again. They must be across the frontier now and over Sweden, though Nesbit had told him with relish that the navigator had to keep to a long and very narrow air corridor, otherwise peace-loving Swedes would open fire with rather more accuracy than the bloodthirsty Huns could manage. He turned his head to see Nesbit, who held up a silver pocket-flask and gestured to their oxygen masks. So that was what he had been extricating from what he was swathed in.

A faint change in the engine note suggested that the Dak might be shedding altitude, and ten minutes later they were freeing themselves from the oxygen supply. 'Phew,' said Nesbit, unscrewing the cap of the flask. 'I got this out forgetting we were piped into the gasworks. You have first swig.' It was neat Scotch, not a drink Pickup often fancied but heaven-sent at this moment.

Along with the hour – 3 a.m. local time, said Nesbit confidently – and the isolation, it encouraged them to relax the elaborate lack of interest in each other's business they had so far feigned. 'If only this damned window weren't masked,' Nesbit grumbled, 'we might be looking down on lighted streets now. That would be something to tell the folks back home.'

'You've been sent out by . . . *Picture Post*, is it?'

'How did you know? – oh, my dropping the name Hulton? Yeah, just on an assignment, though. Not to stay.'

Pickup was familiar with the weekly news magazine *Picture Post* – his father had had it delivered with the papers from the first issue, around the time of the Munich Crisis in 1938, not long before the stupid Munich crisis with a small 'c' that he'd been on. In the mess at Tempsford its pictures and incisive text were much preferred to the scrappy reports in the daily papers.

There was a Fleet Street contingent based in Sweden, Nesbit was coincidentally saying. Their job was mainly to ferret out news from inside the Reich. The Swedish papers still had reporters in Berlin who managed to send out useful stories. Then there were travellers returning from Germany – businessmen, technical reps, the odd diplomat who lets slip a little observation. Likewise sailors, fishermen, a few refugees sneaking across from Norway or Denmark.

Pickup listened politely while wondering whether Nesbit

was photographer or writer, or perhaps both. 'Do you take your own pictures?' he asked.

'No, no. I'll have a Swedish photographer. I've worked with him before, in Finland in 1940. He's good. Officially, the story we'll be covering is the prisoner-of-war exchange in a couple of weeks' time. You've heard of that?' Pickup shook his head. 'Poor bastards on both sides – or lucky bastards, it may be – so maimed or so ill that they can never fight again. The Swedish government and the Red Cross are organizing it. The handover will be at Gothenburg.'

They were interrupted by the steward bringing hot coffee and sandwiches still frozen hard by the passage at high altitude. 'Sorry about these,' he said. 'You can try thawing them out under your jumpers.'

'And it's obviously a very good picture story,' Nesbit continued as soon as the steward had moved on. 'But in this trade you always nurse the hope of something unscheduled falling into your lap.'

'Such as?' Pickup needed to know. Surely he couldn't be hinting at Sly Lander?

'Only straws in the wind. Something might be going to happen in Denmark. Apparently the German occupation was extremely liberal by Nazi standards, but a new bastard has taken over and – well, Copenhagen is within sight of Sweden. Then there are silly-season rumours, like the fishing-boat crew in the Baltic who saw an aeroplane dive into the sea. Very small, seemed to have its engine at the rear. When they searched for survivors they couldn't find any. But you're RAF, you'll know all about that.'

'No, not heard of it.' Pickup was relieved. Nothing to do with his crazy operation, 'Have you been sent anywhere like this before?' he asked idly.

'Not anywhere neutral. But to some funny outposts of war. Finland, Abyssinia, Persia. Even Madagascar, believe it or not. How about you?'

Pickup shook his head again, but without reasoning, just from some instinct to catch Nesbit's interest, said, 'Only France.'

'In 1940?'

'No.' The instinct was in fact a furtive calculation that an unofficial ally might be a help if things went wrong. 'Week before last, as a matter of fact.'

Nesbit made no reply but rummaged under his cocoon of clothing. He brought out a wallet, extracted a visiting card, delved again for his fountain pen, scribbled a number under the name and handed it to Pickup. 'I'm staying at the Grand Hotel, which is also where the Press bureau is sited. Give me a ring whenever you like.'

It was still dark when they landed at Bromma, so they could marvel at last at the lights bathing the scene. 'Jesus! Look over there,' Pickup cried. In a particularly bright pool of radiance was parked a DC-3 almost identical to their Dakota, but with *Lufthansa* painted on the fuselage, and on the blood-red tail fin a bold swastika.

VI

Whatever else service life offered, Pickup was to reflect many times over the next days, sooner or later it suspended you in a little bubble of time and space insulated from all ambitions or fears. This could last a few hours or some weeks. Usually it occurred when being posted to another unit or sent on a course. You would be confined in a depot or transit camp while they tried to find out who you were, why you were sent there, and where the hell you should have gone. But for sheer surrealism, the bubble that now enclosed him was on its own.

The exhilaration of the arrival at Bromma Airport hadn't lasted long. When they finally got through protracted examination by immigration and customs officials, Nesbit invited Pickup to share a taxi into the city. He regretfully had to decline. He was due to be met, and in fact had already spotted someone in a sort of semi-uniform of dark suit and peaked cap waiting on the other side of the baggage hall. Nesbit gave Pickup a quick handshake, murmured, 'Don't forget what I said,' and bustled off.

The peaked cap duly proved to belong to a Legation chauffeur. But after driving only a mile or two towards the beckoning lights of the city, he turned off through quiet suburban streets, then even quieter roads, until they drew up by the side of a lake. He flashed his headlamps in the direction of the dark shape of a boat moored some way offshore, received an answering blink and switched off the engine. Pickup had finally demanded to know what was going on.

'This is Lake Malaren, sir, and that is the *Valkyrie*. They have not told you?' – in perfect English save for a slight lilt.

'No, they have *not*.'

'It is for security, sir. Both the Legation and the offices in Hovlslagaregaten are closely watched by the police and also by the Germans, especially when the plane has come in. So the yacht is used whenever secrecy has to be preserved. You may find it not very comfortable, but usually it is only for a small number of days.'

The driver unloaded Pickup's valise and carried it on to a little wooden jetty. Presently they heard the splash of oars. A dinghy bumped alongside, in it a bleary-eyed man wearing an old reefer jacket on top of his pyjamas. Fifteen minutes later Pickup was brushing his teeth over a tiny wash-basin. The narrow bunk was made up with a blanket and crisp sheets. So near to city lights, bars, adventures, girls, yet so far . . . it could only happen to Michael Prune, alias Pickup. On the other hand, it was four in the morning, and peering through the porthole he fancied the sky was already lightening.

The days that followed maintained the unreality. The boat-man or boat-janitor spoke no English, so their few exchanges were in grunts and stabbings of the hand. He ignored all suggestions Pickup attempted about going ashore. But he dished up quite good, if repetitive, meals and there was always a pot of coffee sitting on the galley stove. There were books left behind by previous captives. Pickup found a pair of binoculars in the saloon and surveyed the lake. It was two or three miles across to the far shores, he reckoned, with an island in the middle and domes poking up above the trees. In the evening, especially, people sailed little boats. A few hardy souls went swimming but no naked beauties, as promised by Tilly. It was already too autumnal, too cold. Never mind, there were bits of life to be observed – a house-painter at work, dogs being taken for walks, a guy in shorts and vest earnestly doddling along the shore road. Pickup sank into the comfy feeling that as long as he was here he was out of harm's way, and the longer that lasted the greater the chance that the Wild Jews Chase would never be needed. They would arrive by boat, grimed with coal dust.

So next morning, just to restore the chill, the Legation car brought him his battledress, as smuggled over in the diplomatic bag, along with a visitor. This was the Assistant Air

Attaché, a smooth squadron-leader, regular commission, ex-Cranwell, whose first words were that there was still no contact with Gdynia. They must assume that Sly Lander was on.

His name was Richard Petty, he had been on ops, early in the war, dropping leaflets on Bremen from a Wimpey until grounded by middle-ear trouble. Here he was responsible for the Legation's clandestine activities connected with aviation. Or rather, he was the twerp who would carry the can if anything went wrong, and be duly expelled while his superior would be left to continue the good work. Apropos of which, if Pickup was wondering why he was cooped up aboard the yacht, it was because a new face at the Legation always attracted attention.

Furthermore, the *Valkyrie* was the only Legation premises they could be sure were absolutely safe from eavesdroppers. Henry, the Naval Attaché, had only just discovered that even his private flat had been wired up with hidden microphones for the last three years. It wasn't the Germans, resourceful as they were, but the Swedish secret police, on behalf of a Swedish government fanatical about any compromise of their neutrality.

Now, about the aeroplane, the Stinson: it had been left behind by an honorary attaché before the war, when rich young fools could pretend to importance by serving unpaid in one of His Majesty's diplomatic establishments abroad. This particular young fool had brought his own aeroplane. He left in the summer of 1939 to get married, and still hadn't retrieved the machine by the time war broke out. When the Germans invaded Norway and Denmark in 1940, it was assumed that Sweden would be next, and the cloak-and-dagger brigade moved in to set up resistance cells, wireless operators and secret landing grounds, in the course of which the Stinson was flown to a private field belonging to a Swedish nobleman who had been recruited. The main operation had ended in discovery, recrimination and even the imprisonment of one British agent, but the plane had escaped notice and was still hidden on the Count's estate.

A reliable air mechanic from Gotaverken, a company which built American light aircraft under licence, maintained it. Back at the Air Ministry in London the Stinson was officially listed as one of three civilian Voyagers, the other two in Britain, which had been impressed by the Royal Air Force. It had been given an RAF number and was being painted black with RAF roundels. Pickup would be on a legitimate military operation as defined by the Geneva convention or whatever. The Swedish government might not agree, of course, but on the political background of the pick-up – with an obligatory wink at the play on his name – Pickup would be briefed by his next visitor. Meanwhile here was the gen on likely landing fields. He handed Pickup a folder.

What sort of distances, Pickup wanted to know. Oh, within the Stinson's range. The mechanic had also fitted an extra fuel tank just in case, but the Count's place was down in the south of Sweden, well placed for a hop across to Poland. And yes, the reception committee at the other end would have been given the exact pattern of guide lights he was used to.

Pickup was leafing through the aerial photographs in the folder, trying to translate the flat daylight photography into the intense black-and-silver version, more like a photo negative than a print, you actually looked down on when the moon was bright. Which reminded him that the moon hadn't so far been mentioned. He said, 'And when is all this supposed to happen?'

'Ah, was coming to that. The Count wants you down at his place by the end of the month, that's next Sunday. Two or three days to try out the Stinson, get the lie of the land, and you could be operational by – what? Night of October the third?'

Pickup shook his head. 'Full moon's not until the thirteenth. We don't fly more than six days either side, seven at a pinch.'

'Sorry, keep forgetting about that. I'll remind Miles Leveret, who is coming to see you next. Officially, he's the Assistant Press Attaché. Though we don't shout it from the rooftops, he is actually number two of the SOE mission here. You'll know all about them.'

Pickup wasn't sure he did, but let it pass. That was about all, except for one small matter.

'You're not married, I believe?'

'No.'

'But you might have a girlfriend you write to?'

Audrey? Dreaming, O my darling love, of you? Hardly. But it would be nice to drop a line to Sarah Friedlander. He said, 'Yes.'

'Then there's your parents, of course. Does anyone know exactly what form your war effort takes?'

'No one.'

'Right, there's notepaper and envelopes in the locker. Write them a couple of letters while you're waiting here. Number the envelopes in pencil so we can send them in the right order. They'll go to Blighty in the diplomatic bag and be sent on with standard overseas Forces Mail franking. You're in Iceland, on a routine communications turn. You don't actually say Iceland, but you drop a few hints. You've been for a swim in some hot springs, ridden across a lava plain, that sort of thing. Okay?'

Okay, except that it wouldn't fool Sarah.

Each day that followed saw a few more escapers brought back after being recaptured. Some were shot immediately, others hanged before our eyes at the evening roll-call. Each time we looked on in terror, lest we should see Zielinski or Spyra. Only when a week had passed did we dare to hope they had got away. Meanwhile the camp returned to some kind of normality, a process hastened by the continuing arrival of transports from Bialystok. Indeed, after a short interruption, the traffic increased dramatically, and among the wretches now were maimed and dying people. We learned from them that the Jews of the Ghetto had risen against their oppressors, as those of Warsaw had done four months before, and the retaliation was just as ruthless. As for Treblinka, the fires of its revolt were quite extinguished. The fires that consumed its human waste flared and stank once again. The pall of smoke blotted out the sun once more.

Then on the eighth day a horse-drawn wagon of the Wehrmacht came into the camp and dumped a load of corpses outside the camp hospital, which had been spared serious damage in the revolt. They had been captured and shot near a village only 60 km short of Gdynia, and their bodies sent back to the camp by an overzealous transport officer. Our ally in the hospital, the chemist Bader, recognized with dismay the remains of Jan Zielinski but thought he saw signs of life in another mangled body. This inert figure proved to be Leo Spyra, so grievously injured that Bader wondered if he had been mistaken in thinking him alive. The same conclusion was reached by the guard who bustled over with a pistol ready to give anyone who moved a bullet in the head. Evidently deciding it would be a waste of valuable ammunition, he turned away. But Bader saw Spyra's eyelids open a fraction, heard a faint sound from his lips and – perhaps by some sixth sense – glanced at the dying man's hand. He was clutching the little packet of film-rolls. Bader prised it from his hand and slipped it into his overall pocket.

Another two days in the time-bubble passed before Miles Leveret was rowed out. He was dressed in casual clothes with a fishing-rod case slung over one shoulder and a catch-bag over the other. He was having a long weekend off if any nosy parker were tracking him, and after they'd had some lunch he would certainly cast a line. After all, it was part of the act. He had some of the same jaunty assurance that Tilly displayed, except that he was older and craftier and seemed to be putting on his man of the world act more consciously, without the trace of playfulness. Before the war, he let slip, he had been in business in Sweden and had travelled all over the Baltic.

The Stockholm Mission embraced a motley collection of news-from-Germany analysts, liaison contacts with Danish and Norwegian resistance, propaganda peddlers, economic-warriors and SIS agents. Under various bogus descriptions they filled the Legation's overflow offices in Hovlslagaregaten. Pickup had already learned from the Consul in London something of the high complexities of Swedish neutrality. Leveret broached the subject at everyday level.

'You'll see a little yellow and black-striped tiger everywhere,' he said. 'Sort of emblem.'

Pickup nodded. He'd noticed a couple at the airport, one in the corner of a poster, another stuck on to a glass door.

'*En Svensk tiger*. It's a play on words. Can mean either a Swedish tiger or a quiet Swede. Some bright government minister dreamed it up to remind everyone of how they are supposed to stay out of the war – on the one hand keep watch, keep mum, avoid careless talk, same as us. Also in their case, don't provoke. On the other hand, be prepared to imitate the actions of the tiger if attacked. "Preparedness" is the watchword. *Beredskap*. You'll hear it all the time.'

He paused. 'For you on this exercise – Slylander, is it? – it's not a bad watchword either. Keep your head down, merge into the crowd, watch out for the dreaded Swedish secret police!' He gave a little laugh. 'Don't worry. They won't come for you with rubber truncheons. No Gestapo stuff. But they are persistent bastards, and they can cause endless trouble at diplomatic level. We'll be aiming to get you down to the Count's unobserved, if possible. Details in a minute. First I'd better fill you in on that gentleman.

'Rather austere, your proverbial gloomy Swede. We've not had too many dealings with him since the 1940 flap when we thought the Germans were going to invade and he was very keen to lead a resistance group. Since then he's become the commander of his local *Hemvarnet*, which is the equivalent of our gallant Home Guard. Officially he is neither pro-German nor pro-our side, but the lot cheering on the Huns, and to a lesser extent the Swedish government, still regard him with deep suspicion. Which is why you have to be careful not to be seen sweeping up to his manor in a Rolls-Bentley with GB plates.'

They were having coffee in the little saloon of the *Valkyrie* – 'Sorry about the Wagnerian name, old boy,' Leveret had said apologetically. Now he pointed to a framed map of Sweden on the bulkhead. 'At the narrowest point of the Oresund – can you see it, down there between the West coast of Sweden and Denmark? – the Germans are just two and a half miles away. We are eight hundred away.'

That was the hard reality the Swedes faced, he said. Many might be sympathetic to the Allied cause, especially since the rumours about the Jews started to percolate through, but they would never risk a downright breach of their neutrality to help us. The one exception to the rule, the one risk worth taking, was this proposal to spirit out an eminent, eloquent Jew from the death camps – better still, two eminent, eloquent Jews – who could proclaim to the world what the Nazis were doing, and perhaps force them to halt the killing. In fact it was a Swedish show, organized by a little group who were in touch with the Polish underground via a radio transmitter on the island of Oland. Only the actual collection was our task, and had to be done without involving anyone or anything Swedish. If the operation went wrong and the Germans brought down a Swedish aircraft or a Swedish airman, all hell would break loose. If it was an RAF pilot in RAF uniform and an RAF plane, Sweden could, and would, disclaim all knowledge of him.

'So where *am* I supposed to have flown from, if the Gestapo ask nicely?'

Leveret winced. 'Yes, we have given that a spot of thought. The most plausible answer would be Denmark. You could have reached Jutland from East Anglia, been refuelled by the Danish underground and flown on to Poland. A Danish chap crossed the North Sea in the other direction in an old Puss Moth. Took off one day with a chum, and landed safely at Newcastle or somewhere.'

'It was a Hornet Moth, actually,' said Pickup.

'If you say so.' Leveret paused. 'You have made yourself familiar with the maps and photographs of the landing zone?'

Pickup nodded guiltily. He hadn't yet. Never believed it would come to that. Still didn't, actually.

'Good. You may not get the actual grid reference until the last minute. We passed on the point about the moonlight to the other end. Now, as to your immediate journey, you'll be going by train. Cars are too easy to monitor, especially when there are precious few of them on the road, and the police know the numbers of all the Legation vehicles. Furthermore, you are not going until Monday now. Less chance of your attracting attention when the train is full of workaday travellers.'

He delved into his briefcase and brought out an envelope. 'This is your ticket – second class, I'm afraid. You're a humble

94

wireless technician, remember? On your way to our consulate in Malmo, if any nosy bugger asks you, though if all goes to plan you'll be alighting at a place called Hassleholm, which is the last stop before Malmo. The Count will meet you there or, more likely, send his chauffeur. There is also five hundred kronor in cash, for which I must have a receipt, I'm afraid, and a ration card which you may not need *chez* the Count, but have it with you if you go to a restaurant. How are you off for cigarettes? They're the most severely rationed item, as you were no doubt informed at Leuchars. I'll get a couple of hundred Players sent over before you go. Oh, we'll have a taxi to take you to the station. Any questions?'

Pickup shook his head dumbly.

'Good. Now – Henry the Naval Attaché keeps a little Dragon-class boat here which he sails on the lake when he's got a free weekend. I crew for him sometimes. He's coming on tomorrow. You can join us if you like. It'll be a change from being cooped up in this hulk.'

So it proved. The Naval Attaché was daunting at first sight, a masterful, clench-jawed and very straight-laced navy Captain. He too was regarded with deep suspicion by the Swedes, Leveret murmured, hence the eavesdropping on his flat. At the helm of his little yacht, he seemed easy-going enough, but every so often would relinquish the tiller in order to study the lake shore through huge naval binoculars. Only when half the day had passed, several perch been caught and many bottles of beer consumed did he frown, refocus on the same spot, and utter a naval curse.

'Who is it?' said Leveret.

'Mister Smith, I think. He ducked away the moment he saw my glasses, but it was his motor car all right.'

'Swedish secret policeman,' Leveret explained for Pickup's benefit. 'We give 'em code names. Mr Smith is so called because Henry thinks he looks like a professional co-respondent. Would always sign the hotel register as John Smith.'

'He is also one of the blighters assigned to keep an eye on yours truly,' said Henry. 'Sorry if I've drawn him here, though I doubt he will have been able to mark you down, Pickup.'

'Just be extra wary tomorrow,' said Leveret with a wry

smile. 'Don't talk to strangers. Especially if they're wearing two-tone shoes.'

To have lost both our messengers in that fashion all but crushed us. Had it not been for the inspiration of Leo Spyra's superhuman gesture, it certainly would have crushed us. Instead, we were more determined than ever to bear witness, and deliver the grim pictorial evidence that he had saved at such cost. In the aftermath of the events of August the second the atmosphere of the camp had changed. The surviving Ukrainian guards still glared and screamed, but the Germans looked on those of us who had made no attempt to escape with something almost approaching friendliness. Besides, they needed us. We were the only workers left and there was much work to be done, repairing the gaps in the fence, shoring up the few remaining buildings, and continuing to receive transports from Bialystok for onward consignment to Heaven.

Tarrutis, or Kurt Westermann, as he now admitted to being, was one who had not tried to escape. He was thus thrown into our company, though only in such a strange season might he have talked about himself. I had contrived, as casually as possible, to work with him when we were ordered to sort, and mostly throw away as waste, the wretched belongings left behind by those who had gone. I made some remark about us resembling characters in some nihilistic film of the System-time, which was the Nazis' curious term for the period of the Weimar Republic. Possibly because this usage touched a nerve with him, he grunted that he had indeed played a part in just such a terrible film. People had been too ready to forget how bad and demoralizing the movies could be then.

I suppressed any surprise I felt to hear such a loyal Third Reich sentiment. After all, Westermann had worked on in the Nazi cinema for seven or eight years before achieving fame in Storm of Steel, *and was not the only Jew or half-Jew to have done so. But acclaim for the film was cut short by the outbreak of war, and a Hollywood contract that Westermann signed met with criticism at home. Even his return to the Fatherland in 1940 did not restore him to favour in the eyes of Josef Goebbels, effectively the overlord of cinema in the*

Third Reich, nor of the producers and directors who danced to his tune. One of them told Westermann that he would have given him a part even if he were Jewish. Equally, he would have given him a part despite any suspicions of disloyalty. But to disregard both difficulties would have been a risk too great.

After nearly two years of being shunned, he was finally rescued by the unpredictable and temperamental director Herbert Selpin, an old drinking mate. Selpin had been assigned to direct Titanic, *a picture about the giant English ocean liner which struck an iceberg and sank with a heavy loss of life, particularly among poor Irish emigrants cooped up in the bowels of the ship. Rich first-class passengers fared much better. This was naturally a theme that appealed strongly to Goebbels, and no expense was to be spared. Selpin wanted Westermann to play a Jewish plutocrat who succeeds in bribing his way into a lifeboat instead of the young Irish woman and her baby who have been allotted the place.*

It was not a large part, nor an heroic one, but obviously a very important one. All went well while the main filming was carried out in the studios in Berlin. Then Selpin and Westermann took the train to Gdynia – Ha! Our own white hope – where a real liner had been adapted for the exterior sequences. A second crew was supposed to have been shooting these over the past weeks. Selpin intended only to direct crucial lifeboat scenes with Westermann. He was outraged to discover that nothing had been achieved, largely because German naval officers acting as 'advisers' had been more interested in sleeping with the young female crowd players than in organizing the necessary maritime manoeuvres. He swore at them in particular, and the Kriegsmarine in general, for using any excuse for skulking in port rather than venturing out to meet the enemy. This was immediately reported to Berlin. Selpin was summoned back to face Goebbels's wrath and, refusing to cringe to an overlord who either cosseted or despised his film workers, but nothing in between, was thrown into prison and shortly afterwards strangled by the SS in his cell.

Convinced that his friendship with Selpin on top of his other handicaps would bring him the same fate, Westermann fled eastwards to Konigsberg, in which vicinity he had been born and brought up, only to discover that those of his surviving relations who hadn't been yet carted off to the camps were so terrified to see him that they slammed the door in his face. However, one of the Lettish women who had been the family servants in his boyhood, and from whom he had acquired a smattering of their language, not only sheltered him but gave him the papers of a kinsman – Tarrutis – who had been lost while fishing in the estuary. After his new identity had been challenged once or twice because of his poor command of the vernacular he decided to head for the old polyglot border-land where this would stand less chance of being noticed. He reached Bialystok, where he found the Jewish quarter still intact, even to its Yiddish theatre. It was too tempting for the great actor! He sewed the yellow star of David on to his raiment and was soon starring in Shulamit.

Maybe because it was closer to the front line, and there-fore less under the control of the civil government of 'Greater Germany', Bialystok remained unpurged of its Jewry for many more months. Indeed, they were beginning to doubt the rumours they heard of wholesale deportation, gas chambers and crematoria. As already noted, their turn came all too thor-oughly. Westermann was in one of the first transports to Treblinka. That he labours under a great grievance is plain. But is it because he has been flung into hell as a Jew or because he has been deprived of his stature as a film star?

The electric train ambled southwards through a landscape that never seemed very far from water of some sort, whether lake or river or glimpse of the sea. From his window seat at the end of a second-class coach Pickup stared resolutely out at the passing scenery, not from any great interest in the forests and fields and occasional signs of habitation but to avoid catching the attention of talkative Swedes who probably spoke English. The taxi-driver, who turned out to be a woman, had been just such a one, though also quite helpful in locating the right platform at the station and passing on details of the jour-ney from the destination board.

The likelihood of being spotted as a foreigner was increased, Pickup had become acutely aware, by his appearance. His civvies, he realized, must look blatantly foreign. Swedish men seemed to go in for jackets with tucks and pleats and half-belts, or at the other extreme, frock coats and starched collars. A worrying example of the first category was parked across the aisle, a couple of rows up. His fancy light suiting was rather at odds with his bullet head, and his shoes were crepe-soled rather than two-tone. But could this be Mr Smith the flash secret policeman? The old chap who had taken the seat opposite Pickup's was the other sort, frock coat and not merely a stiff collar but a wing-collar, which with his scrawny neck and pince-nez made him look rather like the late and unlamented Mr Chamberlain. So far he had been immersed in his copy of *Svenska Dagbladet*. Pickup looked at his watch. Another three hours before this sluggard express was due to reach – where was it again? He took a peek at his ticket. Ah, yes. Hassleholm.

The train was slowing, if it were possible to get any slower, as the buildings of a larger town than usual began to enclose the line. The station name-boards – another little novelty for a traveller from Britain, where they had been ripped down in 1940 lest they helped invading parachutists – proclaimed that this was Norrkoping, which Pickup had worked out was about the half-way point of his journey. The train stopped there for some minutes if he needed to buy anything. As he turned his attention back to the compartment he just caught the bullet-headed man's eyes on him, instantly flicked away again. In the facing seat the Mr Chamberlain-man seemed about to give him a nervous smile, but instead disappeared again behind his newspaper.

On a whim Pickup stood up and also made for the door, partly to stretch his legs, he told himself, partly to see if there might be a newspaper kiosk with, however unlikely, English or American journals on display, partly to test out vague suspicions. As he looked back someone else was about to descend from the train, someone who immediately withdrew again.

Pickup only registered a light-coloured trouser leg and crepe-soled shoe as they were hastily retracted, but that was enough for the moment. Could it really be the shifty but dangerous Mr Smith? On another impulse he started to march purposefully along the platform towards the station exit. It could hardly be a very convincing deception, minus his luggage and mac, but it might settle silly misgivings one way or the other. After a dozen paces he glanced back. Yes, he was following, light suit, bullet head. Pickup took another few paces and spotted a newspaper kiosk at last. There wasn't anything English, just the amazingly thick Swedish newspapers, compared to the four pages you got at home, and a lot of German ones, including a stack of copies of *Signal*, which he'd been told was a Nazi photo-magazine rather like *Picture Post*. He bought one with a note which he hoped was not so big as to arouse attention. Seemed all right. As he pocketed the change and turned to go back, he confronted Bullet-head likewise attracted – or pretending to be attracted – by newsprint.

Back aboard the train, the wing-collared old boy was now reading a book, but looked up to give Pickup what might be another, more distinct nod. At which point Bullet-head returned and pushed by back to his seat across the aisle. It seemed sensible to assume that this was Mr Smith and that he was being dogged. He felt a shiver, not of fear, for he was not in harm's way himself, but of sheer helplessness. He was all alone in a suspicious land where even the small change of existence, like making a phone call or knowing where to find a lavatory, was different and difficult, and one mistake could wreck the whole tricky operation set up for him.

At least he had learned where there was a lavatory on the train, at the end of the coach, by the door. Might as well avail himself of it now. But could he leave his valise untended? Surely, not even a secret policeman would dare rummage through it in full view of the other passengers. He extracted the most incriminating small item, the folder the Assistant Air Attaché had given him, and made his way back along the gangway, aware of all eyes, or so he felt, on his back. As to be expected in super-hygienic Sweden, the lav. turned out to be nice and clean. He composed himself for a little sit and looked again at the Photo Reconnaissance prints of familiar format but bloody unfamiliar territory. Here be dragons.

Where the Stinson was supposed to have started on its journey to these beasts still bothered him. The Denmark story might fool the dreaded Swedish Secret Police, but not the Gestapo. If they threatened him with torture, he would say Erewhon, which he had encountered in School Certificate Eng. Lit. It was 'nowhere' spelled backwards, more or less. Whistling to keep your spirits up, Pickup. All right then, he had been launched from HMS *Erewhon*, an aircraft-carrying submarine such as had actually been tried out before the war. He'd seen pictures of it in the *Modern Boy*. He shivered and shut the folder again, suddenly homesick for the tried and so far trusty hazards of France.

He was washing his hands when there was a great thump on the door. Pickup jerked it open. It was the ticket-inspector, natty uniform, punch-thing in his hand, and no language was necessary to know what he wanted. Pickup went back to his seat. His valise was as he had left it. Mr Smith, if it was Mr Smith, was in his seat across the aisle. The train was running into a subtly different landscape. There were still clumps of trees and scrub, starting to turn yellowy-brown with autumn, but no longer miles and miles of forest. The fields were bigger, and mostly grass, just a few already ploughed. Here and there, straw bales awaited collection. Red barns looked American, or anyway like the barns in cigarette advertisements in American magazines. Other signs of life included power lines striding across country, telegraph poles, all the things that people string up or poke up in the approach path of an innocent sly lander.

Meanwhile, how to elude the Mr Smith character? When the train next stopped, he could ostentatiously disembark with his baggage, vanish into the shadows providing there were shadows available, and nip back on to the train as it was pulling out. But that was Biggles stuff that would never work in real life. Supposing there was a telephone kiosk at the station, would there be time to find out the Count's number and warn him of the possibility that he, Pickup, was being shadowed? Almost certainly not, and in any case it would breach security. He was not even supposed to know the Count's name, but always refer to him simply as 'the Count'. There was another count in the south of Sweden – they were all families ennobled by Napoleon, he'd been told – who supported the Germans, so keeping it ambiguous was a positive advantage.

Mr Chamberlain put his book away, fished out a pocket watch, glanced over his shoulder down the aisle. He seemed to be getting anxious about something. Pickup noticed that the wing-collar was frayed, the frock coat worn shiny at the collar. The toilet flushed in the WC, a woman emerged, and next thing Mr Smith came hurrying down the aisle towards it. Must have got a sudden urge. Or maybe hadn't dared until now to take his eyes off Pickup.

'*Sir!*' It was Mr Chamberlain, leaning forward urgently. 'We must be very quick, while he is in there. You know that he is watching you? I have also kept you observed, but on behalf of your friends in Sweden. He is from the state police. They do not know exactly who you are, or what you are here for, but if they see you with the Count they will be very curious. I shall leave the train at Osby, only a minute or two from now' – indeed the train was already slowing. 'I shall telephone to stop him going to the station, or even sending one of his servants to meet you. They will all be known. You must nonchalantly board the connecting train which will be waiting at Hassleholm. It goes to Ahus, but you must alight one station earlier, at Kristianstad. You have got that? There we will have someone else to meet you, who has been given your description – be sure to be wearing that light blue raincoat. This person will greet you as an old friend. You must respond in the same way, and – but *shhhh!*'

The sound of the flush came again, and at the same time that of the door being unlocked. As the secret policeman emerged, his secret adversary was collecting his things together, old and blank-faced, a judge's clerk arriving to prepare a trial or a lowly tax inspector to investigate a shopkeeper's accounts. The train came to a halt and without a glance in any direction, without hurrying, he left it.

VII

The branch line was evidently not electrified yet. The train was hauled by a wood-burning locomotive that puffed out copious clouds of smoke. Pickup boarded it without noticing – or even caring any longer – whether the policeman did likewise. He was chiefly aware of being suddenly hungry and tired and fed up with trains. This one seemed to be full of young soldiers, presumably conscripts doing their service. Another ticket-inspector came along and after much jabbering and pointing at the destination on the ticket, helped himself to the additional fare from the handful of change that Pickup proffered. It was getting dark as they trundled into a station with the lights of the town on one side and what looked like a little park on the other. Kristianstad, said the sign. Pickup shrugged into his air force mac and alighted. Mr Smith, the secret policeman, emerged from another carriage and drifted towards the exit amid a bunch of soldiers. Pickup was just abreast of them as they reached the gate.

There were only two people waiting. The stern-looking type in army uniform and an armband, Pickup guessed, would be the equivalent of the regimental policeman or senior NCO posted at railway stations back home, especially at night, to check on the brutal and licentious soldiery returning from leave or liberty, pull out the drunks and generally top up the fear of God all round. Hanging back, behind him and to one side, was – Wow! Lilli Marlene. Or the lofty Swedish version thereof. Pickup had barely registered low-cut blouse, red slash of mouth, pink turban enclosing her hair, split skirt and legs all the way up to her arse, before the creature darted forward, threw her arms round him and kissed him passionately. Just in time he remembered the old gentleman's instructions on

103

the train and forced himself to return the greeting in kind. The strongest aversion of all the aversions that dogged his sex-life was to tall predators with bad breath. Actually, this one didn't have bad breath, but a soft, oatmealy aroma. Her lips, too, had a softness at odds with the garish lipstick.

He became aware of envious catcalls from the soldiery. The girl pushed him back to look at him, as in films, and cried 'Peter!' except that she pronounced it 'Pater'.

'Hello' was all he could think of in reply.

'Come,' she said, taking his arm and wheeling him round. Mr Smith was watching them as she marched him out of the station and into the little station square, but did not follow. Pickup saw the long, lighted windows of what was obviously the station buffet, and through the windows people eating as well as drinking. He was suddenly famished, but his captor strode on. They crossed a green open space dominated by a building like a bloody great cathedral rearing up against the fading light. 'Holy Trinity church,' she informed him. 'Dating from the seventeenth century.' Funny thing to hear from a girl like her.

Ahead of them lay a line of huge, uniform, stately buildings. 'Barracks, you call them, I think,' the girl said. 'All full of soldiers. Kristianstad has always been a garrison town. Two whole regiments, one artillery, one cavalry, belong here, and now, in the Preparedness, many engineers and signallers as well.' Another rather scholarly bit of information to be volunteered by a painted hussy unless, of course, troop numbers were all-important to her trade.

'Kristianstad is also where the famous Swedish crisp-bread or *knackerbrod*, as we call it, is made,' she volunteered next. 'And here, more barracks,' indeed another line of them, parallel to the first. 'Excuse me a moment, my shoe hurts.' She stopped and bent low as if to fix it but actually, Pickup noted, to take a peek back the way they had come. The shoes had no buckles or laces or other means of adjustment. They did have three-inch heels and looked painfully tight. Straightening up again, she caught his eye and grinned ruefully. She was a long way from what she pretended to be, this one.

He said, 'In England you would say, "My feet are killing me."'

'Here also.' She was hobbling now, and Pickup shifted his valise to his other hand. It was beginning to weigh heavy. 'Am I going to see the Count?' he asked.

'Soon.'

They left the square, then turned into a narrow back street. She said, 'You are hungry?'

'And how!'

'What is that meaning?'

'That I haven't eaten since breakfast.'

'And I have dragged you past the station restaurant! But we have to be so careful.' She stopped again, placed her finger against her red lips and pressed herself close to him again, as strolling lovers do every time they stop. She was looking back to the corner they had lately rounded, forward to the next intersection. Pickup smelled her oatmealy breath again. Just above them, he noticed with shamefully keener interest, hung a faded sign with words that looked or sounded like 'restaurant' and 'cellar'.

'Okay. In here.' She led the way into what seemed to be the hall of a deserted house, and down a staircase. At the bottom, cooking smells and the muffled sound of voices from behind a heavy old door but the girl – he still didn't know her name – veered away towards the toilets. 'You can wait one or two minutes?' She smiled, 'Even in Sweden a woman does not go into a cellar bar alone.'

'Of course. What's your name, by the way?'

'Katrin.'

'Mine's Michael.'

'Yes, hello.' But her smile was a bit forced, he thought.

When she emerged her face had been wiped clean of lipstick and she had buttoned up her jacket to hide as much as possible of the area exposed by the low-cut blouse. Most strikingly of all, she had freed her hair from the pink turban to reveal neither blonde nor brunette tresses but little fair curls almost as short as Ingrid Bergman's – ah! also Swedish – in *For Whom the Bell Tolls*, pictures from which had been closely studied in the Mess at Tempsford. It made what-was-her-name – Katrin – slightly more desirable on the Pickup scale, if probably down a couple of points on the Tilly – 'Would be like shagging a shorn lamb,' he'd sneered of Bergman. Meanwhile this lady was still wearing the split skirt and the crippling high heels, so there was a momentary lull in the clatter of conversation as they went through the heavy old door.

Stone vaulting, Pickup took in first, together with soft lighting save for a cluster of bright spots above an open grille the other side of the cellar, where a white-clad cook was busy and smoke shimmied up into the glare and the good smells originated. All around were little tables, one long one, with a good sprinkling of uniforms among the clientele, presumably officers. Back home, anyway, this would be an officers' preserve, and the suave gent in a black jacket who was greeting them would have an *ahem* ready for any ranker who strayed in. In fact he was evidently making some ponderous comment on what's-her-name's – Katrin's – appearance, because she launched into a busy passage of Swedish with comic faces and much pointing to her skirt and shoes. 'My disguise,' she said to Pickup in English, 'has surprised people.'

Not a very useful disguise then, Pickup might have grunted, but after a polite bow to him and a welcome in English mine host was leading them to their table and – Christ! Someone was already sitting there, someone in uniform but a different uniform, unsmiling eyes fixed on them. Pickup stopped, looked wildly around to see if there were others waiting in the shadows. After playing schoolboy games all day with illusionary enemies he had allowed himself to be led straight into a trap. He glared at Katrin, but she hadn't even noticed he'd dropped behind. She did now.

'What is wrong?'

'Who's that?'

'A friend.'

'What else?' – but it had already struck him that the uniform might merely be Air Force rather than the prevailing greenish-brown of the soldiers. Ah yes, on the left breast was the wings emblem which in every air force under the sun signified the wearer was a pilot. Mind you, he could still be a snoop charged with finding out what had brought an RAF pilot, if they'd rumbled that, to this corner of their country. He had risen to receive them now, looking more cordially at Pickup if still

106

shooting frowns in Katrin's direction. Maybe it was only her outfit again, or what was left of it.

Katrin said something quick, intense and Swedish to him, then to Pickup, 'Michael, please meet my friend Anders, of the Royal *Swedish* Air Force' – hell's bells, she might have been trying to advertise Pickup's membership of another well-known Royal Air Force. Anders nodded in more or less friendly fashion and stood up to shake hands while simultaneously summoning a youth wearing a sturdy green apron. 'What will you drink?' he asked, and when Pickup looked inquiringly at the tall glass of straw-coloured beer – could it be? – on the table before him, added, 'Yes, our white beer, or wheat beer, is what I would have suggested.'

When his arrived, Pickup downed half of it in one giant draught, couldn't help himself. It was cool, slightly sweet and comforting. 'Ah, you needed that,' said Anders. He had stern, hawkish features under darkish hair that fell off his brow in a lank swatch like those of the poets whose books and likenesses were always in evidence when Pickup used to drop in on Chris and Sarah. Auden, Isherwood, C. Day-Lewis, that bunch.

He passed Pickup a menu and then exclaimed with a frown, 'But we have forgotten! Do you have a ration card, Mr Pickup?' He pronounced it *raytion.*

Katrin put her hand over her mouth in dismay, but Pickup was already reaching into the inside pocket where he kept his new passport and the extra bits and bobs he'd been given in Stockholm. Yep, there was a ration or raytion card, in fact several. Suddenly he felt relaxed again. This was a civilized country not at war, nowt to fear. The Count could wait. They were ordering the food. Anders urged Pickup to try the fried eel, a local speciality. When it came it was big flattened-out fillets, not the tubular creature Pickup had expected. He broke, not very tunefully, into the opening words of the Red Flag as he vaguely remembered them. Anders frowned. Katrin merely turned a puzzled face to him.

'Why the *Internationale?*'

Never mind, it doesn't matter, Pickup would have preferred to reply – even if they'd heard of George Bernard Shaw, which was by no means certain, spelling out the story would be a bore. But for King and country he bored on, 'There is an old writer of ours called Shaw, Bernard Shaw' – Anders nodded – 'who when he heard that tune for the first time he said it sounded like the funeral march for a fried eel.'

They had the grace to smile.

'Then another white beer for your eel to swim in,' Anders proposed. 'And an aquavit apiece for us.' He looked quite different when he was being jovial.

The aquavits came ice-cold in little stemmed glasses already beaded with condensation. Pickup sipped his. It was delicious, flavoured with some kind of spice. Anders had emptied his glass in one gulp. Evidently that was the Swedish custom. The eel was good, too, in a meaty way. Katrin had asked only for some cheese and a glass of wine. Already she was dabbing her mouth with her napkin. She looked at her wristwatch, looked at Anders. He nodded and she got up to go.

'I will be back for you in a half-hour,' she said to Pickup with a big smile. 'Until then you and Anders can talk aeroplanes.'

'But where do we go?' He was worried again.

'To my father's, of course.'

Pickup stared.

Her hand leaped to her mouth again. 'You did not know . . . they did not tell you who would meet you at Kristianstad? That instead of the Count it would be his daughter?'

'No.'

She laughed now, partly in confusion, partly in relief. 'You must have been *mystified* to be seized by such a strange-looking person. The fact is that I am rather well known as the daughter of a nobleman who is also – as you will see when I come back for you – a driver in the Women's Auxiliary Transport Corps. There have been pictures in the newspapers. Mr Pretorius, the old gentleman who spoke to you on the train, was afraid that the policeman would recognize me at once if I were in uniform. So I had to borrow what I could from one of our girls who is married to a soldier here in Kristianstad. She is quite a . . . colourful dresser.' For the benefit of Anders, who smiled and nodded, she added the name, something like Maia. 'Now I really must go.'

When she had, they ate and drank in silence for a minute or two. Pickup said at last, just to say something, 'Are you stationed here?'

Anders shook his head. 'About ten kilometres away, at Everod. Down towards the coast.'

'Fighters?'

'Also dive-bombers. A Swedish speciality, believe it or not. We have the new B-17 – no! not what you are thinking, the American Flying Fortress. Our B-17 is a single-engine dive-bomber. Only the engine is American, a Pratt and Whitney Twin Wasp. It is a very fine warplane. With the fighters there are altogether four squadrons on the base. Katze drives the Commandant. Luckily he is a sober man who rarely goes out, especially at night.'

'Katze?'

'Katrin, really. Everyone calls her Katze. And you? May I ask what you fly?'

'Nothing very interesting. I'm in Communications. Little unarmed jobs.'

'Like the Stinson?' So he knew about that.

'Yeah, like the Stinson.'

'I took her up on her first flight –'

Christ, what next? Pickup's brain went into a spin.

'Her first flight, I should say, since they brought her down to the Count's field and had the guy from Gotaverken check her over.'

Another silence, until Anders cleared his plate, took a drink and after offering the box to Pickup, lit a small cigar. 'I tell you something, Michael. I would give anything to belong to an Air Force engaged in the war instead of one which exists only to keep us out of it.'

'The RAF would be very glad to have you, I guess, if you can get to England.' He couldn't avoid making it sound sarcastic.

'Or the Luftwaffe? They are good, too, eh? And I have only to take the ferry to Sassnitz to join them.' He squinted at Pickup through a fine plume of smoke. 'Okay, I am teasing you a little, just as you tease me. But three/four years ago I was a raw young pilot in our *Flugflottilj 19*. That would be

109

a *wing* in the RAF, yes? Anyway it became rather famous in Sweden as the only navy, army or air force unit to have been in action since – oh, since Napoleon's time. You remember the so-called Winter War after Russia invaded Finland in 1939?'

'Of course. A volunteer force to go to their aid was being raised in Britain but it never got there—'

'The French and the Norwegians also, and again too late. Only the Swedish force has arrived, *Flugflottilj 19* at their head. You know what planes we had? We had biplanes! British biplanes! Gladiator fighters, and Hawker Hart light day-bombers, but both types still useful. We shot down ten or maybe twelve Russian planes, they got six of ours. Some good guys went down.' He paused as if remembering them. 'Me, I only flew on the last two sorties. It was March already, nearly all over. When the Finns surrendered we came home.'

Shouting and laughter came from a table where four young army officers were jumping up and saluting and pretending to fire guns in some impromptu charade. Anders watched them pityingly. 'You know who is the great hero, the most famous soldier, from these barracks? His name was Sixten Sparre, lieutenant of dragoons, and what he did was to leave his wife and children and run off with a circus girl. Such bravery!' He turned his gaze squarely on to Pickup. 'But to get back to what I was just telling you, I would sooner fly against those Soviet bastards than against any German. So it has to be the Luftwaffe.' His smile was now self-mocking but what he had said, Pickup knew, had a core of truth.

They were silent for a minute, then Pickup said, 'Does *Katze* mean cat?'

'Yoh, little cat.'

'She's not so little.'

Anders nodded. 'But she prowls. I think that is it, perhaps. She goes softly but surely through this world. Her father gave her the name when she was a little girl, she told me.'

There was another silent moment. Then Pickup said, 'What's he like, the Count?'

Anders drew on his little cigar. 'He's all right,' he said at last. 'You can trust him. In the morning, anyway.'

110

'What do you mean? You can't at other times?'

'Not always. It depends.'

'On what?'

Anders held up his empty acquavit glass, tilted towards him.

'He drinks?'

'Show me a Swede who doesn't. But he has to. It can make him less of a good guy then. Just watch out for it, that's all. A small warning.'

'Thanks,' said Pickup. 'You're a friend.'

Attracted, maybe, by Anders's gesture with his glass, the waiter sidled up with the acquavit bottle, misted with condensation. Anders grinned. 'Good. Let's drink to that.'

They talked of other things – how the war was going, what the UFA newsreels from Germany were showing, and drifting on from that, the feature films that each had seen lately. Anders was enthusing over a harem scene in the German *Baron Munchausen* when Katrin or Katze returned. He was facing the door, so saw her first and waved without pausing in his account of naked beauties disporting in the pool. Pickup turned and his heart gave a little leap. Was it, he wondered afterwards, because he saw that yes, she trod softly but surely, like a cat? Or was it that in uniform she looked so fresh and appetising compared with before? She wore a skirt and tunic in sleek material, the tunic with big patch pockets and flaring out from the belted waist with an abandon that Tilly would have coveted. Collar, tie and sheer matching stockings a world away from the thick lisle things imposed on our poor ATS girls continued the overall effect, crowned by the cute forage cap sitting rakishly on Katrin's ever more enchanting bubbly curls. She zoomed ten points up on the Pickup scale.

Anders refused aggressively to let Pickup pay his share of the bill. And fish was off the ration, so not even a coupon was needed. Katze leaned over to give him a peck, and they left him. Pickup followed as she led the way to a saloon car with the drab paintwork of a military vehicle and a sort of stove mounted at the rear. Pickup knew from the smell and the heat coming off it that this must be a producer-gas conversion, such as he had heard tell of when on the yacht, and seen

111

from the taxi window on the drive to the station. Charcoal was cooked to yield a gas that would just about turn over a luckless internal combustion engine. This one started second time and they crept fitfully off until, without warning, Katze swung the car abruptly down a side turning. While Pickup was still blinking at the unexpectedness of this manoeuvre she did it again, and then once more before pulling into a patch of darkness between streetlights. She switched off the car lights, and in the comparative silence as the engine idled, kept her eyes on her rear-view mirror. She said, 'We must sit here a little, to see if someone follows.'

'Was there?'

'Was there what?'

'Someone following.'

'It is possible.'

After another two or three minutes she moved off again. They drove past the dark shape of the huge church and out of town on to an unlighted country road. She seemed not to want to talk. Pickup felt tiredness taking over. Well, it had been a long day. And not over yet. He was content to feel his eyelids droop and dream fragments of dream until the next little jolt or gear-change or sharp corner woke him and he could peek sideways at Katze's profile just outlined by the back reflection of the car lights.

We have run out of Jews! My narrative has now caught up with, and overtaken, the shameful exclamation I framed when I first began to compose and memorize these thoughts. I may now venture into the present tense to record that the strange atmosphere of the camp still holds, but the transports from Bialystok have ceased. The last two were on August 18 and 19. Since then there has been nothing. The cremation-fires have burned out, and today we started to dismantle the grills. There has been a visit from a senior SS officer of peculiarly repellent appearance. He and the Commandant, Fritz Stangl, were seen to tour the whole compound with notebooks and plans. The rumour is that the gassing-chambers will be the next to go, then the scaffold, the wall against which people were shot, the watch-towers, the barbed wire. The burial pits which were emptied of the dead have mostly been filled in, and the field will be levelled and raked for the grass to grow again. One of the guards, it is said, has been offered the whole site for nothing if he undertakes to remain behind and turn it into a farm, so that eventually nothing will be left to betray Treblinka's infamous history.

That is good news for the world. It means that the Germans are resigned to retreat, and are desperate to conceal the evidence of their crimes. It is less good new for many Polish people, in that their 'liberators' will be the Soviet forces who four years ago were their invaders. It is bad news, if long expected, for us in Treblinka. As the works are completed we shall be killed and our bodies disposed of. The guards do not bother to deny the supposition. And for those of us who live only to bear witness it is the worst news of all. Just when our testimony becomes even more necessary, we see less and less prospect of delivering it.

In all, scarcely a hundred Jews are left in the camp. Already we are being worked from dawn till dusk. In the estimate of Bader's friend Roman, a former surveyor from Krakow, the reclamation cannot take more than two more months, and well before the end they will have started to decimate us day by day. The one dubious gain is that so many of our Ukrainian guards were lost in the uprising that those who survived have to concentrate their energies on preventing escapes through the damaged wire. They can no longer prowl around looking for suspicious activity or prisoners talking to each other. It is easier to make plans, but ever harder to put them into action.

Who shall be our chief witness in place of Zielinski? Who shall be our natural leader instead of Leo Spyra? The enigmatic, brooding presence of Kurt Westermann seems to be the answer to both questions.

Twice more Katze pulled off the road into a patch of deep shadow and cut the motor and lights, waiting four or five minutes, seemed more, before driving on again. The last time she did not switch on the lights, but steered by the faint luminosity of the stars and – ah! – the moon. It was hardly into its second quarter, let alone operational. He peered at his watch: nearly midnight. A minute or two later Katze braked and turned into a farm road which led to a cluster of low buildings flanking a more imposing one. It alone had a couple of lighted windows and a big door, at the head of a flight of stone steps, which as Pickup took in the scene was opened wide to reveal a figure silhouetted against the brighter light that spilled out. Nearer at hand, someone else was already wrenching the car door open, a swarthy type in a sort of waistcoat. Oh God, were there going to be servants? Pickup was not at ease with servants, and they always sensed it. 'Ah, Johan,' he heard Katze say, and the bloke reply in Swedish as he wrested Pickup's valise from him.

The Count was in full natter at his daughter even as she led the way up the steps. He was tapping a pocket watch he held in one hand with a finger from the other, evidently browned off because they had arrived so late. In reply, Pickup guessed, she was explaining about the security antics. He took the opportunity to get an impression of the Count. He was tall and stooped, with bits of bald head showing through sparse flattened hair, a somehow blurred face and to go with that – so far as you could tell from hearing him in a still unfamiliar language – a slurred delivery. Was he living up to Anders's thumbnail description from the word go? But the next moment he was holding out his hand to Pickup and addressing him in English that didn't sound blurred or slurred at all, just reproachful.

'We had prepared a welcoming meal for you, after your long journey, but Katrin tells me you have already had something in Kristianstad.'

Pickup started to mumble an apology, though God knows it was none of his doing. The Count stopped him short. 'It is not so important. The important thing is that you have arrived at last, and naturally are most welcome. Please excuse the Countess. She was tired and I sent her to bed. She wishes me to give you her apologies.'

By now he was ushering Pickup through double doors into a big room with big pictures on the walls, a suit of armour in one corner and massive furniture, all rather gloomy save for a log fire in the outsize fireplace. Katze followed them in, and the cove in the striped waistcoat closed the doors behind her.

'Now: you are sure you do not wish to eat something?'

Pickup glanced at Katze. She made a little face as if to say she left it to him. 'No thanks. Honestly,' he said lamely.

'Then perhaps a glass of our Swedish punch, to help you sleep?'

Pickup glanced at Katze again. This time she nodded. 'Thank you. That would be nice.'

The Count busied himself at a sideboard, with various bottles and a tall glass beaker such as Pickup had not seen since he abandoned chemistry, or chemistry abandoned him, after School Cert. It seemed that the punch wasn't going to be a hot steaming concoction, as Pickup had seen depicted in books or, somewhere or other, on a pub sign, and which would have been rather welcome at this hour.

'And you were not observed coming here?' the Count asked over his shoulder, in English although the question was obviously intended for Katze.

'No one has followed us,' she said, likewise in English. 'Nor should anyone have seen us turn off the road. We were without lights already.'

'Good.' He turned, holding up the beaker now two-thirds full of liquid. 'So, Lieutenant Pickup –' with the syllables given equal stress – 'would two hundred millilitres be in order for you?'

Christ, the thing was calibrated, Pickup could see the markings. He looked to Katze once more. She smiled and shrugged. He murmured acceptance, trying to remember how much a litre was.

'You will be thinking it strange that one should be so scientific in small matters,' the Count said as he poured, 'but why be otherwise? It is good to be given the amount you require, not too much, not too few –'

Katze made a little noise, a snicker, even a snort. The Count flicked chilly eyes in her direction, then back to his pouring. He offered the almost-full glass to Pickup and glanced again at Katze. She shook her head. 'Not for me, please. Actually, I think I shall go to my room now, if you will excuse me. It is so late, and in the morning I have to drive to Everod by nine o'clock in case the Commandant wishes to go somewhere.'

She gave her father a dutiful kiss, Pickup thought, and extended her hand towards Pickup. On the impulse, not sure why, he took it and kissed it, as in dreary costume films. She looked surprised, but gave him a grin.

The Count was already filling another glass. 'Your health,' he said, raising it.

Pickup took a sip. It would have been better hot, but was nice enough in a sort of Pimms No. 1 way. The Count seemed to be looking along his nose as he drank, as if measuring how much remained in his glass. When he set it down it was precisely half empty. He offered Pickup a small cigar, took one himself and lit them both before leading the way, glass in hand, to seats by the fire.

'You have met Capten Ahlqvist, I gathered from Katrin.'

'The boyfriend?' – stupid bloody idiot! Even as the words popped off his tongue he feared that he was well and truly out of turn. Not an assumption to spring on any father, least of all one with a handle to his name. And who was now regarding him stonily if not actually spitting blood.

Luckily – whew! – it turned out to be pukka gen after all. The Count nodded. 'She is attracted to him, that is clear,' he said. 'I am not sure I would approve of any serious intentions, but the Countess likes him, if only because he is well mannered.' He drew on his cigar. 'He knows how to flatter the ladies. I must share such matters with you because we have been obliged to tell him something of our little plan.'

'He took the Stinson up, he said.'

'The aeroplane? Yes, I was about to tell you so. You shall have your turn in the morning. But of greater importance, he will also keep us informed about patrols from his aero-drome, weather forecasts and the volunteer observers who keep watch on our skies. We have no choice but to trust him.'

'He struck me as okay.'

The Count took a further long pull at his drink. 'I am glad to hear that. As for the details of time and place and so on, all that will be telegraphed, in code of course, from our people who have contact with the Polskis. You have already been given maps and aerial photographs?'

116

'I haven't studied them yet.'

'Another task for tomorrow, please. It could be soon, you see, the . . . shall we call it the *expedition*?'

'How soon?' Pickup felt that little lurch in the guts.

'In two days, perhaps.'

'Not on,' said Pickup. 'Full moon is not until the thirteenth.'

The Count stared at him. 'What has the moon to do with it?'

'Everything. That's how we find the field, and how we land on it. By the light of the silvery moon.' In case the Count knew the song.

Whether he did or not, he was no longer in any mood for pleasantries. 'But they have talked of lights which are to be set up for the aeroplane—'

'Lamps,' said Pickup. 'To line you up. Hardly bloody great floodlights.'

The Count thrust himself up from his chair and crashed over to the sideboard. Pickup heard a clatter rather than a clink of glass on glass. No more for him, he called. The Count turned to glower at him. His face was mottled.

'You are telling me that you cannot fly until you have the full moon, like a witch?'

'No. But not until it's within a week of being full.'

The Count slurped half his refilled glass. He sighed. He actually groaned, it seemed to Pickup. 'We are all prepared,' he said tragically. 'The mechanic from Gotaverken will be here tomorrow. We have lanterns to light the landing path when you return. We have gas for the plane, more precious than gold in Sweden today. We await the signal to go, and you say you cannot.' His eyes were looking a bit muzzy, and when he spoke again the words came out thickly, which was just as well, because what they sounded like was 'Or will not.'

Go to hell, Pickup muttered under his breath. It was bad enough being issued with a gipsy's warning by the likes of the Branch Manager. Damned if he was going to take it from some stuck-up neutral. But all he actually said was something about looking at the calendar again tomorrow. Just now he was tired, and suddenly it really was creeping up him, that sometimes welcome, sometimes not, feeling that you only

117

want to close your eyes and crash. The Count glowered at him anew before ringing for the footman, or whatever he was, in the stripey weskit. Poor blighter, he was probably dying for his pit himself.

The bedroom into which he was shown was as forbidding as anything downstairs, but did have, as the lackey kindly pointed out to him, a fully operational w.c. opening off. He put it to use as soon as he was left alone. The bed looked comfortable and was big enough for two, if not three. Not much chance of anything in that line, unless Swedish girls were as willing as Tilly believed, even when they already had a bloke in tow and, what's more, one who was confident and could make conversation and had decent straight hair. Anyway, there was no knowing where Katze slept, might be on another floor. When the w.c. cistern stopped filling up and all was quiet, he listened for a bit. A little sound came through the wall from the next room, an exhalation or someone shifting on to one side. But it could just as likely be the old Countess as Katze.

He got into bed himself. Yes, very comfy. And Christ, yes, he was tired. So, of course, the willies had to start assembling. It was talk of the job that had set them off, of course, this crazy unreal operation which half the time he simply couldn't believe, like one of those characters in books who were forever having to pinch themselves. Thanks to the Count, no pinching was necessary now. The prospect of flying into the dragon's mouth came pushing in, just as the prospect of gym next day had come and squatted on the bed every Monday and Thursday night in his schooldays. What had been safely in the future was suddenly gibbering at you. The fact that it wasn't possible while the moon was only a slice didn't count. It was all his fault for lacking aggressive instinct.

Out of the nowhere, a wholly new, shameful, tempting thought struck him. He didn't have to do it at all, whether sooner or later. The Swedes couldn't make him, indeed half of them would be out to stop him if they got wind of the plan. The RAF couldn't make him, not in a neutral country. There would be hell to pay if and when he got back to Blighty, of course . . . he'd need to devise a plausible reason, preferably technical, for not going. Or better, he could set out, stooge around over the Baltic for an hour two and then come back with the excuse. Better still, just slip the word to the pro-German gang and they would ensure the whole thing was scuppered. He reached in the darkness for his wallet. Yes, he could feel it safely tucked into the back flap, the card that Nesbit the Newshawk had given him. Meanwhile enjoy whatever was offered. Maybe Katze would come floating in at first light, a vision of loveliness . . .

VIII

No vision of loveliness woke him, just a sweaty night-mare in which he was flying a waggon-load of strangers home in an Airspeed Ferry biplane and he couldn't recognize a single feature of the landscape, let alone the landing field. Later, after dozing off again, it was faint sounds of activity, the rumbling flush of a lavatory and then a manservant, a different one, bringing in a jug of hot water and a clean towel. By the time he'd shaved and dressed and found his way down to breakfast, Katze was in fact about to leave. The servants had kindly lit the charcoal stove on the car for her. Fresh and pretty in her uniform, she introduced Pickup to her mother, who was unsmiling and wore her hair elaborately wound round her head like a schoolmarm. The Count was wearing a kind of pleated tunic over riding britches and knee-length buttoned gaiters, and seemed to have quite forgotten his paddy the night before. He greeted Pickup jovially, smiled fondly as his daughter prattled on and then followed her out, leaving Pickup to the silent disapproval of the Countess.

He listened gloomily to the fitful chug-chug of the motor as it was chivvied into life, drank a cup of lousy coffee and crunched a slice of the knackerbrod Katze had told him was made in Kristianstad, presumably from the knackers of an armadillo. He had just wiped his mouth when the Count returned, rubbing his hands. 'If you have had enough to eat and drink, perhaps you would like to take a look at our little secret, eh?'

'Fine. Whatever you say.'

The Count peered at his jacket and slacks. 'You have brought no riding clothes? I have told Stockholm that you should bring riding clothes.'

'Sorry, no one passed that on to me. Anyway, I'm afraid I don't ride.'

The Count spread his hands. 'Then we must walk.' He scooped a watch out of his top pocket. 'But in that case we should start at once. The mechanic has to come from Goteborg, but he is usually at the field by ten.' The Countess said something in Swedish and he snapped back in a reminder of last night's form. He turned back to Pickup. 'She says we should order her carriage, but I tell her it is a long way round by road. We shall walk.'

In the hall he paused to take a hat from the array of hats and coats. Pickup noticed a military cap on the next peg, and hanging below it a military greatcoat with a single big star embroidered on the epaulette. The Count followed his eye. 'Ha! You see the uniform. Have no fear, it is only mine. For the *Hemvarnet*, which is the same as your Home Guard in England.'

That's exactly why he did have fear, Pickup muttered. Another Major Kerr. But at least he sounded friendlier now. He was saying confidentially, 'Of course, the real reason why we must stay within the estate is that you must not be seen on the road outside. There are sometimes people watching to see who comes and goes.'

In the courtyard a stable boy was holding the reins of two placid-seeming horses. It occurred to Pickup that perhaps he ought to show a bit more willing. To be honest, he had ridden once before. It was with Audrey on an earlier weekend at the Winwicks'. They'd hired mounts from the local riding stables. Audrey had all the right accoutrements, jodhpurs, boots, hacking jacket, hat and little whip thing, but hadn't seemed all that sure in the saddle. 'A girl can ride a bicycle, and a girl can drive a car,' he had quoted to her, 'but a girl who rides on horseback is stretching a thing too far.' Don't be mucky, she'd snapped. They had walked the horses along country lanes and trotted once, which was more alarming, but he had survived with nothing worse than a sore coccyx.

Also, if he fell off now and broke his collar-bone or something, that would neatly put the kybosh on the whole Wild Jews Chase. 'Sir,' he called to the Count, 'I'll try riding if you like. As long as we don't have to gallop.'

121

'Take Asta here. She is old and rather lazy.'

They set off on a path by the side of a formal garden, through a paddock, Pickup supposed it would be, and then along a track through rusty-green woods such as he had seen from the train. The chances of a helpful accident receded as the Count seemed to forget his hurry and became positively chatty, pointing out particular features of the landscape, asking Pickup about his homeland. Guessing that semi-detached, pebble-dashed seaside suburbia might not impress, Pickup borrowed the manor house belonging to the parents of a snob college-mate who had turned out to come from the same part of the world. Pickup had been invited over one Christmas. It was very grand, set on the banks of the estuary with views across the mud-flats to the Welsh hills. For a while, that was where he had lived in his daydreams.

They emerged into a little meadow at the edge of the woods, indeed still hemmed in on two sides and a bit of the third by trees. At one end was what could only be a modest aircraft hangar. From a flagstaff a windsock fluttered listlessly. So this was the field. On acreage, Pickup gauged, it would be plenty enough for any light plane. The Count kicked his horse into a canter and headed for the hangar. Asta seemed content to amble after him at her own pace. By the time Pickup had awkwardly dismounted, the Count had one of the big double doors open. Pickup followed him in.

Hell's bells! What met his eyes looked even more toy-like than the L-5 he'd flown at Bovingdon. Hell's bells squared, it was painted a shiny green with Swedish crowns emblazoned on the wings and tail fin, and a life-size yellow and black striped tiger painted along the fuselage side. He pointed to it, lost for words, dumbstruck.

The Count laughed. 'Don't worry. This is not your aeroplane. This is our Swedish GV-38. I bought it for my son who was crazy about flying, but since two years he has been in our embassy in Washington. So it has become a kind of talisman, you could say. I told you of our Home Guard. I have the honour to command the battalion of this district.' He paused as if to invite a knowing nod. 'And we have made ourselves quite famous as the only *Hemvarnet* unit to have its own air force.

Of course, the high command is not amused and tries to stop us getting petrol for it. But the newspapers made a story about us for a few days, and the government has decided it is rather good for morale, you know. Anders – the friend of my daughter you met – flew it for us at first, unofficially of course, then we found a young reservist who has a pilot's licence and can join us when we have an exercise.

'The importance of which, the real reason for all this –' his voice hardened, the joke was over – 'is that when your aeroplane has to fly, the peasants think that is only the Count and his crazy Home Guard air force. Even the *Lottas* who watch the skies for the air defence – even they are deceived. Especially when the light is not too good, eh?'

As he spoke he was leading the way further into the hangar. Pickup could just see one wing-tip of the Stinson, the rest was hidden behind a canvas sheet suspended like a curtain from the roof-truss. 'This is only since we have painted it in your RAF colours,' the Count explained as they pushed past it. Now the Voyager was in full view. 'You see, both machines have the high wing, is it called? And square fuselage section, and in-line engine.'

He must have learned off these details. Certainly the general arrangement of the two planes was similar. Better still, the Stinson's war-paint would have passed even the Branch Manager's inspection – overall matt black, RAF roundels minus the white ring, regulation service number in place but not too prominent. No Lizzie-type ladder was needed, the little triangular, forward-hung cabin doors were no higher off the ground than a Ford V-8's. The Count cocked his head to one side and listened. 'Ah, I think I hear the mechanic arriving.'

He was riding a little pipsqueak motorbike, which along with aeroplanes, it struck Pickup, were just about the only vehicles the Swedes couldn't convert to charcoal. He stood the bike on its strut, peeled off cap and goggles and revealed himself to be a stocky, freckled type of about forty. 'This is Per,' said the Count and, looking at Pickup, 'By what such name shall we address you?'

'Mickup,' said Pickup. He'd never liked it, but it seemed to fit the requirement. Per nodded to him. He looked steady and reassuring. His technical English was fine, if his every-day vocabulary not so good. They hauled the curtain aside to extricate the Stinson and pushed and pulled it out on to the apron. Per went at once into a systematic check of tyre pres-sures, oil levels and electrics. When he had the engine exposed, Pickup peered hard at it, trying to settle the question which had worried him, on and off, ever since the lanky Yank at Bovingdon had gone on about the original Voyager being under-powered. 'What's the power plant?' he called.

'Uh?'

'Which motor does she have?'

'Franklin.'

Shit, ninety miserable horses, maybe only eighty. 'How many horse-power?'

Per shrugged. 'Ninety, it says in the book.'

'What is it actually?'

Per grinned. 'At Gotaverken we know some tricks.'

'And?'

'We got a hundred and five, maybe a hundred and ten. We have no test equipment here but at take-off I guess you have a hundred-five for certain.'

Thank God for the Taffys and Pers of this world, thought Pickup. 'I'll take her up as soon as you're ready,' he said.

He did a couple of circuits just with Per at the dual controls by his side, then two or three more with the Count, a not very confident passenger in the seat behind. With a light breeze and three aboard, the Stinson still needed all of six hundred feet, he estimated, to come unstuck. In the air she handled nicely enough, and the one landing so far had been a doddle. He turned east with a view to swinging round in a much wider circle so that he would head back to the field on roughly the same vector he would be taking on the return trip from Poland, if ever there was a return trip. That way, he could start now on fixing the pattern of the landscape in which it was located. The morning's nightmare was an old favourite, but one he took to heart.

At which point he felt the Count trying to attract his atten-tion. Not to go too far from the estate, it sounded he was saying. Something about it being too light to be confused with

124

the other plane, something else about petrol. Well, there would be other opportunities. He turned back to line up for the approach. 'If you return when it is still dark,' the Count said, 'we shall have lights to mark the landing strip.'

Beside him, Per whispered, 'Candles!'

So much has happened that I scarcely know how to begin! A month in time and many leagues in distance now separate us from Treblinka in those dark days after Zielinski and Spyra had been brought back dead or on the point of death, and I was brooding over the inertia which seemed to grip us. Only a day later we heard of a desperate escape plan for a small number. A detail of fifteen men was required to work outside the camp, lifting some land-mines which had been laid too far from the perimeter. A government officer's horse was killed when the officer was hunting, and complaints had come from on high. Our new friend Roman, the surveyor, was in charge. He still had to find three workers, The intention, he whispered, was to kill the Ukrainian guard escorting the party and make a run for it.

There was no time for deliberation. Westermann was asked bluntly if he would be our eminence, and agreed. Against my protestations, I was to be the second emissary. Marek would be in reserve and, more importantly, lend practical help to two persons whose lives had been led at some remove from down-to-earth travel and foraging.

I can recall that day only in a series of strident images from which, at the time, I felt detached – the Ukrainian struck dead with one blow from a spade as we were momentarily hidden from all watch-towers by a clump of trees, his body hastily stripped of his uniform for Marek to don, Marek marching us on, shouting and waving the dead man's gun, hoping that no watcher on the towers would notice the diminution of the squad.

Then a sequence of scenes in which we dug up mines, blindly, inexpertly, avoiding death by luck rather than skill. After each prodding and digging we moved on fifty or a hundred metres until suddenly we were quite out of sight of the camp. Marek resumed his own clothes and we stumbled off across fields and through forests as fast as we could. In my case, alas, this was less fast than the others, and for a shorter time. I was soon struggling for breath, my heart was labouring and there was a fierce pain in my side. By night-fall we three had been left behind. Only Roman stayed with us at first, but soon left to head south, towards his home town of Sokolow. He hoped to be sheltered there by old friends.

In vain I pleaded with Westermann and Marek to leave me and press on alone. Marek wouldn't hear of it. Westermann took the same stance, if with a shrug. I think he felt, perhaps rightly, that a small group moving cautiously stood a better chance than a dozen in a hurry. We had lost Spyra's map when he was recaptured and shot, but Roman left us an inferior one. Lest anything worse should happened to me, I now made sure the others both memorized the details that Spyra had entrusted to me, so long ago, of how to find and prove ourselves to the contacts who might lead us to the Gdynia stevedores.

The days that ensued are a blur of contradictions, of sullen silences and cheerful camaraderie, of hope and despair, of bitter nights in cold ditches and exhausted sleep in warm barns. Of farmers who threatened to report us and farmers' wives who gave us food and milk. Of towns we skirted and villages that welcomed us. Once we were carried for 50 km on a lorry loaded with the hides of animals. Another time we had to leap from the only train we boarded. With our hearts in our mouths we crossed into the former Polish Corridor, now once more part of the Reich.

Spyra's instruction was to make for the small town of Starogard, or Stargadt as it had become again, and find a locksmith's shop near the main Christian church. There we were to ask a certain question, and reply correctly to one from the shopkeeper. This we did, and he sent us to wait in the churchyard. After a while an old crone approached carrying a bundle of sticks for the fire. She gestured for us to follow her, but not too closely. She led us into an area of buildings destroyed by bombs or gunfire, and after looking around, down shattered steps into a cellar beneath the ruins.

There a man obviously of some authority awaited us, a lawyer or school director perhaps, but now very agitated.

126

After quickly confirming that we had escaped from Treblinka and were chosen to bear witness of its horrors, he dropped his bombshell. The stevedore organization in Gdynia had been infiltrated by the Gestapo, and all its members arrested and shot. This had happened some weeks ago, but the Germans had cunningly maintained a pretence that all was normal, and several fugitives had walked straight into a trap before the truth reached Starogad, not until the previous day. Nor could they be sure that under torture no one had betrayed the activity here. As soon as a guide for our journey could be mustered, we must be on our way again.

On our way where? Westermann asked, almost the first words he had spoken.

Well, the possibility of an alternative passage to Sweden had arisen, by aeroplane. A number of fugitives and couriers were awaiting just such an opportunity, but the Swedes who were making the arrangements were only interested in Jews who had escaped from one or other of the death camps. We looked at each other in astonishment, even disbelief.

Preferably, he added, these Jews should have stature in the world beyond our ravaged continent. 'Here is Kurt Westermann, the film star,' Marek shouted, pointing. 'And there a famous university professor!' Before I could protest, our inquisitor had asked Marek what his calling was. A barber, an ordinary barber, said Marek.

Westermann and I were then subjected to further questions, adroitly chosen to judge whether we really belonged to the occupations we professed. Westermann, for example, was lobbed one about the American film Gone With the Wind *which had come along on the eve of war. Now the actor came to life, told a story he could only have heard in Hollywood, and let drop the information that it was Dr Goebbels's favourite picture. It was a small performance.*

'Good,' said the inquisitor, who now turned out to be arbiter as well. 'It may be that only two of you can be taken. But all three of you shall set out. You will leave as soon as your guide arrives. You have quite a few long German miles to go, and not much time.'

*   *   *

Dinner that evening was formal. The Count wore a dark suit with a high collar, almost like a military tunic, the Countess a lot of jewellery over a long dress. The guests were the local doctor and his wife and a clear-eyed, open-air type who was evidently the Count's agent, or factor. They addressed the Count familiarly as Bertil. Everyone seemed to be in on the great secret, though abstaining from any direct references, and sometimes breaking off a remark when servants came in to hover round the table, which was often.

'Meet Dr Glas,' the Count had said with an elaborate smile when effecting introductions. Or what sounded like 'Teako' to give him his first name.

The doctor, Pickup saw, was none too pleased about this. 'It is Dr Holmin really,' he said. It was only Bertil's joke to call him Dr Glas. That was the name of the doctor-hero, or doctor-villain, of a notorious Swedish novel, *Doctor Glas*. They did also share the same forename, Tycho, which he spelled for Pickup.

'If the Count should warn you not to accept any pills I dispense, that is just him teasing,' he said wearily. 'I hardly notice it any more.'

He had a kindly, bearded, humorous face. If the conversation touched on the forthcoming mission, or was cut off short because of servants, he would direct a little knowing glance at Pickup. What with the doctor in France only a fortnight previously and now this one, Pickup reflected, doctors seemed to be involved in all his doings. He rather liked and trusted doctors, he decided, not so much for their expertise as their instinctive understanding of what people were worrying about.

The meal was fish soup followed by meat-balls in a spicy sauce, then cheese and stewed fruit, only the fruits were not the apples or pears of home but deep red plums, cherries and berries. There was a little wine for the two ladies, beer and aquavit for the men. The talk, inevitably, was of the war. They would lapse into Swedish, then someone would want to ask Pickup what he thought, and English would be the tongue until the Countess obstinately piped up in Svensk again. Dr Holmin seemed the best informed, though how much of his news was hearsay and how much fact was impossible to tell.

An eminent Danish scientist called Bohr had apparently escaped and was now in Stockholm. The government had suppressed any mention of this in the papers or on the radio; the supposition was that the Allies wanted to smuggle him on to a plane to Britain. Eyes were cocked in Pickup's direction for confirmation, but he could only spread his hands and shrug.

Also from Denmark were rumours that the Nazis were finally rounding up the Jewish population, until now left alone. Several hundred had already been transported to Germany. This was not altogether a troubling rumour, Pickup sensed. If true, it would embarrass the pro-German Swedes who had used the demonstrable survival of these Jews to pour scorn on stories of transportation and death camps elsewhere in Europe. Again, eyes flicked his way.

The one undisputed event was the one of which Pickup had already learned from Nesbit on the flight over. The exchange of prisoners of war too ill or too maimed to fight again was now imminent. The British would be brought on the ferry from Germany to Trelleborg on the south-west tip of the land, and travel by train to Goteborg, where they would board the white-painted ships waiting to carry them home across the North Sea. The Germans would be making the same journey in the opposite direction. While they were in Sweden, both parties would be fed and cared for by the Swedish Red Cross. In all, there would be seven or eight thousand men, Holmin said. With nurses from the little district hospital, he had volunteered to travel on the trains between Trelleborg and Goteborg. 'We shall try to be as sympathetic in one direction as in the other,' he added with a wink.

Pickup had been watching as the butler, or whatever he was, kept the glasses refilled. The Count's had to be topped up more often and more fully than anyone's. His face began to take on the blurred look of the previous evening; his voice got louder and more argumentative. He snapped now at the doctor in Swedish. Holmin frowned back, clearly urging the Count to keep quiet on the matter. As they left the table to have coffee in the big room with the pictures and the armour and the log fire, he drew Pickup aside.

'I have also promised Bertil to be on hand should your . . .

passengers . . . need attention, as he has reminded me just now. Do not worry, should these other great events happen at the same time your mission will still have first claim.'

In a dopey sort of way Pickup was cheered up by both these acquaintances of the day who quietly connived in what had to be done, first the mechanic, now the doctor. He didn't feel quite so alone, quite so subject to the moods of the Count. It lasted until the guests were preparing to leave and the Count was called away by the butler, or whatever, to answer the telephone. When he returned, his face was mottled as well as blurred.

'That was Oland,' he announced to the room. 'The landing is set for tomorrow night, or to be exact, at two hours in the morning of Thursday –' he glared squarely at Pickup – 'if our young Englishman does not find the moonlight too thin.'

Pickup pulled his face into a far from funny smile. If doctors were on the whole reassuring types, bloody old Sunday soldiers – there had been three of them, too – were stinkers.

'So before you go,' slurred the Count – or Cunt from now on, Pickup decided – 'we will drink a toast to the success of our plan.'

Dr Holmin caught Pickup's eye and mouthed a rueful apology.

IX

The co-ordinates didn't arrive until after 10 a.m. Pickup already had the maps and photographs spread out on a table in a little parlour which the Countess was supposed to use for feminine pursuits such as sewing, but rarely did. He'd rustled through them yet again, smoked three fags and chewed his fingers before the phone rang. Mooching into the hall, Pickup heard the Count in his study repeating the figures – they could only be figures – often more than once, each time on an ever-rising inflexion. He was drumming up courage to barge in and ask to get them himself, even if they were in Swedish, when the Count said *Tak* and a moment later there was the jangle of the earpiece being hung up. Pickup was still rooted outside the door as it was jerked open. The Count looked put out.

'So! You are waiting for these?' He waved a bit if paper.

Pickup held out his hand. What else would he be waiting for? But he grunted a *Tak* of his own. It didn't stop the Count from following him into the parlour and standing over him. Pickup located the particular bit of territory on the map and hunted for the batch of photographs which ought to cover that zone. From the Count came a stream of helpful comments.

'They said you should look out for a small lake. See! There it is!' In fact there were several lakes on the map, of which two figured in the photographs, both roughly the same comma-like shape and therefore not of much help unless they could be related to another feature. Pickup became aware of a sweet, tell-tale smell on the Count's breath. He had already been at the beaker, with the sun – had it been visible – still well below the yard-arm. Pickup shuffled back to the big map and checked the reference again. Yep, just about dead on 18

131

degrees east, 54-odd north, providing the Count had got the numbers right. The trouble was that none of the photographs seemed to square up with the geography of the map.

Just as he was about to explode into curses he heard the sound of a car door being slammed, then voices and a servant's footsteps as he made his way out. The Count perked up. 'Ah,' he said. 'They have been able to come actually.'

'Who?

'Anders and my daughter, I think.'

So it proved, Katze leading the way with a big smile and a kiss for her father, Anders searching for Pickup and saluting the moment he spied him. Both were in uniform. Relief filled Pickup. It would be all right now, except that Katze was already explaining in her wayward, tumbling English that Anders had only been able to leave the airfield and have the car by arranging an urgent meeting with his opposite number along the coast at Ronneby. They would have to go on there, but would come to the house again on their way back.

Anders had spotted the maps on the table. As soon as the Countess had appeared and coffee had been served, he caught Pickup's eye, flicked a finger in their direction and whispered something to Katze. 'We must let the two airmen make their studies,' she announced, ushering her mother to the door. 'You also, Father,' and when the Count tried to protest, she hustled him out as well. She had his measure, Pickup thought, if no one else did.

With Anders everything fell into place. He spotted that the Count had transposed a 7 and a 5 in the co-ordinates, shifted to the right square of the map, found the relevant photograph and related them precisely. 'You see, we patrol to within ten kilometres of this coast. We cannot cross it, of course, but we get to know the scenery beyond the coast. Konigsberg, Danzig, Kolberg – I can tell them by their churches and steeples alone. Gdynia, next door to Danzig, is even easier. Gdynia is cranes and tall store-houses and flak-towers. You know about flak-towers, I guess?

'I have heard tell of them.'

Anders grinned. 'Okay. You won't be going too near any of these places. Your target is west of Danzig. I can give you a track to take you straight there, if the wind doesn't change. But I propose you take a course four degrees more southerly. That way you will cross our coast where the spotter maidens will have been given hints not to get too excited by a small monoplane heading out to sea. It will also give you extra clearance as you approach Gdynia. But be careful not to drift too far west as you pass the island of Bornholm, which the Germans occupy with rather a lot of guns and searchlights. What is your cruise speed again?'

'Hundred miles an hour, downhill and with a following wind. Say one-fifty kilometres.'

'Okay. After one hour you will be approaching the German coast just here, see –' His finger marked the spot.

Pickup could hold an interruption back no longer. '*German* coast? I thought it was going to be Poland. No one said anything about plonking down in the bloody Fatherland itself!'

Anders laughed. 'Steady, old chap. It is all Germany again now, *Grosser Deutschland*, as far as Kovno, and then it becomes the *Reichskommissariat Ostland*, which is not so damned different. But this area we are looking at, it was maybe just inside the Polish alley. Certainly it has always had many Polish inhabitants. They were the servants and farm-workers and foresters, and from the messages the Count gets it seems there are still plenty there.'

He took a gulp of coffee before continuing. 'This stretch of the coast has not so many defences as far as we can tell. It is sand-dunes, then woodlands and low hills. On the course I am suggesting, which is the best reason of all for taking it, you will see immediately a large inland sea or lake. Cross it on the same bearing and look out for a river flowing into the lake from the south-east. Follow this river until it is crossed by this railway line here, running east to west. Now you head due south, only a few minutes' – he reached for the photo-graph – 'and you will see all this ahead. Okay?'

Pickup nodded, trying to burn into his memory the shapes of fields and spinneys and buildings just discernible.

'It is farmland but not good farmland,' Anders was saying. 'Mostly it is for growing turnips and potatoes, just a few muddy meadows for cows. Only where there were horses for

133

sport, or for soldiering, are nice grass fields to be found.'

He set down the coffee cup. 'Such as this one here, which is where the lamps will be lit for you. Yes, it is not great, and the ground is rather soft, but that should be no big trouble for a light aeroplane like the Stinson.'

'Thanks.'

Pickup hadn't intended to sound sarky, but Anders perhaps realized that he had been a bit too breezy. He added, 'If the moon is shining, that is.'

'Yeah,' said Pickup. 'The river I follow – would that be *rilera* in Swedish?'

'Could be. Why?'

Pickup embarked on the snatch he could remember of the *Hutsut Rilera* song. Anders looked puzzled for a second, then grinned and joined in. 'That was the big *schlag* last year. Or the year before.' He looked at his watch. 'Now Katze and I must go on. We may call in again on the way back to Everod. In any case we will let you know of any change of the wind. You should get some sleep this afternoon.'

For two days and nights we have been hidden in the stable-loft of a farmhouse some 50 km west of Danzig. The head of the family is of Teutonic stock and his wife a Polish Catholic. The children are at school by day, which is fortunate, they tell us. Young people are less able to keep secrets and, after years of Nazi education and the lure of the Jungvolk *and the* Jungmadel, *likely to be less than sympathetic to wandering Jews. Their assigned Latvian farm workers also cannot be relied upon, so for most of the time we must remain in the loft, grateful for its shelter and warmth but often hungry and thirsty. There is no water within the building, only a pump in the stable yard, and we dare not show ourselves when the children are at home or the Latvians are about. Sometimes we hear one or more of them come into the stable, and must then lie above them without movement, without making the slightest sound, even without breathing if that were possible. Instead of striving to listen to the beat of my heart, I fear its bumpings and hurryings, lest they be audible. Over the weeks Westermann has become friendlier and more talkative, but still spends hours on end frowning in concentration, as if trying to settle some eternal problem of the universe. Marek is ever Marek, touchy, grumbling and helpful.*

The hands of the little travel clock the Count insisted on lending him had hardly moved since Pickup last looked. He'd been down to the field with Per, examined every organ of the Stinson, tested every instrument, topped up the fuel tank to the last cubic centimetre, returned to the schloss, had a late lunch and then tried to follow Anders's advice to get some sleep. Got properly into bed, in his singlet and the wretched floppy underpants he called droopy-drawers. It was no good. He kept going over and over the route he would follow, the descent he would make, as assembled in his imagination from the maps and photographs and what Anders had told him. It was starting to seem quite authentic but all too likely to bear no relation to what would loom up in actual bloody fact.

If he went, that was. The teasing thought wouldn't go away, that there was no absolute necessity to carry out the op. No one could make him, no one could punish him, as long as he stayed in this weird, equivocal land. All he had to do was give himself up to the authorities, claim asylum. But he wouldn't. Barring any last-minute cancellation from afar he would set off an hour after moonrise, as sure as eggs were eggs. Why? Because that's what you did, that's why.

Faintly, he heard motor noises, doors, voices again. Was that a cancellation? A twinge of hope was abandoned as soon as conceived. It could only be Katze and Anders returning as promised. Ordinarily that would have been something to welcome, nice bit of crumpet plus a good bloke, but the light was fast fading from the sky behind the curtains of his window. It was getting dark and he still hadn't slept, still felt tired before he'd even started. When he kipped down at Tangmere before an op., he sometimes had recourse to handiwork, as Tilly put it, with the aid of a *Men Only* or *Esquire* from the pile of tattered magazines that had accumulated in the cottage. Here he'd been obliged to rely on imagination, and imagination hadn't been firing. Visions of Audrey as Audrey inspired no activity at all. Audrey as Anita produced a few stirrings, none urgent. Sarah? That wizard encounter had been cut short before it could endow him with any lurid dreams, just romantic schoolboy ones. As for Katze, she was Anders's, and Anders was around.

He was wondering whether to get up and find them, if it was them, or give sleep one more chance, when he thought he sensed someone outside his door, listening. A servant, or maybe the Countess in person, trying to ascertain if he should be called to take tea. There it was again, the faint creak of someone shifting balance – and then the door was being eased open.

'Who is it?' Pickup called.

'Oh, I have awoken you.' It was Katze's voice, Katze's silhouette against the soft light of the landing, Katze's bubbly curls catching the same light.

'No, I wasn't asleep.'

As he switched on the bedside lamp she crept in, letting the door swing to. 'You must,' she said. 'Anders told me it was important that you should have slept before you . . . before your mission.'

'Hardly worth it now.'

She peered at the travel clock. 'There is still nearly five hours.'

'Where is Anders, anyway?'

'There was the opportunity to get a ride back to Everod this afternoon on a courier plane, so naturally he took it. He was rather uneasy to be away from his duties the whole day. And there he can be of just as much help to you tonight, perhaps more help.'

But not so much comfort. Never mind, there might be compensations. She looked cuter than ever, with her tunic unbelted and unbuttoned as if she had been about to take it off, and her tie loosened. Oh God, he had to be wearing his droopy-drawers. She caught his gaze and said, 'I was on my way to change out of uniform. I shall stay tonight and be here to see you return, as long as once more I am back at the station to say good morning to the Colonel.'

Pickup turned back the corner of the feather bed thing to make a space next to him, and patted it. 'Come in, then,' he said. Never mind the droopy-drawers.

She laughed.

'Seriously. To help me get to sleep.'

Now she was looking at him gravely. 'What do you do habitually?'

'How do you mean?'

'When you fly from your station in England and would sleep first?'

'Oh, there I only fly on errands. Just a taxi-driver!'

She didn't smile at that. 'Anders says that when you were looking at the maps and air photographs together he could tell that you were used to making such landings in such fields, you had done it many times. My father has also told me of the small torch-lights which are all you have to land by. That does not sound like taxi-driving.'

Pickup couldn't think of an answer to that. Anyway, why not play the hero, just this once? Could win the lady's favour.

Sure thing, she leaned over and kissed him on the forehead. 'Last year an RAF bomber crashed on Oland after being hit by the German anti-aircraft guns. The plane was not carrying bombs, but supplies for Polish patriots, also a returning patriot who was to have been dropped by parachute.'

'What happened to him . . . and the crew?'

'All killed, except one man who went to hospital and afterwards was interned.'

Pickup remembered it happening. To one of 138's Polish crews before they were hived off, and a popular bunch. The Joe they were to drop was also a Polish RAF officer, so he'd been invited to the mess in Tempsford. There he was, about to exchange the dalliances of war for the certain danger and hardship of going back into the witches' den, and he was imitating people and telling stories that made even the Branch Manager laugh. But Katze was talking again.

'Anders guessed that people are also landed in occupied countries, and others brought out again, in a small plane. And that is what you do.'

'Maybe.'

'Then you are very brave.'

'Not true.' If his head hadn't been on the pillow he would have shaken it. 'The brave ones are the people we take in.

137

They stay there, we fly back to bacon and eggs. There was a girl I took—' He stopped short, it was the drop-off that still haunted him in the arsehole of the night, that would always haunt him.

'What about her?'

'Nothing.'

'Please.'

'Oh, she was pretty. Very French, very cute. We heard later, over the grapevine, that she'd been caught and tortured – unspeakably tortured – and then killed.'

Katze reached out and switched off the lamp. In the sudden darkness he felt her lips on his brow again. She was cool and fragrant, not just from the expensive scent she would use, but from herself, too. He enfolded her in his arms, only a bit clumsily, and sought to kiss her on the lips.

She twisted away. 'Not for you.'

'Why?'

'For Anders only. For you, this . . .' She took his hand and did a strange but nice thing. She kissed its palm, right in the middle, then folded his fingers over as if to trap the kiss there. It aroused him. He found her knee and slithered his hand up her thigh, but just as he got to the stocking top she stopped him with a giggle. 'Are you armed with your *Beredskap*? Your preparedness?'

'Oh God, no.' He had left them on the bedside table when hastily packing his valise at the Winwicks'. If found by Mrs W. they would have condemned him, with any luck, to disfavour even more enduring than any earned by flooring Mr Winwick.

'Never mind.' Her free hand reached across to stroke the far side of his face, softly and lightly. It moved down his neck, paused on his collarbone and then set off on a slow descent. Pickup felt his limbs going rigid, and willed himself just to relax and enjoy whatever happened. The hand searched for the button that fastened the droopy-drawers, more or less over his navel.

It found it. It unfastened it. Katze's eyes widened in appreciation. 'Ah! It is not a *kraft* I must throw back.'

'What?'

'When we catch *kraftor* at midsummer – crayfish you call them, I think – we must put back any which are smaller than ten centimetres. Yours is more than legal!'

'Glad to hear it.' Audrey had never made mention of such matters.

'But because I do not want a baby, we do something very Swedish instead,' she whispered. The touch of her lips, even lighter and softer and warmer than that of her fingers, joined in on the near side of his body. She was planting little kisses an inch apart, an inch further down. Pickup knew that at last he was about to experience the secret act he'd heard about, had detected oblique hints of in a novel once, but had never dreamed of getting, least of all from a nice girl.

It is to be tonight! The word was brought to us by the Polish wife as soon as the horses had been shut in the stable at dusk and the Latvians had returned to their camp. We must leave this refuge as soon as our guide returns, for there is still a journey of five Teutonic miles across country to the field where the aeroplane will land. Oh, I will believe that happening when I see it. We hear the English and the Americans flying high overhead, we know that they drop supplies, and bomb dockyards and cities, but to alight in enemy territory without attracting notice, and then depart again, that seems so desperate a feat. Marek is ever alert, listening for any new noise. Westermann remains strangely detached, seeming neither elated nor alarmed at the prospect before us. I endeavour to be equally calm, for anxiety is a worse threat to a lame heart than physical exertion. I take slow breaths, make sure my boots are firmly but not tightly fitting, and force myself to live again the hideous business of the camp in its heyday, lest I forget the purpose – the sole purpose – of this journey we have undertaken.

Our guide returns. We bid farewell to the sweet Christians who have risked so much to help us.

The moon hung in the sky as if it had only just got up again after the flu, low and thin and wan, scarcely able to define itself through the cloud. The Count, who had been mugging up the subject in an encyclopaedia, chuntered on about semi-diameters and terminators and how it would be brighter later on, but for Pickup the plain truth was that at this hour, anyway, the moon was about as much help as a glow-worm. What the hell, all he wanted now was to get the next three hours over, one way or the other.

He finished the last of the pre-flight checks and glanced inquiringly at the mechanic Per, who was perched on the seat alongside Pickup's and had been watching every flicker of the dials and gauges. Per nodded, mouthed something about good luck and gave Pickup a friendly slap on the shoulder; he was a good sort as well as a good mechanic. He slithered out, carefully closed the little door and took a couple of steps back to be clear of the tailplane. Behind him, just visible in the gloom, stood the Count and Katze, her arm linked through his, both wrapped against the night air. Pickup waved to them, opened the throttle and released the wheel-brakes.

This bit was uncomplicated. Even with a full tank, but only one body aboard, the Stinson weighed no more than Grandpa Pickup's Austin Seven. She rose demurely into the air. Pickup aimed for a gap in the treetops which, he had worked out, should put him more or less on the correct track. So it proved. As he gained height only a slight adjustment took him on to the compass heading Anders had prescribed. It was bloody dark, though. The moon still hid her light, and no bright stars were on parade. Venus, so courted at Leuchars, was a morning star at present, not likely to be of much help on this trip.

Then the coast slid into view ahead, a wavy ribbon of luminescence across the dark nothing below. No searchlights or Bofors shells, thanks. Over the sea, things got better still. The surface was reflecting what light there was. You could refer to the world down there. At 8,000 feet on the Stinson's altimeter, decently calibrated in Anglo-Yankee measurements, he levelled off. The patchy cloud was a bit lower, say a thousand feet lower, which was useful if he needed to hunt for cloud cover but not so good if it was going to mask the landing area.

It was getting cold in the little cabin and the former attaché's flying jacket had been more fashionable, in its day, than practical. Thank God for the submariner's pullover under his battledress.

Now he could just pick out a humpy land mass to the west. That would be Bornholm, to be given a wide berth, Anders had advised. Okay.

Sixty minutes out, precisely, he sighted recurrent flicks of light ahead to port. Could be from a distant light-buoy or even a lighthouse, though Anders hadn't mentioned such a thing. But his lot would only patrol in daylight, so might not know about them. If they were navigation aids, that suggested that Jerry wasn't too worried about this approach. You saw nothing of that sort en route to France.

Cloud still patchy.

Ah, a line of darkness terminating the faintly silvered seascape before him. Enemy coast ahead, as the bomber crews were supposed to say, poor bastards. For them it was literally true whenever the target was Berlin or Bremen or Hamburg. From open sea, slap over the heartland. Likewise for yours truly in about three minutes from now, and however Anders may have dismissed the difference between the heartland and occupied territories, Pickup couldn't suppress a twinge of funk. If you were forced down in France or Holland or Poland, at least you had a chance of being sheltered by friendly natives.

The band of sea grew narrower, the mass of land drew closer. If there were going to be guns and searchlights, this is where they would be waiting. But only a few degrees east a bank of low cloud straddled the coast at about 3,000 feet, too inviting a chance of cover to forgo. He went into a gentle descent and made for it. After four years of war and a total of twenty months on ops of one sort or another, Flight-Lieutenant Prudence Pickup was finally flying into das Reich, if flying blind at the time.

Emerging into clear air again, he was already over the inland sea or lake, just shimmering in the measly moonlight. But beyond it all he could see was featureless darkness. Of any river running into it, not a glimmer. Must have drifted off course while in the cloud. Then the water was behind him, and still no sign. Don't panic, don't panic. He steered into a wide climbing turn to starboard which should bring him to a

141

second transit of the lake without wasting too much fuel. He hoped. It was a ploy he'd used on Lizzie operations many a time, if with more moonlight and a lot more horse-power on call. You had to make yourself a human autopilot while constantly swivelling every *n*th of attention from left to right and back again, but he did seem to have a useful bump of locality . . . this time, too, please.

He had all but completed the full 360 degrees and was over dry land again, beginning to despair, when he spotted something immediately below. Could this be it? If so, he had drifted further off course than he thought.

Bloody hell, another patch of cloud hid everything. The air was a bit bumpy, must be above hills again. He glanced down to check and there it was, directly below, just catching the starlight as the cloud parted, a glint of water – then another, then a whole ribbon of wet-reflected light. A *rilera* all right, but was it the right *rilera*? A peek at the compass confirmed that the heading was exactly the one Anders had given him. And to settle the matter, in the darkness ahead he could just discern the blacker mass of a plantation of fir trees whose triangular shape was etched on his memory from poring over the photographs. Thanks be.

It was an arduous journey, and one I despaired of ever completing. My confidence in myself soon faded as I struggled to keep up. Eventually my breath came so painfully that I implored Marek to continue without me. He could take my place. Otherwise we might all be too late for the appointment with the aeroplane. Westermann nodded his head in agreement. But Marek would have none of it. 'We must help him,' he cried. But he is but a metre and a half in height, and lightly built. Westermann uttered a snort of contempt, and without ceremony hoisted me over his shoulder, my head hanging down his broad back, my legs in his grasp. We set off again. Even allowing for my modest physique, I could not see that he would be able to carry me thus for the distance remaining. But he must have plodded on for a full hour before the guide motioned to us to halt. 'Wait here,' he whispered, 'I shall be only a wink.' And to Marek, 'You come with me.'

Westermann put me down and I sank to the ground, too dizzy to stand. From smells and sounds borne on the wind I gradually worked out that another farm or riding stables lay close by. Westermann stood facing into the wind, his head back. Maybe he was filling his lungs after his exertions, or maybe trying to pick up the salt tang of the Baltic he had known in his boyhood.

When the others returned, the guide was leading what at first I took to be a small horse. It was in fact a donkey. It had no saddle, but a heavy collar which the guide indicated, as he lifted me on to its back, I could grasp. So it was that, like the Christians' Jesus on his entry to Jerusalem, I completed my momentous journey on the back of an ass.

And now we wait. It is after midnight, I know, but not how many hours. A pale half-moon casts a faint light over the landscape. The brave Polish patriots who awaited us here are already stationed at different points on the field, with the lamps they will light when their leader gives the signal. We look to the north, from where the aeroplane will come. If it ever comes, sneers Westermann. It will be an Englishman of the RAF, we have been told. The English are lazy cowards, he says. Why could we not have had an American, who would at least be on time? I see him in a new light since he rescued me, but wish he would not say such things.

The sky was clearer now, the moonlight a little stronger. Below, the river was reduced to a bright thread, broken ahead by – yes! – the railway line running east–west. But where the hell were the lights? It was a common hazard of the job, not being able to spot them. You could rarely be 100 per cent sure you were over the right patch. Equally, you had no means of telling if something had happened to foul up the reception plan. So you circled around a couple of times, began to flounder off here and there in the blind hope of finding the magic lanterns, and ended up in a panic sweat. The sensible course was to run for home straightaway, which Pickup had done often enough. The penalty was the sour feeling that you had wound yourself up to snapping point for nothing, no score, anticlimax. Plus the possibility of having to go through the whole drill again the next night.

What was that just glimpsed through the starboard rear window before the wing strut blotted it out? He dropped into a tight diving turn to bring it into forward view. The familiar diagram was suddenly laid out ahead, two lights a couple of hundred paces apart, lined up into the wind, a third one sixty or seventy paces abreast of the far one. They must have waited until they heard him before switching on. Pickup crossed the field at 3,000 feet and blipped the engine to signal that he'd seen it. A wide descending circuit brought him on line to land, into the wind and at about the right height.

Few trees, no power cables, not even a road along which a truckload of Panzer Grenadiers might arrive in a hurry, it seemed all too easy. In his mind he rehearsed the immediate action should anything suddenly look wrong – throttle wide open, carry straight on and goodbye. If already down, and there was enough acreage left, same drill and take off again. Meanwhile, concentrate on the landing. At last – well, a heartbeat later – Pickup felt the landing gear kiss grass. Bumps and lurches ensued, the field was no cricket pitch. As soon as he drew level with the second light, Pickup made a ninety-degree turn, taxied the sixty paces and turned again to head back to where he'd touched down. If the Poles had been given the signal-lamp pattern they would also have been told about this standard drill and should be waiting there. They were, three or four dim figures, one of them waving his torch in little circular motions.

Pickup swung the plane round to face into the wind again, throttled back to tick-over and screwed round to unfasten the rear door. Crikey, they had the urgency as well as the drill. As soon as it was yanked open, someone was being bundled into the rear seat. Pickup could only glimpse a bony head, pale face, dulled eyes, before he had to switch his attention to the front passenger door.

The torchlight illuminated for a moment the second arrival. Pickup saw a thickset figure, an expressionless profile, also that he knew about seat-straps and reached for his. Would he also have the sense to keep his hands and feet off the dual controls? From outside, the door was firmly closed.

144

There was no time for assurances, still less for niceties. Pickup waved blindly through his window, opened the throttle and released the brakes. With a full load the Stinson needed its furlong of run, but finally came unstuck. At 6,000 feet he levelled off and set a reverse course to bring him to the coast. He listened carefully to the engine note. Sounded all right. On routine jaunts, if any could ever be thought of as routine, this was the point at which he would light up the first fag. In an aeroplane largely clad in canvas and dope the temptation was weaker. Also, he wasn't separated from the clients. Did he offer them one? He risked a quick peek backwards. The Jew seemed not to have shifted an inch since he was deposited in his seat, but his eyes now met Pickup's with a gaze so intense, so eloquent, so desperate to tell someone something that Pickup flinched.

He turned back. Shit, what was that in the sky far ahead? At this distance tiny and blurred, but unmistakable, two searchlights were poking about the sky. The Stinson must have been seen or heard on the inward passage, and they had been alerted too late. Unless it was some other intruder they were after, maybe one of the Polish Liberators from Tempsford. In which case, thanks, comrades. Either way, the danger was that night-fighters had been scrambled, or mobile flak batteries called in.

Pickup had a sort of hunch, based on Anders's gen, that there weren't a lot of these about, while the heavy ironmongery was definitely concentrated around Gdynia to the east. He decided to incline westwards again and hope for cloud cover or, failing that, make a run for it at daisy-cutter height. Fighter pilots didn't like slow, low targets in poor visibility. One misjudgement and they could be slamming into the deck or the drink at terminal velocity.

It worked all right at first. The two searchlights were well to the starboard as the coast came up. He aimed for some low cloud ahead over the sea. He was actually crossing the coastline when the beam of another bloody searchlight sprang up from nowhere, just snaring the Stinson. Pickup went into the conditioned reflex he'd acquired over northern France, flinging the plane into a steep diving turn away from the light.

This rammed you into your seat at about six times the force of gravity, a bit taxing even if you were used to it, downright alarming if not. Pickup shot a glance at the Jew by his side. His hands were clenched, his mouth open, as he fought to draw breath. From behind there had come only an eerie gasp.

Pickup rolled the Stinson level and reached the cloud just ahead of the searchlight. The manoeuvre seemed to have foxed the operators, an ill turn delivering a good turn.

The cloud held them for four minutes, say seven miles before they emerged into clear air. Pickup swivelled round to look back. The searchlights were all angled too high. The Jew in the back had half-closed eyes, only the whites showing.

Pickup stayed low until Bornholm showed up on the Port quarter, closer and more menacing than on the outward trip. He climbed back to 5,000 feet, by which time he was probably safe, heading for Swedish skies. Only the Swedes to worry about now, efficient bastards. He made a correction to bring him to the Skane coast where he had left it three hours before. Please God, Anders has done his stuff.

He had. Or alternatively, the gunners and aircrew were all in bed with their Lottas.

Fuel gauge registering about an eighth of a tank, more than enough. Beside him, a heavy silence. Behind him, a different sort of silence. Below, a familiar landscape nicely delineated by moonlight that was, at last, of adequate wattage. Pickup allowed himself to start enjoying the best bit of any op., landing in one piece at the end of it.

X

Dr Holmin was better than his word, not merely on call should either escaper need medical help but actually waiting at the field, along with the Count, Katze, the mechanic and two shadowy others. As the engine spluttered into silence, they all crowded round. Pickup's door was wrenched open, the Count was intoning some formal welcome, Katze giving him a hug, but the doctor was looking past him, into the cabin behind. In a moment he had opened it and was peering inside.

Pickup knew with a dull certainty that something was wrong. He slithered out of his seat, discovering that his feet had gone to sleep, as his mum used to say of pins and needles when he was little. He stamped them gently to get the circulation going. Dr Holmin was leaning into the rear cabin, his bearded face close to that of the motionless figure. He reached into his overcoat pocket for a stethoscope. The welcoming chatter had died away.

One of the strangers the other side of the plane seemed familiar, Pickup thought, but in the dimness – Per was already away down the flarepath, extinguishing the lights – he couldn't be sure. The other one, who wore an expensive-looking overcoat with a white silk scarf at the neck, was heading towards them.

The doctor straightened up, shaking his head. He said to Pickup, 'I am sorry. He has had a heart onslaught.'

'Is he . . . ?'

'He is alive but in a perilous condition. Fortunately, I came directly here in my car. I will take him to the hospital. To go to the house and telephone for an ambulance, and then wait for it to find us, would waste more than an hour.'

This last was mainly addressed to White Silk Scarf, as he

came up. Holmin pushed past him to go and fetch the vehicle. Pickup and he eyed each other.

'Gunnar Lingstrom,' the man said, holding out his hand. Pickup guessed he was one of the Swedes who'd organized it all. He had a pink face, silvery hair, gold-rimmed glasses.

'I am sorry this has happened . . .'

'It is unfortunate, but we have your other passenger. He is quite a catch, as I think you say.'

On cue, the other Jew joined them at this point. He had been a strong silent presence on the flight. Now he seemed anxious about something.

Lingstrom said, 'He says that his friend was carrying something that belonged to them both, and we should find it in case it will be lost at the hospital.'

The Jew reached in and began to rifle through the stricken man's pockets. Pickup watched uneasily, it didn't seem right even if it was the Swedes' show now and Lingstrom was looking on calmly.

Lingstrom must have sensed his disapproval. 'These poor men are our guests,' he snapped. 'We do not own them.'

The exchange was interrupted by Dr Holmin backing his car up to the plane.

'*Was machst du?*' Evidently the doctor was also uneasy. Lingstrom snapped at him, too, in Swedish.

'*Alles gut,*' said the man himself, the first words Pickup had heard him utter other than the exclamation when they dived. He pocketed something he had finally found.

Holmin grunted and pointedly asked Pickup, rather than the Swede, to help lift the patient into the car. He was given the easier end, the feet and legs, but couldn't avoid looking at that skull-like, inanimate, strangely gentle face. They laid him on the back seat, covered with a rug. It was a proper petrol car because it was a doctor's car. As it crept slowly to the road Pickup saw the other stranger gazing in his direction, and suddenly realized who it was – Miles Leveret, the cloak-and-dagger merchant from the Legation who'd visited him on the yacht.

He gave Pickup a rueful nod. 'It's damned hard luck, after all you did . . .'

'It was my fault. I went into a corkscrew dive trying to get out of a searchlight.'

'Nonsense. Jolly good show, as I shall tell your masters.' He glanced at the retreating rear lights of the doctor's car. 'As for that poor old Ikey, we'll have to wait and see. If he does pull through, somebody will collect him as soon as the doc gives the word. The other client looks in reasonably good shape. We'll stick to plan and drive him to Stockholm as soon as he's had something to eat.'

They sorted themselves out to go to the manor. Katze took her father and Per. Pickup and the second Jew were to go with Leveret and Lingstrom in the weird-looking but petrol-powered saloon in which they had driven down from Stockholm It was a Swedish make, Leveret murmured, a Volvo. They had borrowed it from a sympathizer because the registration numbers of their own vehicles were known by heart to the police. Only the petrol was HMG's.

As the Count maintained, it was a long way round to the house by road, three sides of a square. Pickup began to feel a craving for bacon, eggs and all the rest. Even at this hour, a servant was waiting to receive them. Pickup clattered upstairs for a pee, and on the impulse changed his battledress blouse for his civvy jacket, just in case any strangers came calling. Down in the big room with the armour and the log fire, the Count was already presiding over his beakers and bottles. No aroma of frying, but a nice smell of coffee. Pickup made for a table which had been laid not too far from the fireplace. On it, alas, was the usual cold platter of herring, sausage and cheese, plus knacker-jarring *knackerbrod*. He chose sausage, also a couple of boiled eggs from a little basket of boiled eggs.

'Not quite your traditional aircrew breakfast, I fear,' said Leveret, pouring himself a cup of coffee.

'It'll do.'

'Our client is attending to the calls of nature, and generally tidying himself up.' Pickup had only done the first. He squinted at his hands. Seemed all right. As he looked up, Katze prowled into the room. That she had washed her hands and face and done her hair was evident. At four in the morning

149

she was as fresh and dewy-eyed as the tennis-club girls he had moped over in his teens. Four in the morning! To think it was just twelve hours since she had performed that wicked rite. To look at her now, listening to Leveret, you would never believe it. He wondered, with a stirring down below, if he might qualify for a reward now the job was done.

Or maybe only half done. Of all the bloody luck, that one poor bugger should flake out as he was about to reach safety.

Ah, the Swede Lingstrom was leading the other chosen type to the table.

'This is Kurt Westermann, the film star,' Lingstrom said triumphantly. 'He is famous everywhere in the world. I am sure you will have seen the great film he has made in Hollywood, *Storm of Steel*.'

Pickup hadn't, though he remembered it being on at the local fleapit just as he was completing flying training, and the last thing he wanted to see was an epic of the mud and blood of the previous war. But he nodded and said, 'Of course.'

'It was not the best-timed of releases,' the man said, in English, as if reading Pickup's thoughts. He seemed strangely composed, for one who had just survived a dicey flight into a strange land, and God knows what hardships and horrors before that. He was about forty-five, Pickup guessed, with a bristle of reddish hair sprouting from his skull, hooded eyes, a rather flattened nose, a lesser stubble around his mouth and jaw. His hands, as he ate and drank, were ingrained with dirt, the nails jagged. He was wearing a garment so crumpled and torn it was hard to tell what it had been, but on his wrist was an obviously expensive gold watch – no, two obviously expensive gold watches.

He caught Pickup's gaze and pushed back his cuff. 'Which do you like? I should give you one to pay for the flight.' His English was a bit American.

Pickup shook his head. 'No charge, guv'nor. I forgot to set the meter.'

The German looked puzzled until the allusion clicked in. 'Ah, as in a cab?' He flashed a small smile, no more than four point two on the rictus scale, as Tilly would have put it. From somewhere far off came the faint ring of the telephone.

150

A servant entered and spoke to the Count, who left the room.

Now Westermann was peering at Pickup's attire. 'Before, you were wearing uniform with a pilot's badge. You are of the RAF?' Pickup nodded. No point in pretending otherwise.

'I, too, was a pilot. In the last war.' He chewed in silence for a minute, then said, 'The RAF were the big heroes when I was leaving Hollywood to return to Germany.'

Pickup couldn't help asking the question. 'Why did you return?'

'Picture was finished.'

'Couldn't you have stayed?'

'Plenty did. Fritz Lortner, Mady Christians, that little fraud Reuss.'

'You chose not to?'

'My country was at war. My place was there.'

'Even though you were Jewish?'

'German first, Jewish second. Or so I thought then.'

Lingstrom had been following the exchange. He broke in now. 'Excuse me, I think that such interrogation must be saved until we have the ear of the whole world. In any case, we must begin our journey to Stockholm as soon as Mr Westermann has had enough to eat.'

Westermann laid down his knife and fork. 'I am ready.' To Pickup he said, 'I should like to have your name, so that one day I may thank you properly.'

'No need to. But it's Pickup, Michael Pickup.'

'How are you spelling that?'

Pickup felt in his pockets. He had a pencil but the only thing to write on he could find was the journalist Nesbit's card. Well, he wouldn't need that now. On the reverse he printed his name and passed it across.

'Thank you. I am sorry you have seen me so dirty and stinking of farm animals.'

Lingstrom broke in again. 'Once we get you to Stockholm you shall live like a king.'

Overhearing this, Leveret turned and gave him a look as if not altogether agreeing. At which moment the Count returned. From his sideboard he rapped for attention. Like the others, most of the time he chose the common tongue, English.

151

'Gentlemen! And my Katze, naturally' – she bobbed in acknowledgement – 'I have exciting news.'

He paused for effect, or maybe to sort out what he was about to say. 'Jews from Denmark have started to reach our shores, smuggled across the Oresund in fishing boats. Yesterday I heard the first rumours from my cousin who is the pastor in Lund. I asked him to pass on any further news he received, whatever the hour. He has just telephoned to say that he has talked to three families, more than twelve persons in all, who have already arrived. They said they had been warned by their Rabbi that they were to be rounded up and deported, and that many others will have set out from other points along the sound. It seems that all the Danish Jews, numbering many thousands, will attempt to make the crossing.'

His eyes sought out, as best they could, first Lingstrom, then Leveret, finally Pickup. He said, 'So our brave messenger –' he raised the glass to Westermann – 'will not be alone in his task of telling the world of the crimes against his people. He will be but one voice in a whole choir of voices.'

There was silence in the big room. Westermann's face was expressionless. Leveret scowled. Katze looked bewildered. Only Lingstrom whispered a few words. 'The Danish Jews? What do they know? They are still virgins.'

He rose to his feet. 'It is indeed wonderful news, and we must all hope that this miraculous delivery will continue until every last Jew from Denmark has reached safety. But with all respect to the Count, whose contribution to our own undertaking has been so vital, these are witnesses of rather a different order. The Danish Jews have not, as far as we know, been herded into camps to be gassed, and their bodies burned. That is the dreadful truth which Kurt Westermann and, we hope, the other messenger will proclaim.'

The Count listened bleakly. 'There was another telephone call,' he said, 'From Dr Holmin. The other messenger cannot travel today.'

The silence in the big room was longer this time. Westermann remained expressionless. Lingstrom said, 'In that case, we should leave without more delay.' He glanced at

Leveret, who nodded. Westermann rose from his seat. Pickup followed suit.

He said, 'I come with you, I presume.'

They stared at him.

'Why not? You have a spare seat in the car now. There is nothing more for me to do here.' To lend a boy-scout justification he added, 'I should get back to the squadron. The moon period is just starting, everyone needed.'

Leveret said smoothly, 'I'm sorry, old boy. Dick Petty, the assistant air attaché – you met him – is looking after your arrangements. I believe the plan is that you will return to Stockholm as unobtrusively as you came. That is, detached from any connection with Mr Lingstrom and myself. We have devised papers to account for Westermann should we be challenged on the road. That story will hardly stand up if we also have an RAF pilot in the car.'

'I'm not an RAF pilot now. I'm a wireless technician if you remember.'

Leveret put on a commanding officer sort of face. 'Please don't make difficulties in front of our allies in this operation. You will stay here as ordered. Squadron-Leader Petty will contact you shortly.'

Pickup watched them go. The Count shook hands stiffly with the three men. Katze provided the warmth, literally in the shape of a woollen lumber-jacket she had found for Westermann. 'It is my brother's,' she whispered to Pickup. 'He is in America and can easily buy another.' That she remained was the only consolation, and even that would vanish when she had to drive back to the aerodrome, probably in a couple of hours. Still, there would be time enough for a little pleasurable winding down. He escorted her back into the house wondering how to propose this politely.

In the hall she yawned and said, 'Now I must go up and put on my uniform.'

'What?'

'My uniform, to make me the smart driver of the Commandant once more.'

'But why now?' He was following her up the great curving staircase.

153

'I need to leave by five thirty at the latest. That is in less than an hour. It is easier to go now. Also, you will be very tired, you must go to bed.'

'I won't sleep.'

'O Lieutenant Michael, you cannot play that card twice!'

'No, really. It's all so . . . unfinished. Supposing he dies, the other Joe.'

'Please! Don't say that!'

'Sorry.'

At the top of the staircase she said, 'I'll come and say good-bye, but that is all.'

Pickup cleaned his teeth at the wash-stand and climbed into bed in his vest and droopy-drawers. O God, the same ones he'd been wearing a thousand hours ago. When she tapped on the door and prowled in, she was in uniform, even to the forage cap that made her so sexy. She'd look really cute in that and nothing else, Pickup thought. He told her so.

'Be quiet! I told you I am only saying goodbye. You will be staying here some days more?'

'Dunno.'

'I shall come again as soon as possible.' She was gone.

As the day grew lighter, Westermann concentrated on what he could see of this strange country which took no side in the conflict that divided almost the whole world. He had been to Stockholm, of course, most recently for the opening there of *Storm of Steel* in 1940 – the Swedes had been very nerv-ous of it because of reports that the author of the book from which it was taken, Ernst Junger, held an official post in occu-pied Paris. But he stared with new interest at the fields and farms and woods, a small deserted town, the empty road stretching ahead. They drove on the left, as in England, but the cars had left-hand drive as in Germany or France or America. Ach, the whole Swedish nation was left-handed. Could he live here? Or was that not the intention of these people, in particular the two Englishmen? Was he to be sent on to London or Washington? He could not suppress a twinge of repulsion at the prospect. Despite everything, he was still German first, Jewish second. If Selpin had not been so damned insulting about the *Kriegsmarine* heroes they would both be back in the UFA studios, putting the final polish on the next masterpiece.

Of course, in America, he would be able to pick up a career in Hollywood again. That was something to be put into whatever calculation was open to him. Of the English film world he knew little except that the writer Emeric Pressburger was working there, likewise the ladies' actor Adolf Wahlbruck. As for the Swedish, it was so narrow and remote that its stars were obliged to leave home to earn fame – Garbo and Bergman to Hollywood, Zarah Leander and Kristina Soderbaum to the Reich, where they still thrived. Women!

In the end, Pickup slept until noon. When he ventured downstairs it was to be told by the Countess that the Count had gone to the coast, where the arrival of the Danish Jews was evidently continuing apace. She was to remind Lieutenant Pickup not to go out of the grounds.

Had there been a telephone call for him?

She thought not but he should ask the Count's agent. The agent shook his head. After the cold-table lunch the Countess called for her carriage in order to visit a sick neighbour, she said. This was his chance, unless the agent was still about. He tapped on the study door, and when there was no reply crept in, closing the door behind him as silently as he could.

The telephone stood on a small table beside the Count's desk. It had no dial. As at home, anywhere outside the big cities, you had to ask the exchange for the number you wanted. The only trouble was that he didn't know the number he wanted, or how to find it. If only he hadn't given Nesbit's card away, that at least had a Stockholm number the journalist had scribbled below his name. He could have rung Nesbit and asked him casually for the Legation number. Stupid bugger, what on earth had possessed him to part with it? Conceit, and post-op. light-headedness.

Wait a minute! In his room there should still be the documents he'd been given for his pretend posting to the consulate in Malmo – he rattled up the stairs two at a time, rummaged in his valise, and hunted through the find as he descended

155

again. Nothing for Stockholm, but appended to the address of the consulate its Malmo number. Back in the study he breathed a prayer and lifted the ear-phone. When the operator answered he said, 'Do you speak English?'

There was a moment's silence, then 'A little.' That usually meant quite a lot.

After some careful enunciation, a little repetition and a desperate search for the number he was ringing from – luckily it was displayed on the instrument – he heard a click and a sort of rattle and an inquiring feminine voice. This time he guessed it was logical to ask directly in English for the Consul.

'He is out.'

'When will he be back?'

'I cannot tell. He is occupied with the Jews coming from Denmark. Mr Porter is also out of the office. Who is calling?'

Pickup hesitated. 'Pickup,' he said, 'I was to come to Malmo as a telegraphist . . .'

'Ah, yes. A moment please.' Pickup heard a whispered exchange in Swedish. 'We understood we were not to expect you after all.'

'That's right. But I need to call the Legation in Stockholm, and don't have the number. Can you give it to me?'

Another consultation, then, 'Okay, it is not so secret.'

Pickup thanked her and nerved himself all over again. When the connection was made he asked for the Assistant Air Attaché rather than Squadron-Leader Petty by name, it seemed more official. Half a minute crept by before a voice said, 'Who's that?' Help, it didn't sound like Petty, perhaps his chief, who would be at least a Wingco –

'It's Sly Lander,' he said softly.

There was silence again, then a bark of 'Wait!'

Pickup suddenly panicked. What was he doing? Better hang up. He was about to when he remembered they would have the Count's number and ring back if he was due to be torn off a strip.

Another voice came on, assured, authoritative. 'Ah, Mr Lysander –' he pronounced it more like *Lusanda*, as if Swedish – 'I'm sorry we haven't been in touch with you again about your visa, but we have not yet heard from London. We will inform you as soon as we have. There is no need to telephone the legation again.' The last bit had a less than diplomatic harshness to it.

In Stockholm, Westermann had been taken directly to the Grand Hotel. He couldn't believe it when he recognized the *torchères* – unlit now to save fuel – alongside the main entrance. This was where he had been given a room for the *Storm of Steel* opening, shared on the second night with an agreeable young reporter who had interviewed him. This time he must share with the fussy Herr Lingstrom, who kept close to him at all times. But the suspicious English would not have allowed him such comfort at all, if they had had their way. They were for keeping him hidden away in some cellar.

As it was, he had slept for ten hours, had a bath, put on clean clothes provided by his hosts, and was now savouring the hotel's good food and drink and warmth. Though a few hotels and restaurants in Berlin had managed to preserve a great deal of luxury, none of them could match the Grand's profusion of waiters, porters and page boys, or the sheer opulence of its Royal Restaurant. The glass roof was five storeys high, the tables stood around a central court which boasted green grass and tanks of goldfish. An organ played.

How unbelievable that it was only two days since he was being hustled through fields and marshes. And before that, dumped among the living few left in a charnel house. How was he able to adjust from one to the other without even trying? Could it be because his life had been spent in the fabricated ordeals and escapades of film-making? You threw yourself into another world when shooting started at seven, and quit it just as easily at the end of the day. No, it was not quite so simple as that. On *Titanic* the story and the making of the story had become grimly intertwined, and he had been torn apart by his inability to switch from real fears to make-believe, or from make-believe back to real.

Lingstrom was busy preparing a document to be wired to all the Swedish newspapers and the broadcasting service, inviting them to send representatives to a Press conference where they would hear a witness to profoundly disturbing events.

For the foreign correspondents in Stockholm there would be no need of such communication, because they were all to be found here, in the Grand Hotel. Two large salons, complete with telephones and secretarial help, were provided for their use by the Foreign Ministry.

Westermann passed by these, he guessed, as he made his way to the ground floor. Through a door he heard voices, the click of typewriters. A moment later he met a tall figure wearing a monocle, and with a carnation in his buttonhole, who gave him a puzzled nod as he made for the same door. There had been a French journalist of that appearance at one of the *Storm of Steel* receptions in Stockholm.

Lingstrom had nodded abstractedly when he said he would like to go down to the bar for a drink, and called after him, 'Put it on my account.' He had added, though, 'Remember, don't talk to anyone. I will join you in a few minutes.'

In the bar Westermann saw someone else who seemed vaguely familiar – much the same age as his own, handsome, well dressed, smiling as if he recognized an old acquaintance. He detached himself from the group he was with and came over. 'Kurt Westermann!' he exclaimed. 'I think you do not remember.' He was speaking in German. 'The grand opening of *Storm of Steel* in New York, what a night that was!'

'Ah, forgive me. You are . . .'

'Thomsen, then of our embassy in Washington.'

'And now?'

'And now? Your ambassador here in Stockholm.'

Next morning Pickup was woken from frowsty sleep by the sound of a car and then, from below, the unbolting of the big door. It could only be the Count. He splashed his face, pulled on his clothes and hurried down. In the breakfast room Dr Holmin was stirring a cup of coffee. 'Ah, good, you are here,' he said. 'You got my message?'

'What message?'

'That I left last night with the Countess?'

'No.'

'Ah, it was late, for her. First, I must tell you with sorrow that our poor invalid died yesterday without recovering consciousness. In the end there was nothing we could do. His heart was worn out, like a machine that has been tested to destruction.'

It was a strange simile to use, Pickup thought, maybe coined by the doctor because he was talking to an airman. He was suddenly stricken by a piercing guilt. He had thought of the two men only as fares – no, not quite that, whatever Tilly said about being taxi-drivers, but as the objects of the exercise rather than as people. It was no better than the time he'd flown the beautiful agent into France and the main emotion he entertained was a morbid lust, as if to have her before it was too late.

'Who was he? I mean, what do we know about him?'

'Almost nothing. Not even his name. He was about fifty years of age. His body bore signs of much ill-treatment latterly, such as a fracture of the right femur which had been very badly reset, if reset at all. His teeth had been well cared for in earlier years, with many gold fillings, but this would not necessarily mean he was a wealthy man. Such dentistry was quite common in central Europe, especially among the Jews. The clothes he was wearing were a strange mixture – heavy trouser and boots as might have been worn by a labourer, what had once been a fine silk shirt, and a suit bearing the label of a tailor in Salonika. Again, I do not think that means he was from Greece. Did not the fellow Westermann mutter something about his garments being all he could find?'

'He also took something from this man's pockets. Something important, he said.'

Holmin nodded. 'I was uneasy about that. We can only hope he will have passed it on to Lingstrom and his friends.'

The obvious occurred to Pickup. 'Ah, they might know who the bloke was.'

'They did not know they had Westermann until he told them.' He paused for a moment. 'But even if we learn the Jew's name there is a difficulty. I must declare his death to the authorities, exactly as in your country, I believe. I must write the certificate of death, just as my namesake in the Count's fancy, Tycho Glas, has to write that of the old parson he has just poisoned. If we do not have his address we are required to notify the police. We could say that he was an unknown stranger, a beggar found by the roadside, but that would stir up the suspicions of those who already distrust the Count. They will come nosing about this place, and watch everyone who comes and goes.'

Pickup nodded glumly. In that case, bang went all chance of his being able to get out.

Holmin was looking at him with shrewd eyes. When he spoke again, his little beard wagged more positively. 'Now, there is something happening which can perhaps be of help to us. The arrival of the Jews from Denmark! – it is a great and welcome happening, of course, which no Swede dare oppose. I am on my way to the coast to see if I can aid any escapers who are ill. The Count is already there, but we may not find him. My other message was that I wished you to come with me.'

Pickup goggled.

'Between us, we should be able to acquire enough small pieces of Danish paper to give our poor corpse a nationality, if not an identity. A few bank notes, a letter or a receipt, even a newspaper of recent date would serve – one cannot expect everyone smuggled aboard a fishing boat to be carrying a passport. If we can pick up some Danish clothing of about the right size, all the better. So! Will you come?'

'I don't think I can.' It sounded awfully wet. 'The Count said I must stay out of sight. Also, there might be a phone call for me from Stockholm . . .'

'I shall tell the Count I needed you. It will be my fault if he is angry. As for any telephone call, the Countess or the agent can make a note of that for you.'

Pickup hesitated, helpless in this land of the glib.

'We will be back tonight, I promise you. I have operations to perform tomorrow.'

'Okay,' said Pickup. What the hell.

XI

There were at least sixty of them, Pickup estimated, men, women and children, just beginning to find their voices again. They were still being ushered into the mission hall as Dr Holmin parked his car above the harbour, and their silence then – save for the crying of babies – reminded Pickup of the desperate surmise which he fancied, sometimes, in the demeanour of a fugitive Resistance hero as he alighted at Tangmere, still not quite sure that he had been transported to another world.

He had stared, a bit unbelieving himself, across the sound to the irregular blur on the skyline which Holmin had told him was Copenhagen – the enemy in occupation, only five miles distant here, even less further up the coast. The boats would load up at little private jetties at the end of people's gardens and sneak out under cover of night or fog. They would carry the usual fishing gear and pretend to be fishing, in case a German patrol boat hove into sight, when the refugees were bundled into the fish-hold and covered with nets and baskets.

This point of disembarkation was a fishing village whose name Pickup hadn't caught. The local doctor was a friend of Holmin's. He had been standing by for seventy-two hours, so Holmin was giving him a break, starting with the escapers just off the boat below. What the young mothers wanted first was to change their babies' nappies, Holmin pointed out. It was always thus. He was fuming over the money the Danish skipper had charged for each passenger. 'Five hundred kroner,' he muttered. 'How could anyone seek to make such profit from the misfortune of his fellow creatures?'

Though he nodded agreement, Pickup couldn't help thinking that the skipper was risking his life, his crew's lives, all their livelihoods. After all, Lysander drivers were paid for their ferrying; not much, perhaps, but it went into your bank account regular as clockwork, up to and including the day your number came up, should that happen.

His gaze roamed again over the arrivals. Apart from smelling of fish, and in some cases wringing fishy water from trouser bottoms or skirt-hems, they could have been a party of Jews much the same as that he remembered seeing at Southport on a family outing before the war, when his father had not failed to make a sneery observation, his mother had protested and he had smirked. Middle-class, well dressed if a bit smoothly dressed, lots of make-up for the ladies, shiny shoes on the children's feet, fleshy noses, tight curls, mostly dark – God, what was he thinking? The sudden piercing image this time was of just such a Jewish couple fleeing *Kristallnacht* five years ago. He and the rest of the gang on that insane Dachau stunt encountered them on the road out of Munich without even thinking of their plight. Until later he, Pickup, had diverted attention to the wretched pair in order to engineer his own gang's escape.

He sought vaguely to make some amends now. Smiled at a rather snazzy-looking girl. She looked away. Patted a little boy on the head. He slunk away. The doctor was busy listening to mums and peering down throats. He caught Pickup's eye and waved him over. 'The clothes in the car, please.' Pickup fetched them. As he got back to the mission hall the first of the families was being claimed by the Swedes who were offering hospitality. In the next hour he and Holmin dished out most of the clothing and accepted a few worn or waterlogged escape garments no longer needed, including an indubitably Danish Navy reefer jacket.

'With this, our poor corpse will certainly pass muster,' the doctor exulted. They had also collected some sodden Danish bills, a letter and – unbelievably – a scribbled receipt for the 500 Kr. crossing fare which one of the party had persuaded the skipper to give him on arrival.

It was when only one family and two elderly couples without children still awaited the doctor's attention that striding into the mission hall came Alec Nesbit.

162

Oh Lord, he must have remembered Pickup's stupid let-slip on the Dakota flight – *knowing* let-slip – about having been in France only a few days earlier. Kurt Westermann had been put up to say his piece, everyone had wondered how he got to Sweden, Nesbit had put two and two together, and here he was on the track of the indiscreet Special Duties flier.

Even as he jumped to these conclusions they crumbled away. Nesbit hadn't yet noticed him, wasn't even looking around. Maybe he was only here to write about the scene in the mission hall – of course that was it! The arrival of the Jews from Denmark. There was a photographer with him, camera bag slung over his shoulder, camera already in his hands as he followed Nesbit's pointing finger and made for the family with the most kids. It wasn't retribution, just the long arm of coincidence, thank God. He felt quite tipsy with relief.

Nesbit spotted him about five minutes later, just as Pickup was trying to decide whether or not to go and accost him. He made a face, waved and came across, every inch a Fleet Street reporter in his belted camel coat and trilby.

'Small world,' Pickup said lamely.

'Getting smaller. What brings you here?'

'Nothing official. Day off from duties, so I'm giving the doctor here a hand.' He introduced them. Holmin eyed Nesbit rather suspiciously, Pickup thought.

Nesbit encompassed the scene with a sweep of his hand. 'This is what I meant by a story dropping into your lap, but never expected to be as good as this.' He directed his gaze at the doctor to add, 'Which doesn't mean that I am just using these people and what they have been through. I feel for them like everyone else. If anyone is exploiting them it is the Danes, charging the poor bastards for bringing them across.'

Holmin launched into angry confirmation of this scandal, all suspicions forgotten. Nesbit jotted down some notes. Pickup left it to them, until Nesbit excused himself to interview the family with children before they were driven away to the home that had been found for them. Another boatload of escapers was already arriving, and it was not until Pickup was loading the doctor's car ready for their own return journey that the reporter sought him out again.

'There's one other thing you might be able to help us with, old boy.'

'What's that?'

Nesbit bit his lip. 'Funny rumours going around Stockholm, concerning Kurt Westermann.'

'*Who?*' Quick thinking.

'The German film star. *Storm of Steel,* if you saw it.'

'Yeah, I remember. What about him?'

'Been seen around the city, people say. But none of the film companies knows anything about him, or why he should be here. Except that apparently he is also Jewish, or half-Jewish anyway.'

'So maybe he escaped too. Sneaked over on the ferry. Or on the Lufthansa flight from Berlin.'

'Not a chance. You saw what the passport control at Bromma is like. And the ferry port will be just as tough, you can bet.' He looked intently at Pickup. 'One of the resident Fleet Street mob, Denis Weaver, came up with the suggestion that Westermann might have done a Rudolf Hess and landed a light plane down these parts. He was a flier in the last war, won a gong – I wondered if you might have heard something . . .'

Pickup shook his head. Nesbit was getting too close for comfort. To make matters worse, Holmin had come out and joined them, head cocked inquisitively as he overheard the last words. 'Hess flew to Scotland back in forty-one, all alone in an Me 110,' Pickup reminded him. 'No one knew why. Or if they did, they weren't saying.'

'We understood he carried some sort of peace offer.'

'A further weird rumour,' said Nesbit, 'is that he has been seen hobnobbing with Hans Thomsen.' When Pickup didn't rise to the name he went on: 'Who is the German minister to Sweden, very shrewd, very suave, a professional bloody charmer and one hundred per cent a Nazi.'

'Sorry, can't help you.'

Nesbit cocked his head to one side. 'If you do hear anything, give us a ring. You've got the number.'

Pickup didn't dare confess that he'd lost it or, rather, given it away.

164

'Which reminds me,' Nesbit added, 'is there one we can reach you on?'

'Not really. It would give my superior shits of the feathers. You know, still the old GPO pen-pushers at heart, please don't talk to those journalist fellows.'

Nesbit gave him a come-off-it look, but Dr Holmin was already tearing a page from his prescription pad. 'Here, sir, take my number. You may call me should you find you have more questions.'

'That's very civil of you, Doctor.' He took the slip and winked at Pickup.

They left the coast without running into the Count. He was already back home by the time Holmin dropped Pickup off at the gates, and he'd crunched up to the door. 'There have been telephone calls for you,' he said accusingly. 'From your legation in Stockholm, I suspect. The second one came just as I arrived back from Lund. I was unable to say where you were, which made me sound foolish.'

'I'm sorry. I did leave word where I was going.'

'He will telephone again, this person. Tomorrow morning, early. Please make yourself ready.'

There was no ceremony of Swedish punch that evening. Pickup went to bed, slept not very well, got up at seven, was grudgingly given some foul tea substitute and *knackerbrod* by a servant, and then hung around, hung around, hung around. The call didn't come until after ten. It was Richard Petty, the assistant air attaché. He said, 'Unless you want a court-martial, old boy, don't ever do that again.'

'What?'

'Ring the legation, as you did yesterday. The Swedes listen in to every call on that line – how the hell did you get hold of it?'

'From the Swedes, as it happens.' He paused for a moment, fingers crossed.

'What was so urgent?'

'Just wanted to know what's happening about . . .' He was going to say about his getting back to the squadron but broke off to ask, 'By the way, I take it that this call is safe?'

Petty sounded slightly more amiable. 'At this end, yes. I'm

165

calling from the Royal Swedish Aero Club. At your end the Count always claims that his connection is not tapped. Apparently it runs across his own land pretty well the whole way from the exchange.'

He paused. Despite all he had said, his voice seemed hushed when he resumed. 'The thing is, there has been a bit of a balls-up concerning your operation.'

'How do you mean?'

'Well, one of the Jews pegged out –'

'I know that!'

'– and apparently there is some snag with the other. Anyway, it looks as if we may have to do another pick-up, if you'll pardon the pun. So you are to stay put – absolutely put – where you are, and await further orders. Got that?'

'*I can't,*' Pickup wanted to cry, but Petty was already forging on.

'You'll have some help this time, though,' he said.

'How do you mean?'

'A visiting fireman flew in on the Mosquito this a.m. Didn't see him myself, he's already on his way to you. You've heard about all the Children of Israel arriving from Denmark? The Germans are screaming but for once the Swedes are standing up to them. Bloody good show. It's also made our travel cover much easier. Miles Leveret is driving down quite openly to report on it for the Office, and on the side pick up any information about enemy movements the refugees might bring. The new chap is with him, in the guise of a special envoy from the Church, if you can believe it. Miles will drop him off at the Count's after they've shown themselves to the multitude a few times. Is he there, by the way?'

'The Count? Yes.' Indeed, he was at the door, scowling impatiently at Pickup. 'Do you want to speak to him?'

'Only to ask him to put a vase of flowers in the spare room and air the bed.'

Pickup's relief that he was not in big trouble quickly gave way to forebodings. The threat of having to do another descent into Witchland curdled everything. With the squadron, what he had hated most were the times he'd had to abandon an operation because no signals from the field showed up, or the

166

moonlight wasn't up to par, or the weather had broken, and so had to go again next night. But it had been his own decision then and usually, to be honest, the only sensible one. Here it would be imposed. The prospect was too harry grimmers to contemplate. At the same time he was illogically troubled by the mysterious visiting fireman who was on his way. What rank? British or Polish? Pilot or navigator? Or might not be aircrew at all, but an army type, probably from the Commandos. It could even be a professional cloak-and-dagger merchant. Either of these would want to take charge of the operation, up till now *his* operation.

He alternated all day between dread and resentment, dread drawing ahead when the Count took a telephone call and informed him that tomorrow night was set for the repeat flight. Details of the exact landing field would follow, and there would be only one poor witness to bring back. He had sent a message to the mechanic Per, who would return at once. And as if seeing Pickup's apprehensions, and at last appreciating them, he added – without an edge, almost with a twinkle – that as the weekend was approaching, Katrin should be home again to help.

It was evening, and dark already, before the awaited sounds of tyres on gravel, opening and shutting car doors and a dog barking brought Pickup hurrying to the hall. The Count was already hovering at the entrance. First came Leveret. Behind him came – no! It couldn't be, it couldn't be, but nor could it be anyone else, even (or especially) in a raffish blazer and spivvy grey trousers, clutching a shiny suitcase, a canvas bag slung over his shoulder, already mouthing something cheery and obscene. It was the most welcome, alarming, unexpected and inevitable arrival that could possibly be conjured up. It was Tilly.

Kurt Westermann lowered himself into the elegant hard chair that passed for comfort in what was to be his home for an uncertain time to come. It was Hans Thomsen's idea, an ingenious solution to the dilemma which had been tearing Westermann asunder. He dared not go back, as Thomsen had urged, to the regime which had ordered the squalid race-annihilation he had finally seen for himself, and which would doubly welcome the opportunity to be rid of someone who had also been associated with the disloyal Herbert Selpin. At the same time his whole being shrank from denouncing the land for which he had flown and fought in the Kaiser war, and the public who had made him a star. He had resolved to surrender to the Stockholm police as an illegal entrant, and spend the rest of the war in internment, but Thomsen had warned him that, with more and more Swedes beginning to believe allied propaganda about so-called death camps, it was still possible that he would be forced to stand up and shout lies and blasphemies about the Fatherland.

That was rich, Westermann thought, coming from a German who was by birth a Norwegian. And who had ignored Westermann's attempts to tell him what he had seen, preferring to ascribe his misfortunes solely to the *Titanic* scandal. 'It was merely your bad luck,' he had ruled, 'and some bad judgement in ever becoming involved with an arrogant film-traitor like Selpin.'

Thomsen had then produced his compromise solution. His predecessor as Minister in Stockholm was an aristocrat-diplomat of the old school, a Prince no less. He had shown no conspicuous enthusiasm for National Socialism, and had finally been replaced by Thomsen some six months ago. He had chosen not to go back to the Reich, but to retire to the palatial villa outside the city he already owned. Noblemen, Thomsen said sardonically, had ways of looking after themselves and each other. The Prince continued to enjoy a degree of diplomatic privilege. He also still had property and family in Germany. It was in his interest to do occasional favours for his successor. He had agreed to take Westermann into his household provided the fugitive were furnished with a diplomatic alias and all the papers to go with it. Ostensibly he would be a clerk seconded from the Legation to help the Prince write an official history of German–Swedish relations since 1940.

If this ruse were to succeed it had to be carried out instantly, before rumours spread, before Westermann could be positively identified by a journalist. And once installed in the villa, he must not venture out, at least not in the foreseeable future. Westermann had agreed. He had little choice. And it would give him time to rest, to recover from the foul realities thrust before him, to refresh his arts of impersonation, and – who knows? – find his way back into the film world which was his only true country.

In the end, the Branch Manager had ordered him to come, Tilly was explaining. Dinner was over, Miles had been persuaded to stay the night by the Count, who knew a toff when he saw one, and now it was time for the late-night Swedish punch ritual, except that Miles had requested brandy instead. He and the Count were getting on splendidly, even the Countess had stayed up, and then – delight upon delight – Katze had arrived home, peered round the door for a moment and said that she would join them when she'd tidied herself. Meanwhile Pickup and Tilly took the opportunity to catch up on each other's tidings. They carried their 200 millilitres apiece over to a couple of chairs a bit away from the bar. Tilly was also carrying a canvas bag which he set down on the floor by his side.

'Yeah, I'm afraid you're not the Branch Manager's favourite counter-clerk,' he said. 'What really pissed him off this time was the way you'd managed to flee the country before he could have you shot for your adventure with the gallant old brown jobs of the Home Guard – the one you felled is okay, by the way, though the odds on his becoming your father-in-law are now somewhat longer, I gather. She got though to the station on the phone, asking for you.'

'Who?'

'Anita or Audrey or whatever. Wanted you to know that what happened was nothing to do with her. Sounded quite tearful. She'll be panting for it next time you see her, you jammy bugger.'

Pickup shook his head. 'No, it was pretty well all over anyway. Incidentally, fleeing the country was not actually of my choosing—'

'Of course it wasn't. Operational necessity, as I told the B-M. The cloak and dagger brigade supported us on that.' He paused for an instant. 'It was also their suggestion that a back-up pilot should be sent out. Apparently this second sortie is a super-duper priority. It's got to succeed.'

'The first one having been a complete bloody failure,' Pickup snapped. The drift of what Tilly was saying was now plain. He was going to do the op. Pickup was taken off it. Sacked.

'No need to be like that,' said Tilly between puffs and match-scratchings as he strove to light an evil cigar the Count had given him. 'They were loud in your praise in Stockholm, those that knew about it. It wasn't your fault that one of the poor buggers died. Still less your fault that the Swedes have gone and lost the other, the film-star bloke. Not that he sounded a very reliable choice.'

There was the sound of tittering from the bar. The Countess and the Count, now distinctly blurred, were looking in their direction. 'We would like to say a prayer now,' intoned the Count, 'and wonder if Pastor Tillotson would lead us.'

The old fool had been much tickled to learn that Tilly had accompanied Leveret as a representative of the Church, and this was about the fourth leaden joke he'd cracked. Well, it made a change from hailing Dr Holmin as Dr Glas. Tilly gallantly waved his arm in a mock benediction.

That done, he leaned close to Pickup. 'You've not been grounded, if that's what you're thinking. You're still our intrepid sly lander. The only difference is that I'm going with you.'

Pickup stared at him, at once flabbergasted and exhilarated.

'We've just the one bod to pick up, so there is room for both of us. You're familiar with that little aeroplane by now, only sensible for you to fly it. I can navigate, keep watch and generally ride shotgun.'

'Eh?'

'What John Wayne did in the picture we saw in Cambridge that time –'

'Ah, *Stagecoach*, you mean? Picking off the Indian braves from the roof?'

Tilly put on a rugged expression and voice. 'You got it, pardner.'

170

'What are you going to use for a shotgun?'

Tilly delved into the canvas bag dumped by the side of his chair. He showed Pickup a squat little weapon seemingly forged from gas piping and old hand-rails. Pickup had seen them around often enough, even old Winwick's home guards had been issued with a few. It was a war-utility machine carbine, as the Pongos would insist on it being classed, or sub-machine gun in ordinary language, said to cost only 13s.6d. to manufacture, and if you weren't careful it would take your fingers off.

'Sten gun, isn't it?'

'Right first time,' said Tilly. 'Cheap but effective. Leveret's lot made me have it. Apparently they had several hundred smuggled in when it looked as if Jerry might move in on Sweden. They were to be distributed to potential resistance groups, but the threat died down again.'

There was a tinny clatter as he rummaged in the bag. 'I've got eight mags, that's about two hundred rounds. Should be enough for any injuns we're likely to encounter.' He rummaged some more, and pulled out an envelope. 'And this is where we encounter them, if we do.'

Pickup blinked. 'The landing zone? We are supposed to get that from the Swedes in the morning.' He looked to the Count for confirmation, but the Count was busy measuring out another metric potion for himself.

'Yes, that's the drill,' said Tilly. 'But as I was around when Leveret and Co. were being consulted on it, they gave me some advance gen. He unfolded the map and photographs. 'I'm afraid it's even more into the lion's den than you had to go.'

'Let's see.'

Tilly passed him the map. Kolberg, which had been the farthest point west on the map last time, was now on the eastern edge. 'The field is somewhere here' – he poked a finger – 'between Kolberg and Swinemund.'

Even with the latter name pronounced as Tilly pronounced it, this was indeed utter Witchland. But the euphoria that had seized Pickup when he learned that he wouldn't be going alone lingered on. 'Actually it's pretty well due south from here,' he said breezily, 'and not too many miles inland. It's mostly water we'll be flying over.'

'What about that island, Bornholm or whatever it's called? Bristling with flak guns and swarming with panzer grenadiers, they said.'

'Give it a wide berth, as they told the giant's wife when her time came.'

Tilly grinned, the old Tilly again. 'That's the spirit.' He looked round. Katze had come back and was smiling and chatting to the others. She had changed into slinky civvies again, and even if Pickup found her more alluring in uniform, she really did look like a film star.

'Wow! You didn't tell me we had a fully certified popsy on the premises. No doubt you have already had your pleasure of her, you swine.'

Pickup let that one go by. He didn't want to defile what had become a sacred-but-profane, or profanely sacred, little memory. Also, *swine* couldn't help but echo the way Tilly had pronounced Swinemund, which already gave him a shiver, however breezy he had been a minute earlier.

She was prowling over to them now. Anders's analysis still fitted. Though she was no beanpole there was a cat-like, wary grace to her movements. As he introduced her to Tilly he was aware of the old familiar feeling from village hop and necking-party days when he would find himself in a threesome, sharing a girl's favours with a friend. It wasn't jealousy, really, nor rivalry, just the dull certainty that sooner or later they would have eyes only for each other, and he would be the spare prick at the wedding. Funny, he hadn't experienced it with Katze and Anders.

They talked inconsequentially. Tilly exercised his palais-de-dance charm. Katze shot some nice fond smiles at Pickup. Then she noticed the Sten gun still at Tilly's side. 'What is that for?'

Tilly stuck his cigar in his mouth, picked up the Sten and cradled it in a crass imitation of the much-published photograph of Churchill wielding a Tommy-gun. 'We'll fight them on the beaches, fight them on the landing field, fight the buggers until the Nazi evil –' he pronounced it 'Narzi' with a soft 'z', just as Churchill did – 'is banished from the world for ever.'

Katze laughed, whether or not she caught the reference. Pickup said sourly, 'Blimey, how many millilitres have you had?'

'Okay, back to habitual British sangfroid. The chances are that we don't find the field, or no one has set out the lights, or if we do get down the Joe won't have turned up. All the same, I think I'll try out this toy before we go.' The last words merged into a prodigious yawn. As they stared, he wilted visibly. After all, as he proceeded to explain to Katze, he had been on the go for the best part of forty-eight hours, with only a chilly snooze on the Dakota and a little nodding off during the car journeys.

'You must go to bed at once,' she declared. 'Come, I will show you your room.'

The Count agreed. 'Yes, you must sleep,' he cried, by now heavily blurred. 'So that this time tomorrow we may celebrate your return with a proper witness at last.'

Well, thanks. Pickup would have buggered off upstairs himself, but Leveret drew him aside. 'Squadron-Leader Tillotson, or Tilly as one calls him, I believe, has been fully briefed. He will pass it all on to you, if he hasn't already. I have to go on to Trelleborg in the morning. That's the ferry port where our chaps will be arriving on the POW exchange next week. It's a good opportunity to mosey round the place and look up our contacts. But I hope to be back by the time you set off, certainly by the time you return, and will take the client directly to the *Valkyrie*. We're not going to risk losing him again. We'll come back for you two as soon as we can get you on a flight, preferably by Mosquito. Anything else?'

Pickup thought. 'Why the Sten gun?'

Leveret smiled. 'Mainly a gesture, old boy.' He turned off the smile. 'True, this excursion is a little more critical than last time, but we have every confidence that you and, er, Tilly will pull it off.'

XII

Katze was to drive them to the field next morning. The Count, still in more or less cordial mood, could not accompany them. The map co-ordinates had not yet been telephoned. He must stay in the house until they came. Pickup was all for telling him they already had them, but Tilly frowned a signal not to. 'Let him,' he whispered. 'Keeps him out of the way. And they just might change.'

That he and Katze had spent a night of shame together was unlikely. Tilly had been too shagged already, and anyway Pickup had heard small solitary sounds from the room next to his which he now knew to be Katze's. All the same, it would be as well to clear the air. She was in uniform, because it was an official car, even if exuding fumes from the charcoal-burner. She ushered them aboard saluting and generally pretending to be a humble auxiliary about to chauffeur senior officers, Pickup put on a gutteral wireless-comedy accent to say, 'Thank you, Lotta. To the flyg-platz, please.'

'Lotta?' said Tilly. 'She was Katze last night.'

'All our Svedish girl-soldiers are called Lotta. Last time she vas not here. I have had to ride to the flyg-platz on a horseback'.

'You know I could not be here,' Katze called over her shoulder. 'I was bringing Anders from Everod. Then we must go on to Ronneby.'

'Anders?' Tilly asked obligingly.

'A friend.'

'He's in the Swedish RAF,' Pickup supplied. 'Flight-Lieutenant, but they call it Captain.'

'*Kapten*,' chipped in Katze.

'Aircrew?'

174

'Naturally.' That was Katze again.

'Good type,' said Pickup. 'Helped me a lot with the flight plan. Knows the coast over there. Wish he could do the same this time.'

'He will,' trilled Katze. 'It is Saturday, he will be off duty later. I am to pick him up in Kristianstad this afternoon.'

Pickup felt another of his lightenings of the heart. Tilly grunted.

It was the long way round, of course. When they reached the field, Per had the Stinson wheeled out and was completing the pre-flight checks. Both tanks were full, he reported, but they didn't have much left over for topping up. Katze went off to park the car out of sight, just in case.

Tilly appraised the Stinson. 'Trim little crate.'

'Just the ticket for the weekend aviator,' said Pickup.

They climbed aboard from opposite sides, Pickup into the pilot's place on the left, Tilly at the dual controls on the right. Pickup took him through such proficiency as he had acquired (a) from the laconic Yank at Bovingdon and (b) the hard way. Tilly liked the neatness of the cabin layout, was surprised at the absence of a radio. As they finished, Katze came back, carrying the Sten.

'Are you wanting this?' she called.

'Thank you, yes.'

'Right,' said Pickup. 'Shall we take her up? Give you a feel of her.'

'Don't be crude, young sir. Oh, the aeroplane, you mean? Yes, we'll take wing, but only a couple of circuits in view of what our friend here says.' He beckoned to Katze. 'I say, would you like to come with us?'

'If you do not mind me, I would love to!' She bubbled with excitement.

Tilly murmured to Pickup, 'Might as well get the feel of her, as you put it, with a full complement aboard.'

He nipped out to open the ratty little rear door for her, with an appreciative eye on her behind as she squeezed in, and stowed the Sten gun under his seat as he resumed his place. Pickup hoped it wouldn't rattle around if they hit any disturbance, or even start firing. He would also have liked to be

175

absolutely sure it was safe to become airborne, no spies with binoculars lurking in the woods. Per had reported nothing, though. They'd have to chance it. Only in stories could people leap into unfamiliar aeroplanes and fly away Peter, fly away Paul.

Tilly took over as soon as they were at a comfy height. He tried a couple of turns, a climb and a descent, but then handed back to Pickup and reached for the Sten gun. Complete, Pickup noticed, with long thin magazine poking out the side. 'What are you doing?' he yelled. They were enclosed in a tight little cabin with no aperture to aim a gun out of, and probably just as well. One haywire squirt forward and you could shatter the prop, one blind one backward and you might blow the tail off.

'All right, all right,' Tilly shouted back. 'Just finding out what's possible and what's not. No aerial combat, that's obvious. It's on landing or taking off again we might need the bloody thing.'

Pickup was wrenched with a sudden impatience. What had they been filling his head with in Stockholm? Tilly of all people, too. The flight commander who had ruled they were taxi-drivers, not bank-robbers, the acting squadron commander who had done forty-four landings and/or pick-ups without the need to play at soldiers. But who was now frigging around with a poor man's Tommy-gun, frightening the passenger and bouncing up and down in his seat as Pickup strove to steady the Stinson for landing. He wished Tilly had never come muscling in on his operation, with his stupid gun and his showing off to Katze.

The moment the wheels touched down he was at it again, wrestling with his door, trying to hold it open with his boot while he pushed the stubby muzzle of the gun out through the crack.

The Stinson rolled to a stop. Pickup sighed a big sigh. From behind, Katze exclaimed, 'That was so exciting and so beautiful. . . .'

'You must have flown with Anders many times,' Pickup said.

She gave them a naughty grin. 'Not in an aeroplane.'

Tilly laughed, but as soon as she had wriggled out, took her place in the back to fiddle with the door and the Sten some more. 'A bit better,' he grunted. 'You could just about take a poop at someone obliging enough to come up astern, likewise from your seat. From that one of mine it's a job even to poke the muzzle out, never mind point it at a target. But I've signed for it, so we'll take the bloody thing.'

'It's only thirteen-and-six if we lose it,' Pickup said sourly. But now they were down, and now that Katze was identified as Anders's popsy, his irritation faded.

Per topped up the fuel tank. As he had forecast, that didn't leave much to spare. He had also seen to the charcoal burner on the car while they were in the air, he said. They helped him wheel the plane back into the hangar, then Tilly suggested a little stroll in the woods before they went back to the house. This was a bit out of Tilloid character, Pickup thought. It was a nice day now, though, cool and crisp with sunlight filtering through the trees. Weird, but not worrying – yet – to reflect that in not so many hours they would be back here to go dicing.

Tilly must have read his mind. 'Going to get your head down this afternoon?' he asked.

Hell's bells, what a googly when Katze was there between them. It could only be a fluke, of course, Tilly couldn't conceivably know what she had done. Nor did she seem to have noticed any innuendo. 'Hope so,' he said lamely. 'You too?'

'I've just slept for ten hours, but I guess so.'

There was a rustle in the underbrush a few yards away. Something scuttled across the path ahead, and close by, so close he could almost feel it, came the flat, percussive ratatat of a burst from the Sten. Katze gasped, Pickup swore. Tilly took no notice.

'Missed him,' he said,

'Missed what, for God's sake?'

'A hare, I think.'

'It was only a rabbit,' said Katze.

'You might have warned us,' Pickup added. 'We're frightened of guns.'

'Go on with you. At least I've fired the damned thing now. The cue for a little formal practice, I think.' He signalled them to come to a halt and pointed the Sten at a young silver birch. He fired another little burst and a splinter of wood flashed white in the sunlight as it was clipped from the trunk.

'Your turn now, Mickup. This little apology for a butt tucks under your right elbow,' he demonstrated. 'The mag rests on your left forearm, close the hand round the stock, if you can call that bit of perforated gas pipe a stock. The thing to remember is not to let your fingers stray into the ejection port on the other side, because if you do the bolt will take them off.'

'That's handy.' Pickup had in fact heard it before, from an agent he'd ferried into France who had just been on a small-arms course. He cradled the Sten as Tilly had shown him, then twisting it to be able to see the ejection port. His fingers were certainly quite close, but as long as they curled round and gripped the stock they were safe enough. He copied the crouching stance Tilly had adopted, the gun tucked in at waist level, aimed simply by looking at the target

'Okay, at the tree, in your own time . . . fire!'

Pickup squeezed the trigger. There was no recoil, just a sort of vibration and the splutter of noise. He'd let go no more than five or six rounds, but there was a *thwack-thwack* as two slugs hit the trunk and the top of the poor harmless silver birch sagged forward.

'There you are!' whooped Tilly. 'Born gangster, if ever I saw one.'

Pickup was tilting the gun over again to check his grasp. He'd caught a flash of brass as the stubby 9 mm cartridge cases were ejected, he'd heard and felt the impact of the bolt as it slammed back to scoop up the next round. Just to imagine getting your fingers in the way gave him a little shiver in the groin. A practical point also occurred to him as he handed, the Sten back to Tilly.

'What if you're left-handed?'

'Good question. I've been thinking, that would make all the difference in that starboard seat of mine. If I tuck the stock in here under the left arm – see? – with this little finger on the trigger, my left foot holding the door open, and my right hand round the stock, I'd have fifty or sixty degrees of traverse, I reckon.'

He went into the crouch again, swivelling to swing the gun from pointing obliquely forward to obliquely back. The target was another tree. There was a last flat ratatat burst, the tree duly shivered, but from Tilly came a single wordless screech, the Sten fell to the ground, he seemed to be falling too, but steadied himself somehow and began to scream profanities, just the words spattered out as the Sten had spattered bullets, *fuck* and *Christ* and *Jesus* and *fuck* and *fuck* again. He turned and stared at Pickup and Katze aghast, holding his right arm out. Blood was spurting from his thumb, or where his thumb was now nearly severed. The end, red and squat, stuck out at an angle, the nail catching the light as it flopped from side to side.

Tilly looked again as if he might fall. Pickup was heaving up, couldn't help it. It was the nail. So Katze acted first. She grabbed Tilly's right wrist and wrapped the thumb in a handkerchief the same colour as her uniform, until almost immediately it was reddened with blood. 'Quick! To the car.'

Between them they steered Tilly back towards the hangar. He had gone pale and was sweating profusely, but after a few yards he shook off their support and tried to stumble along unaided.

Per had already emerged, maybe made curious by the sound of the shots. He started towards them, evidently saw the crimson wrapping to Tilly's hand and shot back into the hangar. As they reached it he was sifting through the contents of a first-aid box. He tore open a paper packet and brought out a big lint dressing. Pickup swallowed hard as Katze peeled off the sodden service hanky, the hanging end of thumb nearly coming away with it, blood still pumping out.

She said, 'We should stop the bleeding, but I don't know which artery it is. Do you?'

No one did. 'I don't think it is as bad as it was,' said Pickup. Just get him to the doctor was what he wanted, get him to a hospital.

Katze nodded. She enfolded the whole palm of the hand in the dressing and tied it into place with a bandage. Per

179

volunteered to ride up to the manor and have them ring Dr
Holmin to warn him. The Count didn't allow motor vehicles
to use the bridle paths, but this was an emergency. Katze
hurried away to start the car. Pickup was left alone with Tilly.
He sat him down on a stool.

'It'll be all right,' he grunted periodically, or 'It's nothing
serious' followed in either case by 'I'll be okay for tonight,
don't worry.' Then his head would loll forward until he jerked
it back again. He held his right arm out in front of him, the
swathed hand supported on his other wrist. The dressing was
already showing crimson, and blood had leaked on to his
blazer and flannels.

It was only a little more than one Swedish mile, Katze said
– four or five English miles – to Alvarstorp, where Dr Holmin
had his practice and was also in attendance at the local hospital. She was driving a bit faster than before but it was still
another ten minutes before the houses of a small town, or big
village, began to show up. The hospital was long and low and
not very big. Dr Holmin, thank God, was waiting for them.
The call from Per had caught him just as he had been about
to set off on his rounds, he said. There was also a man in a
white overall behind a wheelchair, which the doctor insisted
Tilly should use, and supervised his transfer into it.

Inside the building Holmin invited Katze and Pickup to wait
while he had a preliminary look at the injury.

'It was my fault,' Pickup moaned. 'Should never have raised
that hare about what if you were left-handed.'

'Hare? It was only—'

'I should never have *mentioned* being left-handed. He had
to go and try, knew his finger would be out of the way now,
forgot about his thumb.'

'Always you say it is your fault. It was the same with the
poor Jewish man who died.' Her eyes were angry. 'It was no
one's fault. It was bad chance. It is bad chance again. You
say these things only to make people tell you that.'

He must have looked so abject that she softened at once,
and reached out to take his hand. Hers was a soft, warm,
smooth feminine hand such as he had valued above all other
contacts when a gawky teenager. 'Sorry,' he said.

180

'No more *sorries!*' she exclaimed, but smiling.

He squeezed her hand, she squeezed his in response. There were streaks of drying, darkening blood on her uniform skirt and one sleeve of the tunic. She caught his glance, made a grimace and nodded pointedly to his clothes. They bore the same stains. 'When we get back we give them to Fru Stiller, the housekeeper. She has tricks.'

They talked, or just sat together, hands still joined, in silent communion until they saw Holmin approaching. From his expression it was unlikely that he brought very good tidings. He said, 'He is as well as may be expected. He has lost quite some blood, but not to any danger. The small artery that was severed had already begun to stem itself. I have tried to rejoin the bone that was fractured. If it will knit we cannot tell yet. He has shock, naturally, and was in great pain. We have given him morphine, also an injection against Tetanus.'

'He must stay in here?'

'Oh yes.'

'How long?'

'Until tomorrow at the very earliest.'

Pickup saw Katze willing him to challenge that. He said, 'How about tonight?'

'You mean, to make the flight?' So Holmin knew who Tilly was. Unless he had just guessed.

'Yes.'

Holmin shook his head. 'I am sorry. I would like to say yes. But he has had morphine, you will know what that means. Also, he has lost blood and the altitude could start the bleeding again. Most important of all, he must not move the thumb by the breadth of a hair if it is to start to knit. At first, in fact, he must not try to use the hand at all.'

'Will it get better?' Pickup asked. For a moment, the idea that Tilly might never pilot a plane again outweighed the dismal confirmation that, after all, he would be on his own again that night.

'If all goes well, your friend can start to move his hand again quite soon. But the thumb must be held firm until it is healed. And until that time he will not be able to handle the controls of an aeroplane, because it is with the thumb –' he

181

demonstrated with his own hand – 'that we grip or hold or twist.'

'Thank you.'

Holmin held out his hand in farewell. His eyes were fixed on Pickup's. His little beard wagged as he said, 'You must excuse me now. I will be at the field in the night, as before, to see your return.' He nodded to Katze and trotted away.

Katze looked at her watch. 'I must collect Anders from Kristianstad, but I can go round by the manor to let you off—'

'No, I'll come with you.' The last thing Pickup wanted was to rattle round the bloody manor with only the Count to talk to, and only the night's work to think about and dread.

It was the first time he had seen Kristianstad by day, and a fine day at that. As they approached the station where she had met him before, Katze turned in through a gate and parked the car. She switched off the engine and led Pickup into a sort of public garden with trees and paths and little wooden houses like witches' houses and a bigger, arty-crafty building painted green and white. The general effect reminded Pickup of some snooty seaside place he'd been taken to as a boy.

'This is our Tivoli,' she said. 'It is nicest in summer when you can sit and eat or drink outdoors, but the theatre café is always nice, and I can wait for Anders alone if he has been held up. You see, when I am off duty we meet in Kristianstad because if I take the car all the way to Everode they might find some task for me . . .' Her voice trailed off in bubbly giggles at the chain of circumstances and excuses.

They went into the café, which was light and airy and already had people, both military and civilian, sitting at tables. She chose one by a big window overlooking the greensward. Unless Anders arrived very soon, she said, they would be too late for lunch at the manor, the servants had Saturday afternoon free. But they could have something here, meanwhile would he like a drink?

Yes, said Pickup, but on him. He ordered white wine, because that's what she liked and he still had most of the kroner he'd been dished out with, which was just as well when

182

he came to pay. He hadn't much experience of wine, other than those booby-trapped bottles of red he'd brought back from France last time. This white turned out to be a golden yellow, and not too dry, a far remove from the acid gut-rot old Winwick had served on Pickup's first visit.

'Chablis,' sighed Katze after the first sip. 'In Sweden we love it especially because in winter, when it is dark for nearly all day, we can see sunlight in each glass.'

Oh, he could fall for her, and in the nicest way, too. She didn't plunge him into the Eeyore gloom to which he was usually prone when he was smitten. True, he'd been mildly jealous of Tilly when Tilly had arrived firing on all cylinders, but he felt nothing of the same about Anders, indeed was actually looking forward to his arrival. It was like those long-gone days of Sarah and Chris, poor bugger, across the landing on Staircase S. Two's company, people said, but three was easier. On which cue, Anders came striding in.

He was in uniform and a bit hot and bothered, Pickup thought. He kissed Katze's hand, wrung Pickup's and said, 'Excuse me if I have kept you waiting but . . . well . . .'

They looked at him expectantly.

He sat down, sweeping off his cap. 'I guess it's okay to tell you. The Americans have been bombing Gdynia. Big raid. We were on standby in case they headed for our coast to get away from fighters, but our guys on patrol didn't see any great fighter activity. They reported a lot of flak, though, and at least one Flying Fortress going down.' He looked at Pickup. 'Shouldn't affect you tonight. Could even help, if they start reinforcing the defences round there from other sites along the coast. Do you know exactly where you're going yet?'

'Unless they've changed it in the last twenty-four hours, yeah.'

'You have a co-pilot this time, Katze told me.'

'I did have. Not any more.' Pickup caught Katze's eye. She nodded. He told Anders what had happened, baldly at first, then letting the Tom and Jerry cartoon element emerge. After all, it was a loony accident to have happened to anyone, a comic self-inflicted wound. 'He can't thumb a lift with me

183

tonight after all,' he ended, holding up his hand so that only the four fingers showed. 'Got no thumb.'

'It is not lost yet.' Katze protested. Anders grinned and ordered another carafe of Chablis.

'Hey, not for me. I'm driving tonight.'

'Oh, you will have time to sleep first. It will help you to be calm, and anyway we are now going to eat something, and as the French say, a meal without wine is like a day without sunshine.'

Even as Anders prattled the waiter was setting down a dish of cold fish in a sort of jelly with other bits and pieces, and a salad, all looking very delish. Tilly aside – if it were ever possible to set Tilly aside – it was suddenly a day replete with sunshine. Tasting the wine and savouring the food, basking in the company of the wild, bubbly Katze and the poetic-looking but good egg Anders, Pickup was filled with an irrational, semi-blotto contentment. All he wanted was for it to last for ever.

It lasted precisely until Katze drew up outside the manor. The Count was waiting for them, face like thunder. Why had he not been kept informed about poor Major Tillotson's accident, nor been given any explanation of how it had been allowed to happen on his, the Count's, land? What if the police were to make enquiries? – just when their presence could jeopardize an all-important appointment which brave Poles were risking their lives to keep. On which subject, when the map reference had still not arrived he had taken the risk of telephoning Oland, only to be told that the English airmen already had it. They gave him the co-ordinates again but it made him look foolish. And with a final glare at Katze in particular, equally discourteous was the failure to send word that they would not be here for lunch. The Countess was much vexed, especially as two servants had been prevailed upon, needlessly, to give up their half-day off.

Pickup shouldered the apologies, laying as much of the blame as he could on Tilly. It was a lousy trick but tactically necessary, and anyway it would all be water under the bridge by the time Tilly was back on the scene.

Katze took over with lots of repentant darling daughter stuff.

As soon as the old grump seemed to be simmering down, Anders led Pickup away to the library to sort out the route for him. Once more he spread out the map and photographs. Again he frowned at what he saw. 'We don't patrol this far. Beyond Kolberg, when there is only occupied territory to the north, the Germans regard the Baltic as their sea. They run the ferries, the air lanes are all theirs. We stay clear.'

Pickup's spirits, already sinking, went into a steeper dive.

'All the same, I know this part of the world,' Anders was saying. 'Pomerania, they call it. Next to Prussia, and not so different. Big estates, noble farmers, stand aside when the Freiherr goes by. My grandfather was one.'

'*What?*'

'My mother's father was Ulrich, Freiherr von Damitz. He died, my uncle Gerhard is now head of the family, also a colonel in the *Wehrmacht*. I have a cousin in the *Waffen SS*. We used to go there every summer, sometimes also at Christmas. Gingerbread, candles on the Tannenbaum, trumpets sounding from the church tower.'

He had reached for the slip of paper with the co-ordinates as he reminisced. He located the landing field, gave a whistle of surprise and riffled through the aerial photographs. 'You will not believe this but ... here we are! You will not be putting down exactly on their estate, that would be too much like a cheap-paper novel. But it is not more than five kilometres away. See! That is the church I just told you of, where the trumpeters played from the tower on Christmas Day.'

He peered at the photo again, this time with a magnifying glass. 'I think I have been in your field. We rode that way when they made us go riding, my sister and me. We were city children, brought up in Stockholm, and thought it very boring as well as making our bottoms sore. Yes, there is the *Schutzenhaus*, which the local regiment would ride out to for exercises and shooting practice – we saw them once, charging up and down on their horses, and smoke coming from the chimney of the hut as their dinner was cooking.'

'Is that the field where I'm going?' Pickup wanted to know, urgently.

Anders hesitated. 'Yes, it is,' he said finally. 'Which is quite good, I think. About three hundred metres long, two hundred wide at one end, a little less at the other, Screened by trees on three sides but not too high. No road to it, no houses for miles.'

'Except the Shooting House.'

'Only a Sunday hut for Sunday soldiers. No one lives there.' He peered once more through the magnifying glass. 'Or anyway, I see no signs of anyone living there.' He paused. 'There is, perhaps, a track to it from the road to Koslin over there – see? But it does not look well used.'

'Okay,' said Pickup.

Anders was examining another detail now, a smile on his face. 'And this that looks like a low wall across the other end of the field, can you guess what it is?'

Pickup shook his head. The Chablis was beginning to catch up on him. He felt muzzy and tired.

'I remember it well. There were several such walls and remains of old forts. My cousins called them the Swedish Fortifications, a reminder of the days when we cruel, warlike Swedes occupied this piece of Germany! But we must decide on your route.'

'Later,' said Pickup. 'Must get my head down for a while.'

Kurt Westermann sat alone in the Prince's library, an old-fashioned reading stand on the table before him. The book it held was a novel by Ernst Junger, the same who had written *Stahlgewittern*, or *Storm of Steel* in English. Westermann hadn't come across it before, because he had been in Hollywood making the film of that title when this new one was published in the Reich in 1939, and by the time he returned in 1940 it had been withdrawn from the bookshops. Apparently it contained oblique criticism of Nazi rule, though not of its ideals. It was called *Auf den Marmorklippen*, *On the Marble Cliffs*, and he was impressed by what he had read so far of it.

Was this not a pointer to the way one should behave, especially if one had been a front-line soldier or airman? One continued to play one's part while maintaining one's reservations. Junger, as was well known, held an important

186

cultural-military post in Paris. He, Kurt Westermann, part-Jew, would have played his part in an important propaganda film but for the vanity and obstinacy of the director. Even his aristocratic new employer who declined to return to the Reich had been its forceful representative, he gathered, throughout many squabbles over German troop transit or English blockade-running.

He would stay here, help the Prince as best he could, refuse to forgive or forget the hellish treatment of alien Jews he had seen – even if it had been mostly at the hands of Ukrainians and Latvians – but betray his old comrades in arms? Never.

Pickup woke up stickily, reluctantly, to the sound of whispers, giggles, once the slap of hand on bare flesh, from the next room. It could only be Katze and Anders, just what he needed to drive him finally to cut his throat. No, not that, God wouldn't approve, but it was certainly the cue to get the bloody flight over, one way or the other. He'd closed the curtains, the room was dark. In a panic he fumbled for his watch, couldn't see it, found it on his wrist. Okay, still only 7 p.m.

He was just reaching for a cigarette when there was a tap on the door, another giggle. The door was thrust open, and in came – it couldn't possibly be, but for an instant he was fooled. The flared tunic, heavily pressed trousers and crumpled peaked cap could only be Tilly's. He almost came out with a rude, astonished greeting. It emerged instead as a squawk of recognition.

'Anders! What the hell are you playing at?'

'Fits me very well, don't you think?' Anders advanced into the room, grinning a wide grin, placing his feet as a male model might mince along. Pickup couldn't help laughing, at least until Katze followed him in, because she was wearing a sort of lacy dressing gown with nothing much, he guessed, beneath it.

'We found it hanging in the room poor Tilly has,' she said. 'Ready for tonight.'

'He always goes on ops in it, as an officer and a gentleman – or on this job, as he amended it, an officer and a gentile.'

187

Anders seemed not to get that. 'Only the hat is too small,' he said. It was perching absurdly on his head. 'We also had difficulty with the collar, until we looked for the studs – that is the word? – to fasten it to the shirt.'

He studied his reflection in the cheval glass which Pickup's room boasted.

'So smart,' said Katze.

'I still prefer the Luftwaffe outfit with the open neck, the short jacket, the britches and boots, the side cap – that is really stylish, eh? And no fiddling with collar studs that leap from your fingers to disappear. These medal ribbons I am wearing – this one with diagonal stripes I have seen in photographs.'

'DFC,' said Pickup. 'Distinguished Flying Cross.'

'And the next, with thinner stripes of the same colour?'

'Distinguished Flying Medal.'

'Ah, for less distinguished flying?'

'Not at all. It's for non-commissioned aircrew, that's the only difference. Tilly won it when he was still sergeant-pilot, the other one since he became an officer.' He was tired of this dressing-up game, surprised that Anders should go in for it. He said, 'Now, if you don't mind, get back into your own togs while I get my uniform on, and we'll sort out my route for tonight.'

Anders and Katze exchanged glances. Then Anders said stiffly. 'That will not be necessary.'

'What do you mean?'

'Because I am going to navigate. I shall fly with you.'

Pickup goggled. Nothing had prepared him for one between the eyes like this. He said, 'Don't be so bloody silly. If anything goes wrong and the Jerries find a Swede involved it'll be goodbye to cosy neutrality for you. They'll come storming in.'

'But they will not find a Swede involved.' Anders spread his arms to display the two and a half rings on the cuffs of his tunic, the wings and ribbons on his breast. 'They will find only Squadron-Leader Tillotson as you see him before you. I am even wearing his strange underpants that say they are made in England.'

Katze hid her face, they must have been the cause of her

giggles. Pickup was going to protest that the uniform wasn't enough in itself, he'd need dog tags, but suddenly he was captivated by this crazy proposition, he couldn't bear to sink it out of hand, and anyway Anders was forging on.

'As you explained to us last time, or as I learned in Finland, aircrew carry no documents when on operations. All we are required to give our captors is our name, rank and number.'

'We don't know Tilly's number.' He had to say that, it was only fair.

Katze said, 'I can telephone the hospital and ask them to ask him.' She started towards the door.

'Wait!' There was something more if he were going to play fair.

'Yes?'

'You really need his identity discs.' He reached down inside his shirt and tugged up his own, threaded on to a bit of glittery string that Audrey had pulled out of one of her Windmill costumes, she said.

'He would have been wearing them this morning?' Anders wanted to know.

'He shouldn't have been, not while he's supposed to be someone else, and someone from the Church at that. But he might have hung 'em round his neck when he got up this morning, ready for tonight. Or they could be tucked away in his bag.'

'I will search.'

When he'd gone, Katze sat down on the end of his bed, which was nice but tantalizing, because the tea gown, or whatever it was, parted to reveal a length of creamy thigh. This was the cue, he guessed, for some mutual heart-searching.

'Look,' he said. 'Anders is a good type plus. I'm really grateful – in fact overflowing with grate – for his offer to come with me. But it could go wrong, and even if doesn't it would be a court-martial if his high-ups got to hear of it. You're his girlfriend. Tell him to be sensible.'

She shook her head. She was quiet and serious now. 'We talked about it all the time you were sleeping. Anders would not think of going with you if it were for the war. Maybe for comradeship or – what is the phrase? – just for the hell of it?

189

But then I would play hell with him. No, it is something else. It is because of what we believe, at last, is being done to people only because they are Jews. We have seen them arriving from Denmark. All right, they have not been chained up or seen their families murdered, but their faces when they could know they were safe is something I can never forget.'

Pickup thought he saw a tear glisten in the corner of one eye.

'Then that poor man you brought last time who was so ill, and died. His head was only a *skull*. His eyes when they opened, just for a few moments as I looked down at him, were aching to tell me something.'

Now there was a palpable tear.

'How could that other one have vanished? It does not make sense! But it makes us all the more determined to see this third tale-bearer brought to our country tonight.' Anders chose this moment to re-enter. 'And that is why my Anders will come with you.'

'Also just for the hell of it,' he said cheerfully.

She wrenched off a slipper and flung it at him. They all laughed.

'Did you find the dog-tags?' Pickup asked.

He shook his head.

'He'll have them with him, then.'

Katze said, 'I will telephone Dr Holmin. He can bring them when he comes.'

'That'll do,' said Pickup, and to Anders, 'Make sure you have nothing in your pockets that be traced. No letters, no money.'

Anders held up what looked like an overgrown red penknife. 'Is it all right if I carry this?'

'What is it?'

'Swiss army knife.' He pulled out various blades, a screwdriver, a little saw. 'A Red Cross guy from Switzerland gave it to me. Said we neutrals should support each other. A joke, I guess. But I carry it when I fly, for good luck, you know?'

'Sure,' said Pickup. 'A Swede in the English air force armed with a Swiss knife – that'll really fox them.'

XIII

The moon hung in the sky bigger and better lit than five nights before. As forecast by Anders's air force weathermen, a light wind had got up from the south-west, which was all to the good. They had to allow a little extra time for the outward trip but would be helped home correspondingly.

The Stinson was already pointing in the right direction, full to overflowing in every receptacle. The flare-path was lit. Pickup was in his battledress and submariner's pullover, his old forage cap on his head. Anders was wearing the helmet said to have been left in the plane by the original owner, and over Tilly's chain-store service dress a flying jacket that could have been any air force's. The Count, looming all over the place, wore his Home Guard greatcoat, giant star of his rank prominent. Katze was looking cute in civvy slacks and a short fur garment. Per was quietly keeping an eye on technical matters. The trouble was that ten minutes before take-off Dr Holmin had still not shown up, but Miles Leveret had.

Pickup had seen the dim lights of a car turning into the field and breathed a sigh of relief. It would be the doctor bearing the dog-tags without which Anders would be at risk of ending up in front of a firing squad. Then the car itself came into vision and it wasn't Holmin's. It was the American job – a Dodge according to Tilly – in which he and Leveret had arrived the previous night. They had spent the whole day together prior to that. There was no chance of fooling a cloak-and-dagger merchant for more than an instant. The only hope was to take off at once.

'Get in the plane!' he hissed to Anders. 'Pretend you're busy. Don't look at him.'

In the event, and thanks be to God, the Count was lying in

wait to buttonhole his new chum. Pickup clambered into his own seat and started on the pre-flight checks. He hoped Leveret wouldn't know enough about aeroplanes to spot that the senior officer was occupying the second pilot's place. They could be away in a couple of minutes – but that would certainly mean Anders minus identity discs. He was overcome by a panic of indecision. Give me a sign, God. What should I do?

God obligingly sent another vehicle bouncing into the field. Tycho Holmin! All was saved. 'Okay, start up.' The motor fired first time. He opened his door and held out his hand. The doctor hurried up, shaking his head. 'He was not wearing such things,' he shouted. 'Nor could we find any in the pockets of his clothes. I am sorry.'

Christ, what now? To make the worst still worster, Leveret came sauntering up, carrying what looked like that bloody Sten gun. Pickup had noticed it, still in the hangar where they'd left it after the accident, but deliberately didn't retrieve it. Luckily, as it turned out, his side of the plane was the one Leveret approached. To be heard over the noise of the engine Leveret had only to raise his normal I'm-in-charge voice by a decibel or two.

'You're just off then? Sorry I couldn't get here earlier, but the briefing is unchanged. He called across to Anders, 'All fit, Squadron-Leader?'

Anders waved vigorously, map in hand to mask his features.

'Well, good luck. We'll be waiting for you with a bottle of the right stuff.'

Hadn't they better own up here and now? Let the professionals take the responsibility for whatever would happen if the Germans nabbed an RAF squadron-leader with a Swedish accent, Swedish tooth-stoppings and no identification? But Leveret had remembered something. With his free hand he fumbled in his pocket and brought them out – red and green, threaded on a bit of orderly-room string, Tilly's dog-tags!

'Oh, I nearly forgot. He left these in the cubby-hole of the Dodge. Just as well to have 'em.' He tossed them to Anders. 'And you were about to go without this.'

This was indeed the wretched Sten gun, of course. The SOE's pet contribution to the success of the operation, and they had been going to leave it behind! Well, thanks a million, old boy. Never mind, his bringing the discs excused all. Pickup chucked the gun into the back, mouthed a genuine thank-you, yanked the door shut and opened the throttle.

At 60 mph on the clock they lifted off into the moon-night. Now they had only the easy bit, to fly into the maw of the Reich, land in a field frequented by sharpshooters and collect a trick Ishmaelite who might actually perform.

Anders gave him the heading to take them over the same part of the Swedish coast as before, where he knew the location of the observer posts and anti-aircraft batteries. Once they were out at sea he set a much more westerly course. It was a longer way round, but would take them past Bornholm on the west side rather than the east. If the Germans there had spotted Pickup last time, in their Teutonic single-mindedness they would be watching the same bit of sky for any further passage by a small unidentified monoplane.

The sea below reflected the moon and stars. In front the little motor sang. Bornholm slid by on the port bow, dark as ever until a searchlight beam stabbed out, then another and another, but all over on the far side, their source hidden behind the hump of the hinterland. Anders corrected their course to take them due south.

Sixty-five minutes out, Pickup could see enemy coast ahead again, except it wasn't enemy as far as Anders was concerned, merely ancestral. Pickup glanced sideways at him. He'd clawed off the helmet to let his lank poet's hair fall aslant his forehead. The map rested on his lap. His head and eyes strayed continually up, down, forward, sideways, all ways, in the instinctive routine that was acquired only from flying in the knowledge that a predator, in one quarter or another, could be lining you up in his sights. Must have been his spell in the Winter War.

Now they were over the coast, bright line of surf, crescents of sand just showing, then big lakes or pools of still water separated from the sea only by skeins of land. And still no flak, no searchlights. Anders's concentration flicked between the map and what could be seen of the ground. 'Now go towards that line of trees' or 'Follow this river until I say.'

193

For Pickup it was so much easier than having to drive and navigate as well that time began to drag its feet. Surely they must be getting close to the target zone soon? In the tensions of worrying about dog-tags and having to be wary of Leveret, he had omitted to sneak away for a last-minute leak. He began to fear, just from thinking about it, that he wouldn't be able to last out until they landed. Not that he would have much opportunity then, if things were at all dicey on the ground.

At last Anders said, 'Okay, start to lose height. Five degrees starboard – head for that escarpment.' Pickup began to discern evidences of life, isolated farms, a church, sometimes a gleam of light. Did the bomber crews see such things? Only the Pathfinders, probably, who went in ahead and much lower to mark the targets. The poor sods aboard the Lancs and Halifaxes would be too high to see on whom or on what they were dumping their load.

'Okay, now to port . . . and straighten up.' Anders was working from the photograph now. 'See that tower on the skyline ahead . . . if that's what I think it is, we are right on course. Keep same rate of descent for the moment.'

'Look out for the lights,' Pickup interjected. That was one thing Anders wouldn't have experienced, trying to spot a trio of little pin-pricks that stood out about as noticeably, Tilly had once said, as a fly-button in a brothel. You really needed to look vertically down. With too oblique an angle they could be masked by the lie of the land. Supposing that there were any lights, of course.

'I guess we have missed them,' Anders was saying when crikey, there they were, right below, first time. Pickup revved up to signal he had seen them and went into a wide turn to come round again. 'Bullseye!' he cried to Anders. Hundred and fifty miles, detours to avoid this and that, and you bring us in plonk over the spot.'

He made it a very wide turn to give himself a nice long approach, with time to have a look at the field. It was of trapeze shape, with the shorter side at the far end, towards which they would roll on landing, and before which they had to unstick on take-off. There was some sort of embankment they would have to clear then – ah, yes, the Swedish fortifications – but no trees. The trees were along both sides, tall and pretty dense, so it was a bit of a funnel. The near end, now looming up fast, was bounded by the rough road Anders had detected. There were trees along it but spindly, with plenty of gaps. He couldn't see any shooting hut, or whatever it was. Okay. Reduce power, turn into the final approach and Bob's your—

Jesus Christ, what was that? They were just passing over the road when he felt the Stinson shudder, the nose dip for an instant. He could squirt on the power and climb away, or he could complete the landing. Instinct, or something, was already doing that. The wheels touched once, then again and stayed down. They seemed to be rolling freely but Pickup had to stick on some rudder to counteract a yaw to starboard.

'We snagged something,' he said to Anders.

'Yoh. I felt it. Telephone line, maybe.'

At taxi-ing speed the slew was barely noticeable, but whatever they had collected would have to be shed before taking off again. Meanwhile the set pattern back to the rendezvous point was bringing them to the moment which always made Pickup's heart thump and stomach contract. Would it be the Joe waiting for you, in this case a poor yid with hunted eyes? Or would it be some Gestapo thug emerging from the shadows with a razor smile?

In fact it was one man alone, running towards them, waving his arms. Get out the bloody way, Ikey. Got to swing the plane round to point back up the field for take-off. That was the absolute golden rule of this club. He throttled the motor back to ticking over, jumped out and shot round to the tail. Anders had guessed aright. It was signal cable, yards of it, hooked round the tail-wheel and somehow embedded into the mounting. He tugged it forwards but it was stuck. It had also wrenched the wheel out of true.

The bloke had nobbled Anders and was spluttering at him in urgent German. Anders was listening and trying to calm him while working round to examine the tail disaster. 'He says there are soldiers very close. He heard voices shouting and then lights coming this way.'

'We got to get this off first.' He pulled and pulled at one

195

of the two loose ends, then the other, feeling the wire cut into his palms. Neither budged.

'Keep pulling, keep it tight pulled.' It was Anders. He went down on his knees to saw at the wire, close to where it was jammed into the metalwork, with his Swiss army knife.

Pickup shut his eyes and willed himself to pull, never mind the pain. He fancied he heard shouting and the sound of a motor vehicle, hard to be sure with the Stinson's engine throbbing away. Suddenly the wire came free, he nearly fell back.

Anders gave a grunt of satisfaction. 'Now the other!' he hissed.

Pickup glanced over his shoulder down the track or what was visible of it. He saw steel-helmeted figures lumbering in their direction. Hurry, hurry! It was no good, he could no longer hold the cable tightly with hands on fire, fingers slippery with sweat or blood. He'd get something – ah the wretched Sten gun would do – to act as a windlass.

'Hold it,' he shouted. But even as he straightened up the Joe, or Jew, hurried up with a bit of a branch of a tree in his hand and the same idea. He wound and wound the wire around it and pulled with all his weight. It gave Pickup his first real look at him – about forty, fair-haired, good leather coat. Anders was hacking away again, but on the wind came shouts, much closer, and what sounded like a motor vehicle, hard to be sure with the Stinson's engine turning over only feet away. Pickup reached for the Sten anyway, it might be needed in another capacity.

Then from Anders came a gasp, this time, of success. The ratty little rear door was still open. Pickup bundled the Joe into the seat, banged it shut and scrambled into his own place with a last look back – Shit! It *was* a vehicle, a little truck of some sort turning off the track into the field at this very moment.

Anders was already at his controls, must have slipped Swedishly into his seat without agitation. Pickup released the brakes, pushed the throttle open, urged the plane to gather speed, but the tail was nowhere near up when they heard a shot, then another. He took another peek astern. The truck was coming up fast behind and abaft them, would catch up in seconds.

'Take her,' he said to Anders.

'Sure.'

He cocked the Sten, pushed his door, held it open with his foot as Tilly had demonstrated only twelve hours or twenty years ago, and poked the gun through the gap. The crazy little vehicle was close, bouncing and bucking. There was only one wheel at the front, it was a three-wheeler for God's sake. The rear was canvas covered, flapping in the wind. The driving compartment was open, with the driver hunched over the wheel and another man taking pot-shots with a revolver. He was being thrown around too much to hit anything that mattered, but in a moment they would draw level.

Pickup fired, one long burst. He saw the driver jerk back, the other one reach across to grab the wheel. The vehicle swerved abruptly, was over-corrected, lurched from side to side until finally it turned over and crumpled into the ground.

'Got them!' Anders shouted.

'Hope so.'

'And you have fingers still?'

'Think so.'

'Ready to take her again?'

'No, you keep her.' He didn't know why he wanted that, he just did. For the moment anyway. They would be airborne any second – they were! He could tell at once that Anders had the touch. You feel it through the seat of your pants, as the Yanks would say. Anders also knew the way home. Pickup could sit back. At the back of his mind he was registering something. He had at last been required to fire shots in anger in this war. And one of them had slugged the driver of the three-wheeler right between the eyes. He could still see his glasses split into two halves, a hole in the head where they had been, the mouth open as if in astonishment. Well, it was them or us. But he wished they hadn't both looked like granddads.

They reached the coast and crossed it without drawing any searchlights. Perhaps the enemy really had moved them in the aftermath of the raid on Gdynia. Over the sea Anders throttled back to normal cruise speed to conserve fuel. If the old Jerries had been able to get word to the air defence, as they almost certainly would have done, the big risk now was from fighters. Pickup screwed round in his seat to look astern but even on his own side the arc of vision was scarcely better than the arc of fire with the Sten. He caught the eye of the Joe or Jew and gestured to him to keep a watch the other side. The man stared back without seeming to grasp the message, until Anders spoke to him in German and he nodded. He didn't look all that starved or beaten. But nor had the survivor of the first pair, the bugger who had disappeared.

This one was speaking some more, telling Anders things. Pickup waited for a translation.

'He says he did not hear of any Luftwaffe airfield around here while he was waiting, only a seaplane station. This coast is not heavily fortified because it is enclosed both on the west and east, and to the north there is Bornholm. Those soldiers who chased after us were *Volksturmers*, like your Home Guard – or ours.'

So they were granddads. Pickup reflected again on how this whole operation had been precipitated by one pair of ancient part-time soldiers, and just now was bloody near terminated by another. Not to mention the Count and his comic air force, which made comings and goings at his field marginally less suspicious. He needed a cigarette, whatever resolutions he had made last time. He had a packet of Players in his left breast pocket, as likely to be found in the possession of any raff type. He stuck one in his mouth and offered the packet to Anders.

'No, thank you.' Anders sounded distinctly narky.

'Mind if I have one?'

'It is not permitted in our aircraft.'

'Nor ours, but we do.'

'Then I will ask you not to. The smoke stings my eyes.'

That was reasonable, but still a bit preachy. He glanced sideways and met Anders's glance. Anders winked and they both grinned. It was no time for high horses.

'Actually,' said Anders, 'we are going to need all our eyesight in three minutes from now. We have to go east of

Bornholm this time. If you look at the fuel gauge' – Pickup had already done so – 'you'll see one reason. The other is the old rule that burglars follow: never leave by the way you came in.'

Did they? Never mind. Pickup nodded. Seated on the port side, he had the better view of the island as it loomed up, the sea breaking whitely against cliffs, the low hump of the interior dark against the sky, but the sky not nearly so light as it had been earlier. Cloud must have been piling in from the West while they were busy elsewhere. The moon was only a blur.

At which point the darkness ahead was slashed by tracer. Next instant came the roar of twin engines and a shudder of turbulence as the Me 110 swept overhead. It would go round in a circle and come again, this time lined up for the kill.

'Down, down!' he was barking but had already, unforgivably, grabbed the controls and pushed the Stinson into a dive. He could feel Anders's touch still, only feather-light, conceding command while ready to take over again if necessary. That was good and sensible. He grunted approval.

At what might have been five hundred feet he started to pull out, suddenly scared that he had left it too late, but the little plane responded gamely. He levelled off as low as he dared, with the white wave caps just discernible but the sea dark enough otherwise to make the black-painted Stinson hard to spot from on high. He risked a flick of the eyes to his right. Anders had just his fingertips on the wheel, his forward gaze at max. intensity, his lips parted. He sensed Pickup's reciprocal need for approval and mouthed an okay.

The Messerschmitt could be on their tail again in a minute and a half or so, depending on the radius of its circle. Time enough to deviate sharply one way or another in an effort to throw off the bastard, but they'd need to gain height first and then bank into the turn, with the risk that if it was too steep the wings might just flash in the moonlight, poor as that was – better to keep it a shallow turn, pile on the revs and pray.

With the Franklin motor at full throttle, they didn't get the sound of the Me 110 again until it was overhead, except – and Pickup allowed himself a little spasm of optimism – it didn't seem to be directly above them, but some way to port. If the Jerry had managed to lose sight of them on his turn he'd probably have to ascend and start his search all over again. Oh for a nice clump of low cloud now. The best he could see was a layer of stratus two miles ahead, some way off the northern point of the island. It might at least blot out a bit more moonlight.

He glanced again at Anders. He had spotted it, too. He pointed a finger in its direction, and then at the fuel gauge. Pickup throttled back to cruise revs and made for the shadowed waters. Meanwhile, maintain an all-round look-out, or as near to all-round as the Stinson's cramped little cabin permitted. He took a quick shufti to the rear. The passenger was craning his head to look out and up, as if looking for the attacker. Way back behind them, much too late, searchlights were combing the sky. Someone would be up before the Kommandant in the morning.

They would be out of this particular cover all too soon, but there was other patchy stuff lying in wait. With the southwest wind now behind them it would be an easy flight home, if the Jerry really had lost them. Only an utter Pilot-Officer Prune, or however that translated into Deutsch, could have made such a cock-up, though.

Another minute passed. Dare he hope? At least he dared to regain a little altitude, and thereby reduce the risk of slapping into the drink when distracted. It was Anders who finally said it. 'I guess we may have given him the slip.'

'He must have been Leutnant Prune, thank goodness.'

'Who?'

'Prune. The name we give to airmen who haven't a clue.'

'What means a prune?'

'It's a sort of dried plum. What's that in German?'

'*Backpflaume.*'

'Leutnant Backpflaume, then.'

Anders still didn't get it, and why should he? Pointless joke, anyway. It would serve Pickup right if Leutnant Backpflaume blasted them out of the sky there and then. Whereupon, that's exactly what he tried. The rant of the Me 110's two bloody great Daimler-Benz engines came up behind them twice as suddenly, twice as loud and from a much lower altitude. Tracer and cannon-shells were ripping into the sea ahead, but keeping pace with the Stinson, in fact edging further ahead – it was all happening so quickly that even as Pickup silently swore he could see that the old tortoise-and-hare story, low-flying version, was still valid. The sheer momentum of this big clumsy warplane closing in at 300 mph and minimum altitude, made any pass at a shadowy little bug skimming along at wave-top height difficult, if not suicidal.

It whooshed over them and climbed away. There was still its rear-mounted machine gun to elude – streaks of tracer duly flicked overhead and abaft. On an Me 110, luckily, there was only an upper fuselage mounting, impossible to depress adequately in circumstances like this. Thank goodness it was an Me 110 and not the other Jerry night-fighter, the Ju-88, which had a downward-firing MG131 poking out of its rear end.

What to do now? Anders was gesturing to turn to starboard. Yes, that could work If the Jerry crew lost sight of them again on this circle round, they might waste time chasing up and down the expected course.

So it proved, though it was five minutes – no, more like seven – before Pickup allowed himself a small ray of hope. He'd been too cheery too soon last time. But on a 60-degree deviation they could now be eight miles east of where Jerry was looking. In fact it was time to think about getting back on course if they were to make the landfall Anders planned or, come to that, make any landfall while they still had fuel in the tank. The gauge had dipped, thanks to the shenanigans around Bornholm. He handed the plane back to Anders. Anders knew this slice of the Baltic, and the friendly Swedish coast that lay ahead of it, like the back of his hand.

Friendly coast it was not, this time. They were still three or four miles out when searchlights pierced the dark as unwelcomingly as those of Ack-Ack Command on the Sussex shore when you were returning from a particularly lousy taxi-run to Orleans. Except that there you could always fire the colours of the night from a Verey pistol in the hope of persuading the dumb soldiery you were about the King's business. Here you could only turn on the navigation lights.

Anders had veered considerably eastwards in his evasion manoeuvre, and was now correcting his course, staring intently ahead as he sought private landmarks. Satisfied, he reached out and duly flicked the switch. With the searchlight beams floodlighting the sky he might just as well have stuck a glowworm on the tail-fin, Pickup thought, but if his little Lottas had been well briefed they would be looking out for sparkles of red and green.

They were over land a couple of minutes later, keeping fairly low but not so low as to attract attention. Pickup could at last relax, except that in the scramble to free the plane from the wire it had gathered, and take off again ahead of the old soldiers, he had quite forgotten the need to pee which had beset him on the way out. Now it was back, and acute. When Anders asked if he wanted to take over yet, he shook his head, gave him an anguished smile and said no, Anders had done most of the flying, he should finish it. This was no longer Operation Sly Lander, it was Sly Anders.

On Lancasters and Liberators the bomber crews had Elsan toilets, lucky devils.

They must be getting close to home now. Anders was whistling softly through his teeth as he started his descent.

Close eyes and think of desert sands.

Anders was turning into the circuit that would take them round and bring him in to land into the wind. Good! That meant they would roll to the far end of the field from the reception committee. There would be a chance to nip out and have a slash before taxi-ing back up.

Close eyes again. This is something Tilly will relish – how Mickup flew into the heart of Nazi Germany, fought a regiment of storm-troopers, picked up a very important Jewish person, tangled with an Me 110 and could think of nothing but his bursting bladder. On second thoughts, might Tilly fail to appreciate it after being retired hurt from the same fixture?

Hey, and what about Anders having gone in his stead? If Miles Leveret was waiting with the rest of them, as he had promised, he was bound to discover the deception now. Well, he'd have to accept it. They'd done the job, brought back the prize, without causing a single diplomatic squawk. No one outside the little circle assembled in the field need ever know.

The improvised flare-path lay before them. You could scarcely feel the touchdown. He was a wizard pilot, was Anders. They should lure him to 161 Squadron, providing he hadn't already been signed up by the Luftwaffe.

They were rolling towards a halt. He didn't open his eyes until Anders braked suddenly. Forty yards ahead in the dimness beyond the flarepath was someone signalling with a little electric torch, someone hurrying towards them. Looked like Miles Leveret. Crikey, it was Miles Leveret. He came to Pickup's side again and peered through the window to see if there was a passenger. 'Well done, damned good show,' he spluttered. 'Sorry about this interception, but there has been a bit of a flap while you were away. Secret police nosing around, etcetera. The others will tell you.' He'd wrenched the rear door open, and the passenger stumbled out. Pickup followed, tugging at his flies.

Leveret grabbed the bloke's arm in rather a policemanly grip of his own, it seemed to Pickup, insofar as he could notice anything in his hopping-about urgency. 'So I brought my car up this end in case they come back,' Leveret was rattling on. The other side of the hedge Pickup could just discern the dull black gleam of the Dodge. 'That's the back road to Knislinge. I'm taking our friend straight on to Stockholm. He'll be on the Mosquito to Leuchars tonight. Any questions?'

'Don't think so.' He would have asked about Tilly and him going home, but that would almost certainly have given the game away on the great impersonation, which now – thanks to the flap – might never be rumbled. Besides, he could wait no longer. Turning away from them, he surrendered at last to blessed relief, only to be interrupted by Leveret's voice again.

'Oh, Pickup? Is Tillotson all right? He didn't have much to say.'

'He's fine. Was busy saying his prayers, I expect.'

'Of course. We'll get you two away on the next available flight. Richard Petty will phone you at the Manor. Goodnight.'

XIV

Through the putter-putter of the Stinson's engine ticking over, Pickup listened to the car drive off. Anders joined him for a pee, or whatever the nursery word was in Svensk. 'Ah, now we may meet everyone without dancing,' he said. They climbed back into the plane – after the fresh night air it suddenly smelled sour in the cabin. Pickup noticed – and taxied up the field to the hangar.

They were all looking a bit strained there, Per, the Count, Dr Holmin and Katze, whose feline prowl turned into a cat-like spring to embrace Anders and kiss him. There was one for Pickup, too, if fond rather than passionate. Questions flew in each direction, bouncing off each other without striking answers, until the Count bullied everyone except Per into Katze's fumy vehicle. Per was to stay behind and paint out all RAF markings on the Stinson. Whether the paint could dry before any snooper turned up was another matter.

What had happened, they learned on the journey back to the manor, was no longer as alarming as it had seemed at the time. A car had turned up at the house about an hour after Anders and Pickup had taken off. Mr Leveret knew from the number plate that it belonged to the police, and kept out of sight. The inspector it carried, along with a subordinate, had been respectful to the Count but firm in his suspicions. For the third or fourth time in a few days there had been reports of light aircraft flying at night over this part of Skane. The Count, as was well known, operated such an aircraft semi-officially in connection with his command of the local *Hemvarnet*, but he had not notified the authorities of any flights, as was required. Could he confirm that his machine had not been aloft? The Count did so. In that case, would he

204

kindly accompany the inspector to his private airfield to make sure someone else had not taken the plane up.

This had been rather good luck. The little GV-38 was sitting innocently in the hangar, its engine stone-cold. Per had tidied away all evidence of the Stinson. The amateur flare-path was accepted as essential to the Home Guard air force. The inspector had been mollified, even confiding to the Count, as he drove him home again, that the mysterious aeroplane might not have been Swedish at all, but a German machine on a secret errand from the Reich – their Fieseler *Storch* was a similar small monoplane. Stockholm was full of rumours that some important German had been flown into the country only to disappear again.

The Count paused at this point, as if waiting for someone to relate such rumours to the mystery surrounding the actor Westermann, but by now Katze was turning into the Manor courtyard. The inspector had gone on his way, the Count finished lamely, with apologies for troubling him.

Within, the table was laid again for the aircrew breakfast, Swedish version, if reduced in numbers and subdued in temper. Pickup and Anders were the only ones to tuck into the fish soup and potatoes. They also had large whiskies apiece, Miles Leveret having left them a bottle of Hankey Bannister from the Legation cellars. For once the Countess was present, despite the hour, and acting as hostess. But no sign nor mention of the figure Pickup half yearned and half dreaded to see, Tilly.

The questions were all about the flight – dodged with modest understatement – and the passenger Anders and Pickup had brought in. What was he like, this third and last witness to unspeakable crimes against his people? What did he have to say? Anders looked at Pickup, Pickup shrugged his shoulders and said they'd hardly had any opportunity to speak to him. He was a good deal younger and fitter than the poor Jew who had died. He was also practical, Pickup remembered. He told the story of the cable which got wrapped round the Stinson's tail-wheel strut, and how this man had helped Anders saw through it.

Katze was gazing at Anders with love and pride in her

eyes. That was all right, he wouldn't dream of making another pass at her himself, after what he and Anders had been through together. Not while Anders was around, anyway. The Count and Countess also looked fondly on their daughter's suitor, lean and intelligent even in Tilly's flashy service dress. As for Dr Holmin, he was nodding his head busily as if to approve the wisdom of those beings the other side of the Baltic who had at last sent a messenger with the stamina to endure such a journey.

Pickup couldn't put it off any longer. 'What news of Tilly?' he demanded.

'Oh, I am so sorry. Of course you have been worrying. A little septicaemia had developed, nothing serious but enough to keep him in overnight. You see –' he exchanged a conspiratorial smile with Katze – 'I gathered from Miss Katrin that it would be better if Mr Leveret did not find him here while he was supposed to be with you over Germany.'

Gosh, yes. 'You were right. Both of you, thanks.'

'You must also thank the Count and Countess for observing the secret. No one need ever know that a peace-loving Swede went on such a mission instead of a hero of the RAF. Your friend is fine. You shall see him in the morning, after we have all had a little sleep, eh?'

Kurt Westermann had woken before dawn. He lay in his bed in the Prince's villa, turning revived uncertainties over and over in his mind. He had been quite sure that his decision to wait and see was the right one. Then last evening Hans Thomsen had dropped by, ostensibly to bring the Prince official greetings on his birthday, in fact to pass on strange rumours in circulation.

The Press attaché at the Legation had been fending off enquiries from journalists all day. They had heard that a very senior Nazi had flown secretly to Sweden. Was it Goering? He had Swedish connections. Or von Ribbentrop, the once powerful, now out-of-favour Foreign Minister? He could be trying to set up a last desperate deal with the English and Americans against the Russians, or with the Russians against the English and Americans. Either proposition had been aired often enough.

All nonsense, of course. Unfortunately, on this occasion the nonsense was inspired by Herr Westermann's brief sojourn at the Grand Hotel. It was none of his doing, but the fault of the pious busybodies who had organized a crazy scheme to bring in a witness to the alleged extermination of the Jews. Having found one – or so they supposed – they then lodged him in the one place in Stockholm where his presence was bound to be noted, and his subsequent disappearance even more so. If the Swedes began to look extra closely at diplomatic establishments, including those of retired diplomats, his discovery might be rather embarrassing.

What was the alternative? Thomsen had been at his most charming. He could always be put on the ferry to Sassnitz, the Swedes had never paid much attention to warring nationals departing, only those arriving. Or he could stay where he was in exchange for an undertaking to proclaim the real truth if and when the Legation required him to do so. He would stand up and testify that as a Jew he had neither suffered nor witnessed any persecution. He had travelled widely in Poland and Czechoslovakia, as well as the Fatherland, and had seen no 'death camps'. His own flight to Sweden had been solely – and needlessly – to escape his association with the traitor Herbert Selpin. As a surety, he must write a full version of this testimony in his own hand, to be attested by a Swedish lawyer and deposited in a Stockholm bank.

The Minister had departed with a last smile and the assurance that Westermann was free to make up his own mind, but his answer should be ready by the time the Legation opened in the morning.

He knew which way his instinct drew him. To stay safely in Sweden was still the better option. No other witnesses had reached enemy or neutral lands as far as he knew, no first-hand accounts of life and death in Treblinka or Belzec or elsewhere had appeared. His 'testimony' might never be needed. Once it was in the Legation's hands, however, it was a landmine which could go off when least expected. Suppose the unpleasant facts about the camps emerged just as Hollywood or Babelsberg were beckoning again. His prospects would be ruined.

He had armed himself with his own little bargaining counter when, with a presence of mind that still surprised him, he had taken from the pocket of his stricken fellow traveller the packet containing three small roll-films. They were said to record the full horrors of Treblinka. If so, they constituted irrefutable evidence, a last resort with which to buy freedom or indemnity or a passage to America. But not so good if Thomsen produced his affidavit to expose him as a two-timer. Should the austere professor recover from his heart attack, that was a more immediate danger. He was sure to make a fuss over the loss of the films. Finally, there was the one who had been left behind, the fellow called Marek – he had been determined to follow them if the aeroplane were to return for another witness. He also knew about the films. No, Kurt Westermann, you must choose one path or the other – for the prosecution or for the defence, Jewish victim or German patriot, nothing in between.

Tilly was waiting in the entrance hall of the little hospital. His blazer and slacks had been cleaned of blood stains and neatly pressed. His thumb – Pickup couldn't stop his eyes from seeking it out straightaway – was bandaged to the rest of his hand, so that you couldn't see whether it was complete or not. He gave Pickup a guarded look.

Pickup stuck out his hand in greeting, knowing as he did so that this could be seen as a bit tactless, but to hold back woodenly would be worse. Tilly took it in his left hand, with a rueful grimace.

'Wotcher, Nelson?' said Pickup. It was the caption to a cartoon in *Lilliput* that had made them laugh, a Cockney newspaper-seller addressing a formidable Wren officer with an eye-patch and her arm in a sling.

'Wotcher, yourself. I'm not too bad, other than being pissed off with this bloody country and its prissy doctors. I'd have been perfectly fit to fly if they hadn't stuffed me full of morphine and anti-Tetanus serum and God knows what else. I've been hallucinating as if I was in a Boris Karloff film.'

For all the figures of speech, his voice didn't quite have the Tilly breeziness you usually got, whether he was briefing you or borrowing ten bob. Well, he had missed a caper that he could have worked up into a great yarn to entertain the others, back in the mess at Tempsford. Might even be a bit jealous. Mustn't let him know about Anders. At all costs, keep Anders out of this.

'Anyway,' Tilly was saying. 'I gather you came back with the extra Joe, and Miles Leveret bore him off straightaway.'

'Yeah. They were going to get him on to a Mozzy to Leuchars tonight.'

'What was he like?'

'Oh, stocky, quiet, not too old.' What else? Tilly wasn't usually interested in the passengers. But this was rather special, Pickup could see – the last chance of doing the job and bringing out a witness, at least by this route. However affable the police inspector may have been, the Count's airfield would be under surveillance from now on.

Tilly was still looking at him attentively. As long as he avoided any reference to Anders, he could tell the story of sawing through the telephone wire, to show that this chap was no old crock or pansy actor but someone with a practical side to him. For luck, he threw in the breathless take-off just ahead of the Jerry soldiers, without the detail that they were old-timers but also omitting his feat with the Sten gun, because (a) it would have touched Tilly on a sore spot and (b) who then would have been flying the plane?

'Any other lines worth shooting?' Tilly asked cordially. That was more like him.

'One or two. Such as being waylaid by an Me 110 on the way back.'

'That could have been nasty.'

'Nearly was. He missed with the fixed artillery but we would have been a sitting duck for the rear-gunner if he'd been able to depress. We were just able to scoot down and hide in the waves while they were faffing round the sky at three hundred knots to come again.'

'Lucky it wasn't a Ju-88 with that underslung machine gun pointing backwards, like a camel's prick.'

'Yeah. Would have been a cruel stroke of fate to be bagged by a Ju when ferrying in a *Jude*.'

'Eh?'

As a rule, Tilly liked Pickup's strained jokes. Now he looked distracted. Pickup spelled it out. *Jude* was German for 'Jew', though actually pronounced *Yude*. Tilly grunted and, as if making a conscious attempt to buck up, fished for something rude. 'I trust you enjoyed a brave airman's welcome home from Katze.'

Pickup was genuinely startled. '*What?*'

'Oh, come off it. You were undressing her with your eyes all that evening, and next morning, too.'

'That's as far as it got, then. Anyway, Anders was there' – he couldn't keep Anders out of everything. 'He came for the weekend, though not until after I'd set off. He'd had to stay on duty because the Yanks were raiding Gdynia. Did you hear—'

'Stop pissing about, Pickup.' Tilly's face was stony. 'Anders flew with you.'

Pickup was never very good at downright lies, least of all to Tilly. 'What makes you think that?'

'Why else should the nurse have been hunting for my dog-tags?'

Pickup was stunned. He had forgotten.

'You might as well come clean,' Tilly said.

'I don't think I could have coped without him.'

Tilly relaxed about one notch. He said, 'In fact I'd lost them somewhere, the tags.'

'You left them in Leveret's car. He produced them at the last minute. They've been to Pomerania and back, likewise your number two service dress. Not the hat, though. Didn't fit.'

'Sorry about that. So Leveret knows about all this?'

'No. He thought Anders was you.'

'That's torn it.' Tilly regressed to unease.

'How?'

'Because it wasn't me. I didn't go.'

'Who's to know?'

'Me. I will know. Anyway, how could I have flown like this? He held up his left hand, bandaged into one stiff white mitt.

'You could have done that on the op!'

Tilly brushed that aside. 'I'd swear you went alone, but Leveret will already have sent his report. The Joe is already on his way. He'll be well and truly debriefed. If the truth gets out now, all hell will break loose. Swedish ace flies on RAF operation. Imagine how the Foreign Office will react. Or the Swedish government, come to that.'

'Why? It's not as if was a military operation. Strictly humanitarian, bringing out a poor bloody Jew.'

Tilly gave him the reflective scrutiny Pickup had last noticed when he was being weighed up at the end of that night out in Cambridge, the very first hint of an inkling of this whole bizarre operation. He said at last, 'Okay, *True Confessions* time all round. This Joe was not a Jew. Or *is* not a Jew, I should say.'

Pickup goggled, aware only of a huge shock of the unexpected but vaguely feared.

'Don't get all righteous. He is something much more valuable. His name is Husser, he's a Czech, an engineer, and he worked on some secret weapons Jerry is developing. Rockets or pilotless aircraft, maybe both. Apparently we got wind of them a while ago. Bomber Command raided the site back in August, and the Huns moved the whole shooting match to some other part of the Reich. Husser sneaked off after the raid, fell in with some Polish workers on the run and through them eventually made contact with MI6 here.'

'So it was all a bloody great confidence trick!' Pickup couldn't help it, he'd been duped, deceived, strung along. 'Why didn't you tell me, why couldn't you trust me, for Chrissake?'

'Steady on, Mickup. For a start, I didn't know myself until they sent me after you. More to the point, when you were briefed in London, you couldn't have been told any different, because the Political Warfare people hadn't been told either. You have to believe me – theirs was a genuine plan they'd hatched with Lingstrom and his crowd to bring out a Jew or two. The first trip you made was absolutely *kosher*, to use the appropriate lingo. No one could know the other end had picked a couple of duds.

'MI6 in London had just learned about Husser when you

reached Stockholm, and were for concentrating solely on getting him out. Leveret argued that this would mean jettisoning Lingstrom and Co., without whose co-operation the whole exercise was impossible. Once you had done the Jew run, though, it wouldn't look suspicious if we wanted to collect an extra bod, just in case. That's when I was despatched. Meanwhile you got back safely from the first op. only to have one passenger die on you, and the other vanish, which was a king-size bonus for Leveret. The Swedes couldn't possibly object now, having been the trusting souls who lost him. Lingstrom didn't seem to mind even when Miles took over the running of the second trip.'

He glanced down at his hand before continuing. 'You know the rest, better than I do.' Pickup must have continued to scowl. Tilly bridled. 'Oh, for God's sake, take that look off your face. We'll be home in a couple of days with any luck.'

'*What?*'

'You didn't know?'

Pickup shook his head, bewildered.

'The Count rang here, to pass on the message from the air attaché cove. I assumed he had already told you. We catch the Stockholm train tomorrow. We're booked on the next Mozzie flight, whenever that is, just you and me tucked up together in the bomb bay. That's something to look forward to, surely?'

'It would have been, if we'd got just one Jew out –'

'Oh, stop binding, Mickup. With that bloke Husser's help we shall be able to devise defences against the bloody things he was working on, even make our own versions of them. You have probably done a vital bit to win this war. What's wrong with that?'

Before Pickup could answer, if ever he could have answered, there was an interruption. It was Dr Holmin, still clad in his operating-theatre togs, Pickup deduced, and wiggling a finger to summon him. In his office the doctor said conspiratorially, 'That English correspondent we met in Lund, I gave him my office number –'

'Nesbit, Alec Nesbit. What about him?'

'He has telephoned an hour ago, asking if I knew where to

find you. I did not know what to tell him, and anyway I was about to operate. So he said that if I did see you, would you please call him at this number in Stockholm.'

'Thank you. I will in a moment.' And with much to tell him.

'Meanwhile there is another little duty we owe the poor man,' said the doctor. He led the way back into the ante-room, where Tilly was looking aggrieved. 'Ah, Katrin will be here shortly to take you both back to the manor.' He held Pickup's arm companionably. 'While you wait, I wonder if you would care to join us in a little ceremony we are about to hold. It is for the poor soul Michael brought in but who died. We never discovered his name or station. So, as Michael knows, we borrowed some belongings from one of the Jews who have been escaping from Denmark, and pretended that he was such a refugee, for whom the journey had been too much. Now we may lay him to rest in the burial ground. But first we have someone to say the *kaddish*, or prayer for the dead. It will only take a few minutes . . .'

'I would like to come,' said Pickup.

'Why not?' said Tilly.

The coffin of plain, unvarnished wood was resting on a trestle in a narrow room with no windows and a tiled floor. Pickup saw at once that it was still open, which gave him a twinge of unease. At all funerals he had attended – Granny Pickup's last year and a few RAF ones – the lid had always been decently in place. A nurse in uniform stood behind the coffin, alongside a man in black wearing a little cap to cover the crown of his head. Holmin ushered Pickup into the place opposite the nurse, with himself next, then Tilly. He nodded to the man in black, who began to intone the prayer, his voice rising and falling in a language which might have been Hebrew, or maybe Yiddish.

Pickup had only seen three dead bodies ever, and one was a dog. He shrank from the odour of death, the corruption of the flesh. This one had been lying for four or five days now. There could be maggots. He had to steel himself to look down upon the face of the man he had last seen being lifted out of the Stinson. During the flight he had been only a silent

213

presence in the seat behind, until at last there came that dreadful gasp when Pickup went into the dive. Oh, and that most vivid memory of all, when just after take-off he twisted round to look back, and met the man's desperate gaze, as if he lived only to deliver his testament.

He had been cheated of that by death and/or Michael Pickup, and now was cheated of having the word delivered by anyone else, thanks to Leveret and his plots. That would be something to tell Nesbit.

Who was he, who was he? He looked older than the fifty years estimated by the doctor, but that could be the bony head, the sparse grey hairs curling from his neck, the deep hollows in which the eyes were now closed. To have been chosen for his ill-fated mission he must have had eminence of some sort. Musician? Scientist? Architect? Inventor? One day it would be known, when the war was won. He would be mourned, he would be honoured.

If the war is won. Aye, there's the rub. Tilly was right. Husser, the stowaway on Operation Sly Anders, would do more to bring that about than this old boy could ever have done. As Churchill said to Sarah's father – or he had said to Churchill – winning the war was the surest way to save his people. It was still a lousy conspiracy, but he wouldn't stir things up. He wouldn't return Nesbit's call. For one thing, he was too bloody scared. Just imagine the Branch Manager's reaction.

The prayer had finished. The man in black made a little bow and led the way out. Pickup looked down into the coffin a last time. There was no corruption, only stillness, a kind of peace. He reached in and clasped a cold hand in farewell.

Kurt Westermann held the package in his hand, three small cylindrical objects sealed in a square of silk against the risk of rain or immersion – the Eljy film-rolls and whatever images slept in the strips of emulsion within. In the movie studios he had been impressed by the confidence with which the camera crews handled the cans of raw celluloid. One mistake and they could have fogged the film before the next scene was shot or, worse still, after it was shot. They never did, they knew what

214

they were doing. What he was doing he wasn't sure. All he knew was that while the rolls were in his possession he could not feel safe in this refuge. Either he must contrive to get them to the Swedish idealists who had engineered his escape from his enemies, or he must surrender them to Thomsen.

The Prince had been summoned to play tennis with old King Gustav, Westermann was alone in the study, supposed to be reading through some old files. But he really couldn't waste this opportunity to do something with the rolls of film. He took one of the Prince's crested envelopes. It was just big enough to hold the little package. He could put it with the rest of the post the Legation messenger would collect at five o'clock. He unscrewed the cap of the fountain pen the Prince had allotted him. But to whom should he address the missive?

The Swede Lingstrom was the obvious choice, and probably the right one. He didn't take to the sharp Englishman who'd driven with them through the small hours. How about the other Englishman, the young one who'd piloted the plane? He and Westermann were both airmen, and airmen respected each other. This one also had a rather nice, shy smile. He searched his pockets for the card the pilot had given him during the meal at the nobleman's house.

The name printed on front was Alec H. Nesbit, but scrawled on the reverse was the one he remembered: Michael Pickup. In a different hand and different ink was a telephone number, a Stockholm telephone number. The Prince's phone rested on its elaborate cradle close to hand. It would be a moment's work to call that number and ask for Mr Nesbit. But also dangerous. It was likely that the Prince's calls were monitored. He turned the card over again. Below Nesbit's name, in italic script, were the words *Picture Post*. So the fellow was a journalist, and had he not seen for himself the foreign journalists' abode located within the Grand Hotel?

Without conscious intent he had been turning the package over and over, until it became undone. Inside, the rolls had been repacked in their light-proof wrappers, just as he remembered doing with the films for the Rolleiflex he had owned in a happier era, except that they had been about four times bigger than these. He unwrapped one of them. The black flange

215

at each end of the spool, the red backing paper, the little adhesive tail you licked and stuck down to stop the finished roll unwinding – all that was just the same, but in miniature.

Idly he inserted his thumbnail under the seal as if to slit it. He had once watched a vain old actor – was it Jannings? – do this very thing when he spied a foolish make-up girl taking unauthorized snaps on the set. He hadn't smashed her camera or anything like that, merely opened the back, taken out the film and let it unwind. Westermann had actually seen it turn opaque, he had fancied. Would this not be the safest and most elegant solution to his problem? It was quite likely that these little rolls were already fogged or faded with age.

They waited in the waiting room at Bromma, just the two of them in a hall that could have accommodated twenty or more travellers. They had been through all the formalities of producing passports and having luggage examined and documents studied, again just for two. Luckily, a very sound bloke from the Legation had come with them to sort out any difficulties with the Swedes. Why had Mr Pickup stayed for such a short time after arriving to serve as a telegraphist? Sadly, he was recalled on compassionate grounds. His wife had been injured in an air raid. Mr Tillotson's stay had been even shorter. Oh, he had seen how unstintingly the Swedish people were welcoming the Jews from Denmark, and had now to report to the Archbishop.

They had spent one last night at the manor house. Neither Katze nor Anders could be there, but she had telephoned, and the Count was still in jovial mood over the success, at last, of their humanitarian undertaking. If only . . .

The next night they had been aboard the *Valkyrie*, ferried there directly from the railway station. Tonight, likewise, they had been driven directly to the airport. And waited and waited, not talking much. They hadn't talked much since the tiff in Holmin's little hospital. Tilly was still brooding over the question of who had flown and who hadn't flown on Sly Lander 2. Couldn't bear the prospect of getting credit for something he hadn't done.

There was the sound of Merlin engines spluttering into

silence outside, and renewed activity within the building. The Mosquito had landed, bringing a King's Messenger – according to the Legation man – and Dr Malcolm Sargent, who was due to conduct the Stockholm Philharmonic in a programme of British music. How had conductor and upper-crust courier got on together, Pickup wondered, in the little pit for two horizontal bodies that was the passenger accommodation on a Mozzy?

The turn-around wouldn't take long, said the Legation man. They should soon be off. He bustled away to look after his new charges. Even at this ungodly hour, with just two passengers coming in, two going out, the place fidgeted. Figures moved to and fro in the shadows, or conversed in the pools of light. Pickup identified a British Airways bod, sundry Swedish officials, some in uniform, and a knot of policemen, some not in uniform.

Now a recognizable character was bearing down on them. Oh God, it was Alec Nesbit, whom Pickup had so far refrained from mentioning to Tilly.

'Lucky I spotted you,' he called to Pickup. 'You're on the plane tonight?'

Pickup frowned a sort of affirmative. 'This is Squadron-Leader Tillotson,' he said, hoping that mention of his rank would tip the wink to Nesbit to be careful. To Tilly he said, 'Alec Nesbit. We sat next to each other on the Dak on the way over. He's from *Picture Post.*'

'For Christ's sake, what are you doing?' Tilly hissed to Pickup.

'It's all right,' said Nesbit breezily, 'I'm here only to get my pictures and story of the Danish Jews on to the flight. Which is done. But a little bird said that the passengers out tonight were a couple of RAF officers, and I hoped one of them might be a certain M. Pickup.' With a bit of a flourish he produced a small white packet.

'What is it?'

'Delivered to you, care of me, at the Foreign Press bureau in the Grand Hotel. Doesn't say who it's from, or anyway not on the envelope. As to what's inside, I have a sneaky feeling that if I were not such an upright British journalist I should have kept quiet, taken a look and quite possibly found the makings of a very good story.'

He cocked a challenging eye at Pickup. Pickup shrugged.

Nesbit wiggled the packet between his fingers. 'It could be two or three little roll-films, smaller even than vest-pocket. Either that or little sticks of dynamite. Here!' He tossed it to Pickup. 'If I'm right, and they turn out be of something that would astonish the world but not get you into the shit – well, don't forget the silly arse who brought them to you. I'll be back in London by the end of next week if the prisoner exchange goes ahead on time. You know the address. Shoe Lane, E.C.4.'

Pickup suddenly found voice and sentiment. 'I don't know how to thank you –'

'No need, old boy. I've left a taxi waiting, so I must go now. Oh, there's one other thing.' He reached into his coat pocket again. 'Remembering how cold it was in a proper airliner, and having been told that a Mosquito flies at twice the height, I thought the two of you might need this. I've filled it up.'

It was the silver flask he had produced on the outward flight. 'But you can't give us *that*,' Pickup protested.

'It's only plate. You can give it me back along with the photographs. Cheerio!' He was gone.

'I could do with a mouthful of that now,' said Tilly.

'Good idea,' said Pickup, unscrewing the cap. In a minute the British Airways man would bring flying suits and helmets and lead them to the plane. In two and a half hours they could be on the final approach into Leuchars. They would have the day there before catching the sleeper south. While Tilly had his hand looked at, he would go and see Sarah, and show her the little rolls of film and ask her what he should do with them. Hand them over to the Political Warfare people? Leave them with her to give to her father, and thus to Mr Churchill? Or sneak them to the Press? She would know. Then he would hold her tight and kiss her, please God. He glanced at Tilly. 'Hey, my turn, skipper.'

Tilly passed him the flask and gave him an old-fashioned Tilly grin. 'Good show, young Pickup. Don't know how I could have done it without you.'

218